MAGES OF THE ARCANE

Riders of Dark Dragons Book III

C.K. RIEKE

Books by C.K. Rieke

Riders of Dark Dragons I: Mystics on the Mountain
Riders of Dark Dragons II: The Majestic Wilds
Riders of Dark Dragons III: Mages of the Arcane
Riders of Dark Dragons IV: The Fallen and the Flames
Riders of Dark Dragons V: War of the Mystics

The Dragon Sands I: Assassin Born
The Dragon Sands II: Revenge Song
The Dragon Sands III: Serpentine Risen
The Dragon Sands IV: War Dragons
The Dragon Sands V: War's End

The Path of Zaan I: The Road to Light
The Path of Zaan II: The Crooked Knight
The Path of Zaan III: The Devil King

By Sword and Sea: A Novella

This novel was published by Crimson Cro Publishing
Copyright © 2020 Hierarchy LLC

All Rights Reserved.

Cover by GetCovers Dot Com.

All characters and events in this book are fictitious.
Printed in the United States of America. No part of this book may be used or reproduced in any manner whatsoever without written permission except in the case of brief quotations embodied in critical articles or reviews. This book is a work of fiction. Names, characters, businesses, organizations, places, events and incidents either are the product of the author's imagination or are used fictitiously. Any resemblance to actual persons, living or dead, events, or locales is entirely coincidental.

Please don't pirate this book.

Sign up to join the Reader's Group
CKRieke.com

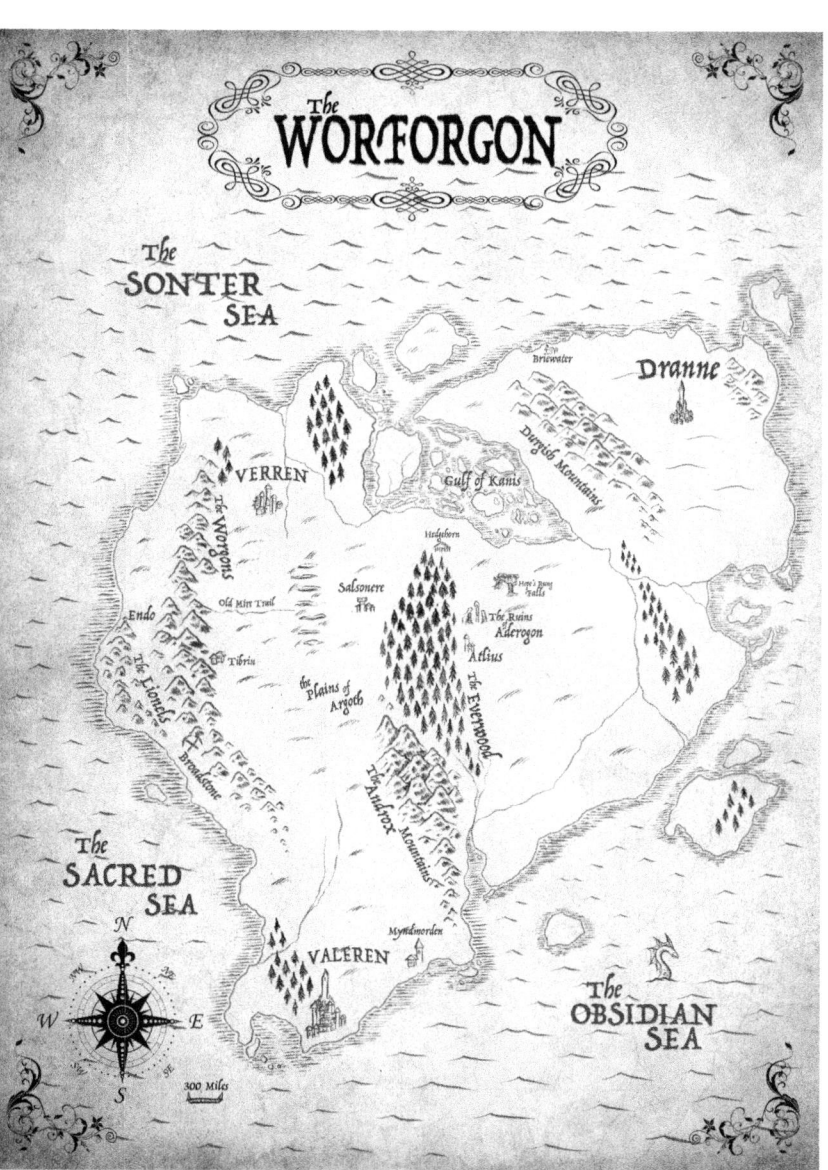

PART I
A VILE PROPOSAL

Chapter One

"What do you mean, *Stone?*" Stone said with his brow furrowed, and a firm sea breeze brushing past. *They want me to decide what we do next?*

"You're the one who's supposed to be the one to save us all," Adler said with his arms folded over his chest and his short brown hair tussling in the wind. "You decide—do we take Gracelyn to Endo? Or do we go after Marilyn, who's supposedly still alive?"

"She is still alive," Gracelyn said in a flat, serious tone. Her flowing brown hair brushed about her shoulders and her knowing hazel eyes beamed from the moonlight. "I'm certain she is. I can feel her."

Adler added, "If she *is* alive. What do you want to do?"

"Why is it up to him?" Ceres piped in, with her mossy green eyes radiating in the moonlight, and her golden hair flowing past her back in the breeze. "Shouldn't it be up to all of us? We loved Marilyn. She saved us a few times. She even sacrificed herself to save us. We can't just abandon her. But gettin' Gracelyn back up the mountain is our priority. We've got to get her safe! This should be a group decision. There's more at stake than that. Wouldn't ya say, Corvaire?"

"Aye," Corvaire said in a low tone. "If my sister is alive, I've got a duty to get her back. I will go. And I will go alone. You all escort Gracelyn to Endo. I will meet you there later."

"But what if we find another Old Mother?" Stone asked. "What if Ceres feels the birth of a new Majestic Wild? What then? We'll need you. We can't split up like this . . ."

"Is that your decision then? To stay together?" Adler asked.

"I didn't say that."

"You kinda did," Adler said.

"Just give me a moment," Stone said.

"I'm going after my kin," Corvaire said. "Lucik and Hydrangea will go with you to Endo. Not to mention Gracelyn's magical ability seems far adequate. Just keep your heads on your shoulders and you should be fine." He pulled the reins of his horse to the side, back southeast.

They were at the break between where the rolling foothills that eventually turned into the great Worgon mountain range met with the shores of the crisp Sonter Sea, and they had a long way to travel back down south to get to the ancient city of Endo Valaire.

"We should be moving," Lucik said with her tussled gray hair pulled back and the broad, aged burn on her right brow and cheek showing brightly in the moonlight. "Who knows how long those two Neferian will stay locked up in that ice Gracelyn summoned. If Corvaire must be off, then away he should go—as should we!"

Corvaire responded with furrowed brow with his thick, black eyebrows, "I will return to you as quickly as I—"

Mud growled then. His canine instincts seemed to kick in, and he growled down the beach to the south. The hair on his back stiffened and his head dropped. Each of them drew their swords.

"See anything?" Stone asked, still with all of them up on their horses. But the dog continued to growl low.

"No," Hydrangea said, with her sky-blue eyes peering out in the same direction as Mud.

"There's something out there," Corvaire grumbled.

Stone saw something then along the shore. It was the dark silhouette of a single figure on horseback, basked in shadow.

"Gracelyn," Stone said. "You've got magic enough for one more go?"

She nodded. "I believe I do."

Each of them stayed up on their horses in a row, each with their swords drawn, and those of them who could use magic were readying it.

All the while, Stone thought, *I know which magic set I am now. I can practice and learn it finally, but I've got to have some time to get to know and use it. I'm not ready yet, but I will be, given time. I will be . . .*

The figure approached, and the first thing Stone noticed was the large headdress topped with bones that curled in, like a rib cage raised upward, and a long thick cloak flowing behind it.

"Be wary," Corvaire said. "There are more than just this one out there."

"Why now?" Ceres scratched her neck. "We just barely escaped with our necks from the battle with the two dark dragons. Can't we have a little rest? Is that too much to ask?"

"I fear we're not going to get much rest with Arken after us," Stone said with his Masummand Steel sword swaying at his side.

The figure cast in shadow approached as they waited, as Adler nervously scratched his thigh and Ceres' heel tapped. His large bony headdress swayed from side to side as the horse brought him closer and closer.

"That's far enough," Corvaire said in a commanding voice, and his black hair whipped at his shoulder in the salty wind.

"Greetings," the man said as he stopped a dozen feet away. He stood there like a man who hadn't a fear in the world—tall with his bony shoulders back, his tan face almost at a full sneer, and a crooked grin showing the tips of his teeth a gleaming white showing between his thin lips. His dull, cold, black eyes looked deeply into them under his crown of interwoven cracked bone and pure ivory that rose to sharp, inwardly curled points. "Fine evening we have here."

"Who are you?" Stone said while the wind whipped and the waves crashed.

"You don't know?" he asked in a grim voice.

"I know who he is," Gracelyn said in an equally grim voice.

"Who's this bastard then?" Ceres asked.

"He's Salus Greyhorn himself," she said. "The Vile King has come to us."

Corvaire leaped down from his horse with the sharp point of his sword aiming at the king's heart. "Get down off your steed," Corvaire yelled. "You'll not take another step closer. I said get down!"

Salus raised his hands in the air, but not without a smug confidence in himself. "Drâon Corvaire," he said in a slimy tone. "I've not come in contest. I've come to meet these people before me. After all, these are the ones destined to change the future, and send the Dark King away from these lands. I wish a truce upon us—an allegiance even."

An allegiance? He tried to kill both King Roderix II and King Tritus while we stood in the halls of Verren. He can't be serious . . .

"We have no need of a friendship with you," Lucik said. "Go back from whence you came."

"I've come far." Salus stroked his sharp chin. "I only wish a few words. After all, those two Neferian seem to be frozen solid —thanks to her." His dark eyes beamed at Gracelyn. "Everyone seems to yearn for her nowadays."

"Keep your creepy eyes off her," Stone said.

"Well, well, well," Salus said. "Quite the enchantment we have for her, don't we, Stone?"

"What do you want? Let us here so that we may be done with this," Corvaire said with both his feet on the grass just off the beach's sands. "You're a long way from the southern coasts."

Stone heard Hydrangea whisper to Gracelyn. "If his lips move to cast a spell, we'll be dead quicker than a cricket chirps. You'll have to cast quicker. Do you understand?"

"I want what you want," the Vile King said with his head cocked to the side, and a thin smile irking on the side of his tanned face. "We all want the same things here."

"And what is that?" Adler asked. "You want a warm bison steak and fresh rolls like us? Oh, and more than a couple hours of real shuteye?"

"Adler," Corvaire groaned. "Keep your lips sown. This is not the time."

"Hmpf." Salus laughed with a paltry sneer. "I wouldn't mind a bit of those things, but if you wouldn't mind shutting your childish mouth while the adults talk so that I don't cut your tongue from your eager mouth?"

Stone leaped from his saddle, pointing his sword eagerly at Salus.

"Don't you expect us to trust you in the slightest! You tried to murder us when you attempted to assassinate the king in Verren. We could've died, and you would've succeeded, but we killed your wizards instead. Why in the Dark Realm would we trust you with anything?"

The Vile King's feet spread wide in a powerful stance as his thick cape whipped in the cool wind under the star-filled sky. "I don't expect you to trust me, but in time . . . I think you will."

"Doubt it," Adler said as Mud growled.

"The reason is," Salus said. "I can help you get what you want, and you can help me get mine."

"Let's just cut him down and be rid of one less—" Adler said quickly.

"Arken has a weakness."

Each of them glared at the Vile King, unsure of what to think, but certainly intrigued by the idea.

"Eager to hear more?" Salus sneered. "I thought so. He's survived many ages, far past that of a mere mortal." He paced back and forth, looking down at the scattered grass along the beach, and his long shadow cast out from the moonlight. "But there's something no one knows about him. Something only I know. Something that can point you in the direction of how to defeat him."

"Tell us," Stone said. "Be out with it."

"Now why would I do such a thing?" the Vile King said with a wretched smile from his thin lips. "Why would I spoil the ending?"

"How do ya know this?" Ceres said, with her horse Angelix stamping from side to side. "You're lying, aren't ya?"

"The name the Vile King was bestowed upon me by my enemies. It is another lie, just like the name the kings bestowed upon the Runtue. I am king. I must protect my people. That is my vow. So I am here to speak to you about how we can both protect our people."

"You're not alone, are you?" Corvaire asked.

The Vile King dropped his head with a snicker. "Why would a king ever travel without an escort?"

Corvaire pulled back into their ranks and glared out into the wilderness.

"So . . . do you want to hear my proposition?" Salus asked with a slight hiss.

"Let us hear," Stone said. "But expect nothing from us. As we expect nothing but lies from you."

"It's simple really," Salus said, brushing his shoulder. "I give you the secret to killing Arken, and you give me the power of the Majestic Wilds once he's gone."

"You're out of your mind!" Ceres said, as Mud barked wildly at him.

"Whoa there," Salus said. "Keep in mind here, that in times of peace the mothers are left in peace too. They're almost forgotten about as time rolls on. And I only wish to be friends with them. I would not pass on any control over them. There are meant to be *wild* after all."

"So, what?" Adler asked. "We give you a friend's introduction to Gracelyn, and you give us the secret to killing Arken? I think not."

"Yes," Salus said, as his dark steed neighed behind him. "It's as simple as that."

"What do you want with the Majestic Wilds?" Corvaire glowered at him.

"I want to share our knowledge."

"What knowledge do you have that I would ask for?" Gracelyn leaned forward on her horse with pursed lips.

"It's everything," Salus said. "Everything."

There was a long pause there. Each of them letting the gravity of that roll through their minds.

"What do you know?" Adler laughed, throwing his head back toward the night sky. "You don't know shite!"

"I've lived a long time, orphan," he said snidely. "I know more than you can ever imagine. Together, the Majestic Wilds and the Arcane King will defeat Arken and end this idiotic civil war. We can reunite the Worforgon. These lands have been war-ravaged for far too long. We can unite and save countless lives. Will you not hear my plea? We can save this world, but only together." He raised his clenched fists.

"I find it hard to trust someone called the Vile King," Ceres gawked.

"He is telling the truth," Gracelyn said, breaking her silence. "In his own mind."

"We can't trust him," Stone said, turning back to her. "Can we?"

"No," Gracelyn snapped. "No, but you don't need a Majestic Wild to tell you that."

"Be gone with you," Corvaire said. "If it's a fight you want, bring those around you down, and let's have at it. Or be off with you!"

Salus' head slunk, and he sighed. "You're not seeing the depth of which I speak. I don't expect you to trust me. But I expect you to trust that you need to kill Arken. Those frozen Neferian aren't going to stay that way forever. You've got to find out how to kill him. And I may be the only person alive who can teach you this. If it's out of necessity that you will listen to me. And if you don't . . . then I'll just send my people down here, and we can have a real discussion, with not only words, but steel!"

Chapter Two

"Threatening us then?" Adler pointed his sword out at the Vile King as the white moonlight gleamed off his new Masummand Steel sword. "That's not really a way to get on our good side."

"I'm not here to be your friend." Salus Greyhorn glared down his crooked, thin nose at Adler. "I'm here to help you survive Arken, kill him, and end this war."

"And in exchange," Stone said, "all you want is Gracelyn. Not going to happen. Not now. Not ever!"

"I don't want *her*," the Vile King hissed. "I want what's *inside* of her. I want the knowledge. I want the tools to build a better world. I know your mere mortal minds can't wrap around the future further than what you're going to shove down your throats next. But we can't create another Arken. There must be a lasting peace to beget a better, brighter future. These lands have known war too long . . . pain too long . . ."

"And you're the one to create a better world?" Stone asked. "You, the *Vile King* is going to create a better world?"

"I told you," he said. "The bitter kings here gave me that

name. There's nothing vile about me. I've only ever protected my people."

"That sounds awfully familiar," Ceres quipped. "Isn't that the same thing Arken said he was doing?"

"How far would you go to protect your families?" Salus sneered. "How far would you go to protect the ones you love? Pretty far I'd imagine."

"I'd do anything." Stone petted his growling dog's head with his free hand.

"You see?" Salus said with his thin arms outstretched, and a biting sea wind whipped through, causing his black robes to waft at his side. "You and I are the same. Except I have far more people to protect than you. I have a village, while you have a tribe."

"We're not the same," Ceres said with a biting tone. "We use the Elessior, and you use Arcanica magic. Our powers come from our Indiema, through our ancestors. Corvaire says your strength comes from killing, and death."

"This is true, unfortunately," the Vile King said. "But we all weren't blessed with kind magic like you. Me and my people use the gift we have to survive, though. Do you apologize to those animals you ingest, after you've shit them out? Do you feel regret for being the prime predators?"

"That's different," Adler said.

"Is it?" Salus glowered at him. "Is your life worth more than a bird's? In the eye of Crysinthian, is it?"

Adler didn't know what to say.

"So," Salus said. "What say, you?"

Each of them seemed to look to Stone, but then all eyes fell upon Gracelyn.

"Do you know if he's telling the truth?" Stone asked her.

She squinted at the Vile King, tall with his crown of bones and ivory creeping high.

"As far as he thinks—yes, he speaks the truth. But the truth is always in the eye of the beholder. I don't trust him."

"That's how I feel," Ceres said. "He creeps me out."

"I've lived far too many years to trust the Vile King," Corvaire said. "You've raided too many camps at night, slit too many innocent throats. You're a monster. Now be gone with you."

"I don't think you're quite understanding what I'm saying," Salus said ends of his mouth curling down. "I offered you my help to defeat the Dark King, but I'm not bargaining with you for *her*. She's going to help me attain my greatest self. Her and the other two Majestic Wilds, will help me, and I'll help them to become more powerful than Seretha and the others ever dreamt."

"If it's a fight you want," Stone said, pressing his boots firmly into the sandy shore.

"No, no, no," Salus said. "This is only the beginning of our relationship. I've lived a long life, young orphans. I have patience. Whether you all live, or die tomorrow, the Majestic Wilds always find a way to survive. If she falls, I can wait for the next. But if you live, you will see me again. Mark my words. And, if you ever decide that you would like my help to kill Arken, and end all this suffering, say these words—*Arcanium Violiant*. Say them three times and I will appear at the dying light of the third day after."

"Give me one reason why we shouldn't strike you down this very night," Corvaire said. "And end your bloody reign in the south."

Salus sneered. "You could try. And you would die."

Mud growled, and then barked, causing his front paws to leave the ground.

Stone looked around and found over a dozen of Salus' men rose, seemingly out of the ground itself behind the Vile King.

Each of them wore long, black robes, and each wielded a long staff, and a thin sword.

"Your meek magic is no match for our combined Arcanica. You know I speak the truth. You'd no faster be able to raise your sword then you would find your intestines brimming with infection, rot, and worms burrowing through. I'm not here to fight you. In fact, I wish you to succeed, that is why I've come." He turned and mounted his tall, brown steed with gleaming muscles.

STONE WAS unsure what to do. He felt as if he should attack him, kill one more rotten king in these lands. But if Salus was telling the truth about the might of his magic, he didn't want to test him—at least not until Stone had some magic of his own.

"Remember what I said," Salus said as his horse walked off, back southbound. "Say the words three times and I'll appear at last light on the third day."

His followers faded back into the dark ground, disappearing as quickly as they appeared—like wet sand washing away back out to sea.

They all stood there, with their horses softly neighing and Mud scratching his ear. They sheathed their swords.

"Did that really just happen?" Adler asked.

"I believe it did," Stone said.

Corvaire spat in the Vile King's direction. "We'll find our own way to kill Arken."

Why would I ever choose to ask for the Vile King's help? What would drive me far enough to give Gracelyn off to him?

After ten minutes of riding, Ceres finally broke the silence —where each of them had many thoughts surely filling their heads. "Well? What's next? How far are we from Endo?"

"I'd say we're nearly a month away at a good pace." Adler rolled his wet sleeves up.

"A month?" Stone asked him, wide-eyed. Adler nodded.

"I'm going after my sister," Corvaire said. "I'll ride for Atlius at first light."

"Atlius is almost two months' ride," Lucik said.

"But if I leave now, I'll ride around the Worgons. It'll save me crucial time—time I don't have."

"You can't leave us," Ceres said. "What if the Runtue come back? What if another Neferian comes?"

He groaned. "We saw what Gracelyn is capable of. You'll be in better hands with her than you'd even be in with me."

"Let's travel to Endo together," Stone said. "We can get Gracelyn there safely, and once we do, we can all ride after Marilyn together."

"No," Corvaire said. "That would take too much time. If she's alive—like Gracelyn suggested—then I'm going after her, now."

"Well," Stone said. "I'm going with you."

Corvaire shook his head with a cold glare, and his wet black hair dripping on his shoulders. "It's just me."

"I'll go," Ceres said in a soft tone.

"What?" Stone asked, thinking of separating their group left a sour taste in his mouth.

"I'll go with him," Ceres said. "After all, I'm a better rider than you, Stone. I If I sense another Majestic Wild awaken, it may be better to be back out in the midlands, and not on the coast."

"She makes a valid point," Hydrangea said.

"Can you get Gracelyn to our home?" Corvaire asked, looking at Stone, Lucik, Adler, and Hydrangea.

"I believe we can," Lucik said.

Wait, I'm not comfortable splitting up like this.

After all, Stone had hardly known a waking moment without Ceres—since she pulled him from the cold grave.

"I'll go with you," Adler said to Corvaire.

"What?" Stone said—he could hardly believe his ears.

"With your sword skills, and Gracelyn's magic," he said. "They may need me more out there than with her. It's a long way, and they may need my help."

"As long as you promise to keep your mouth shut," Ceres said with a smirk atop her horse.

"I don't like any of this," Stone said. "We won't see each other for months. Who knows what's going to happen in that time?"

"But you care for Marilyn," Ceres said. "As we all do. She needs our help. We'd all do the same if it was any of us captured. You know I'm right when I say that."

Stone sighed. He did know she was telling the truth.

"Use the time to practice your magic." Ceres winked.

"But how will I learn?" he asked. "Without Corvaire's tutelage?"

"You're of the Wendren set, just like Gracelyn, and you've heard nearly all of my lessons to Ceres. She may be new to this, but I'm sure together, you'll be able to learn as she does. But don't get disparaged when you don't turn out to be as powerful as her—"

Stone didn't know what else to say. He almost wanted to offer to go off with them.

"I know what you're thinking," Adler said, leaning down with his forearms on Hedron's strong neck. "You're staying with Gracelyn. We'll be fine off on our own, with each other."

"She may give you insight into how to defeat Arken," Ceres said. "Seems like she's gonna learn things pretty quick from here on out. Especially when you get to the mountain under Endo."

"Don't worry," Adler said. "I can tell by that look in your

eyes that this makes you sad. But we won't be off until first light."

"We can make camp here tonight," Lucik said.

"Shouldn't we be worried about Salus and his cronies?" Stone asked.

"I don't trust him," Gracelyn said with wise eyes reflecting the moon's rays off the sea. "But I believe him when he says he's not looking to make us his enemies. He wants my power more than anything. But I don't think he wants to take it by force. The Vile King wants to make a long-lasting allegiance with the Majestic Wilds. I don't feel you will see him again until you speak the words, he told you."

"I certainly hope we never see him again," Corvaire said. "But yes, let us make camp. And pray to Crysinthian that those Neferian stay frozen for the foreseeable future."

"Won't it melt, though?" Stone asked. "Especially when the sun rises? Those dragons are fierce enough to shatter stone."

"That's no normal ice," Corvaire said. "That's a spell cast by one of the mothers herself. If anything will hold them for a good while, it'll be that."

Each of them dismounted and dropped their bags and unrolled their blankets. Adler made the fire, and Stone's weary mind was completely wiped from all that had gone on in the last few hours. He was overwhelmed by the thought of his friends leaving, too, but he was at the brink of exhaustion, and found it difficult to keep his eyes open.

"It's all right," Ceres said to him with her sweet, mossy green eyes. "You can get some rest. We'll see each other in the morning before we go off."

He nodded, and as he felt the warmth of the fire reach his arm, spreading to his chest, he fell into a deep, warm slumber.

Chapter Three

The low flames of the smoldering fire hissed under the low lights of the overcast day—a sky filled with opaque, thick clouds and the low rumbling of thunder out over the dark waters of the Sonter.

As Stone awoke, he rested his head on his blanket, not wanting to say goodbye to the ones he cared about most. He didn't want to go to the city on the mountain without them— nor did he want them going off into the war-stricken lands without his protection. But it had already been decided— whether he like the idea of it, or not.

For the first time since he could remember, he was the first one awake as he rolled up off the ground, looking around at all his friends slumbering soundly around him. Even Mud was sprawled out, letting out those whimpering barks as if chasing a hare off in his dream.

He couldn't find Ceres, so he stood and saw her golden hair quickly as she was over in the pack of horses, dipping her head to Angelix and whispering in her ear. With his blanket draped over his shoulders he walked over to her. Plumes of mist rose from her mouth in the chilly morning air.

She turned to him and smiled. "Mornin'."

"Good morning," he said. "Did you not sleep?"

"I slept until it was my turn for watch," she said. "Only a couple o' hours ago. What're you doin' up this early? You're not usually the early riser."

"Don't know, I'm feeling as rested up as I could hope though. Although I feel like each of us could use another week to fully recover from all we've been through."

"Agree," she said, stroking Angelix's mane.

"Listen, Ceres, before the others wake up . . . I just wanted to—"

"You're not gonna get all sappy on me, are ya?"

"N—no, I just wanted to say . . ."

"I'll miss ya too," she said. "Never thought I'd say those words." She laughed. "But we're friends, and that's what friends are for. I know you want to look out for me and Adler while we're gone. But we'll be all right. And we'll see each other again before we know it!"

"I don't think it's going to be that quick," he said. "A lot can happen in a short span. I think we've already seen that."

"True, but we've gotten through it all so far, and there's so much more to go," she said. "We can't stop now, not until we know how this story ends."

"It ends with us all laughing to Adler's quips in a small, dark pub with wine a' flowing!" he said.

"I like to think that too," she said. "It'll be more than us three at the end of all this, I reckon. We're getting new allies day by day it feels like."

"Yes," he said, looking back at the rest of the party still sleeping soundly with a golden hue cascading on the rippling waters, as the sun trod its way through the clouds. "We're going to need a lot of allies if we're going to war like we are."

"Stone," she asked, turning toward him, yet leaving her

fingers in the horse's course mane. "You been thinkin' about what Gracelyn said to you? About . . . your father?"

"All of the time."

"What do you think about it? You think she's right?"

"She's a Majestic Wild," he said with a playful tone in his voice. "She's one of the most powerful people alive. Hard not to believe her. I suppose—I feel . . . *hope*."

"Hope? Well, that's good! That's not an easy thing to come by in these times . . ."

"I'm hopeful she's right. But I can't say I feel this *urge* that he's out there. Maybe he is, and maybe he'd know why I was buried in the ground like I was. Maybe he'd have all of the answers I need, but there's more pressing things to get to. I can't be thinking about myself too much. I'm too concerned for you, and Gracelyn getting to the mountain."

"Stone," she said with a kind voice and moving her hand onto his upper arm. "You're sweet and caring." She took a quick step forward and pressed her lips against his cheek. Pulling her head back she had a caring smile. "But I'm going to be fine. You don't have to worry about me. If anything, I feel I need to worry about you." She giggled. "I think I may have saved you more times than you have me, but who's counting." He returned the laugh. "Gracelyn and you are what really matter in all of this. You're the one the prophecy spoke of, and she's the one who's going to find all our paths forward in this war. Be strong, Stone. We'll be back before ya know it. And we'll bring back Marilyn, too. Soon we'll be so powerful, and united again, that Arken wouldn't dare come flying at us himself. He'll be shitting his trousers at the thought of it."

"I don't know if you're right about that," he said. "But I like the sentiment. I suppose you're right. This is just temporary. We'll rejoin in not too long a span. I'm at least glad Corvaire will be with you, and you with him."

"If there's anything you should be certain of—" she said.

"It's that you too are far too sentimental!" Adler interjected from behind. He walked over quickly behind Stone, folded his arms over the other side of the horse and snickered at both of them. "What? You don't have to quit sulking just because I'm here."

"Adler, please," Stone said. "Can't you be serious for once?"

"Nope. Anyways, I am going to miss you, partner. You're always good a distraction when a distraction is needed. And you're good with a sword too, *and* I suppose you'll be a wizard now, *and* that dog of yours is always good for scaring off dragons."

"Yeah," Stone said. "Mud is staying with me."

Ceres grinned at them. "Look at us—what was it you called us before?"

"The Orphan Drifters Trio," Adler and Stone said together.

"But Stone isn't an orphan anymore," Ceres said.

"When and if I find a father," Stone said. "That'll be the day I have a family. Until then, it's just *us*."

"Ugh," Adler spat. "I wish we had something to cheer with right now. It's a perfect opportunity!"

"The sun is hardly up." Stone winced. "You really are one of a kind."

"Sun up, sundown, what's the difference?"

They all laughed.

"Next we meet," Stone said. "We'll have ourselves a ruckus! We'll laugh until the sun does come up!" He walked over around the horse, and he and Adler embraced with a loud clap on each other's backs.

"I will miss ya," Adler said. "We are as close to a family as I've had in a long, long time."

Ceres walked around and they opened up for her to share in their embrace.

They were huddled up, with each of their heads touching and their arms over one another.

"Here we are," Adler said. "Three orphans just trying to save the world."

"I wouldn't rather be with anyone else," Ceres said. "Well, maybe someone a bit more mature, and someone who remembers anything at all."

"Saying your goodbyes?" they heard Gracelyn say, walking up to them.

Stone nodded as they released their huddle.

"I didn't want to interrupt," she said. "I know you all are great friends and splitting up is not something that's desired. I wanted to apologize though, for part of it is because of me. I'd go with you to save your friend if that was an option, but I don't believe it is . . ."

"Please," Ceres said. "Don't apologize. It isn't because o' you. None of us are really in control of our destinies now. It ain't your fault you became what you are. Stone didn't choose to be the foretold like he was. I didn't choose to unearth him either, and none of us would've picked Adler to join us."

"Your jokes are starting to sound a lot like mine," Adler said, brushing his hand through his hair. "You're welcome for that."

Ceres sighed, rolling her eyes.

"Either way," Gracelyn said, with her hazel eyes kindly gazing at each of them. "I'm sorry. Whatever I can do to help you in this fight, I will do my best."

"I believe you already have," Stone said.

Ceres gave a quick, icy glare at her. "You watch out for him. He's not the brightest when it comes to being rational. He's hot-headed, impetuous and, just flat-out stupid sometimes." Stone's jaw dropped. "I'm not kiddin'. You know I'm right."

"Yup," Adler nodded. "Yup. She didn't say you're not brave, though. I think heroically foolish might be a good term for it."

Gracelyn laughed, covering her mouth shyly. "I will do my best."

"That's all we're gonna need from ya," Ceres said.

Stone could tell the others were stirring.

"I suppose it's breakfast," Adler said, "and then we'll be off on our separate paths."

"Breakfast?" Ceres asked. "What do we have?"

"Gotta go find it," he said. "Haven't seen Mud in a minute, maybe he's off hunting."

"I'll go too," Ceres said, taking her bow and quiver down from Angelix's back.

"Wait," Stone said. "Look." He pointed to a feral pig shuffling off in the tall grass inland. It was a good hundred yards away.

"I see it," Ceres said, walking off quickly, yet low.

They felt a strong chill in the air. But it was not normal sea breeze. They looked back and saw Gracelyn with icy, shimmering eyes with her hands outstretched and her fingers curled up tightly. She muttered words too softly for them to hear, but they heard a sharp crack out in the area of the pig, and it shrieked loudly.

The pig was lifted off the ground by what looked like a sharp shard of translucent ice, skewering it. It oinked in pain, thrashing for only two or three seconds before its pierced heart gave out, and it fell limp. Mud appeared quickly and galloped over the tall grass to it, sniffing.

"Hah," Adler said. "I wish getting a meal was this easy every time. You sure you don't want to come with us to Atlius?"

WITH THEIR BELLIES FULL, and the warmth of the sun warming their skin, they readied to split up for the first time since Stone awoke from his grave. Corvaire was over talking to Lucik and Hydrangea as Stone helped Adler get his bags strapped up to Hedron.

They didn't talk much, as they'd already said their good-byes. Now Stone had that nervous gut-feeling he was doing the wrong thing by letting them go off on their own.

Adler feigned a smile, somehow showing to Stone he was feeling the same thing. "It'll be all right," Adler said—half-belief in his voice. He went and hugged Gracelyn, who was standing next to Stone, and then they hugged one last time. Adler mounted his horse, as he'd already said his goodbyes to Lucik and Hydrangea—his comrades of the Assassin's Guild.

Corvaire came over to them, and Ceres gave a quick nod, shuffling up to Angelix's saddle, evidently tired of saying their goodbyes and eager to get back on their way.

"Farewell," Corvaire said with his hand out to Stone. "Take care on the long path ahead. Trust your gut and keep your sword within grasp at all times."

Not sure you want to tell me to trust my gut right now . . .

"Thanks for everything," Stone said. "Bring your sister safely back to us. And watch out for them."

Corvaire nodded, taking his hand back, and then kneeling to Gracelyn, lowering his head.

"I will return to you," he said. "May Crysinthian hasten your passage to the knowledge buried under the rocks of Endo Valaire."

"I await your return," she said. "The strength of the blood that runs in you and your sister's veins will be needed in the war to come. May your ride be veiled by deep shadow and your horses' hooves as silent as the night."

He nodded and rose. Corvaire mounted his horse, and with one last look at Stone, he kicked the horse's sides and was off. Adler and Ceres glanced at each of them, and then nodded to each other, and were off behind Corvaire.

Goodbye, my friends. Until we meet again.

Chapter Four

❦

His normally pulled back hair was down, brushing about his chest as the horses took them down the coast. The seagulls didn't sound the same to him, the golden hue of the sunlight on the beach didn't look the same, and the powerful—yet calming—crashing of the waves didn't have the same impact on him.

All he could think about was them.

Lucik rode first, then Gracelyn after her, and Hydrangea rode behind him in a single file down the grassy knolls just off the sands' edge.

He was with them, but he didn't remember the last time he'd felt so alone.

I should've gone with them. I shouldn't have left them. Those were the words that repeated in his head.

They were his only family, and they were gone.

I've got a job to do. This duty outweighs my thoughts. But I can't help it. I miss them already.

He wondered if they were thinking about him. He wondered if they were just on the other side of the foothills of the Worgons to his left.

The sun was overhead then, with a colony of seagulls flying over them, casting down hundreds of darting shadows. A red crab scuttled underneath Grave, moving quickly to avoid the large hooves.

I should've gone with them. I shouldn't have left them alone . . .

Gracelyn's horse slowed, pulling back to ride at his right.

"Getting warmer," she said, with her back straight and shoulders back, letting her then-dry black locks flow behind her in the breeze.

"Yup."

"Do you want to talk about it?" she asked.

"No."

She sighed softly. "How about a song then?"

"I'm fine," he said. "Just don't really feel like talking, is all."

"You don't have to talk to listen to a tune," she said with a smile, showing her pearly white teeth.

"I'd like to hear one," Hydrangea said from behind.

"May I?" Gracelyn asked Stone. "I don't want to upset your silence . . ."

"Go ahead," he said, perking back up. "Don't remember the last song I've heard."

She cleared her throat gently. "Which one would be appropriate for now?" Her fingers caressed her chin, as she pursed her lips. "Oh, I know. This is one my aunt used to sing to me when I was a girl, usually when I cut my finger or fell down on the stones."

Lucik had turned around to listen.

As she sang, Stone found himself entranced quickly. Her voice was delicate, whimsical—yet powerful when it needed to be. He couldn't take his eyes off her. The whole world slowed as he watched her sing.

"WITH THE WIND *of the mountain cold,*

And the breeze of the sea foretold,

KARIIN CLIMBED WITH FINGERS BARE,
　Away from beast with eyes a flare,

SHARP TEETH it had and claws of stone,
　The tiger wished to lick her bones,

A CAVERN she found from the whipping wind,
　Dark and dreadful, she still went in,

SQUEEZE THROUGH SHE DID, her body pawed through,
　In the still darkness, her loneliness grew,

THE TIGER STRODE PAST,
　Growling, roaring, his shadow was cast,

INTO THE MOUNTAIN SHE CRAWLED,
　Deeper, deeper, into the black fog,

ALONE SHE WAS with terror so gripping,
　Kariin's footsteps echoing, her feet slipping,

YET IN THE darkness a light did glow,
　Inch by inch, she crept quite low,

　　　　　　　　. . .

Humming, floating a lantern she did find,
 Behind it, a pointy-eared elf quite blind,

'Who goes there, lass, to visit me this deep?
 So alone I've been, so lost, so weak,'

My name is Kariln, by a tiger I was chased,
 Until this cave I found, I'm glad I escaped,

'Alone I'm no longer, and pleased I am,
 For together, may we find sunshine again,'

Far they went through the mountain,
 The blind elf's lantern a warm beacon,

The sunlight they did find,
 On the mountain's other side,

Under the sun's warmth and glee,
 A frightening sight they did see,

The tiger flashed its wicked teeth,
 Snarling, growling with her terror deep,

Back we must go, into the cave we must,

For the tiger is hunting with wicked lust,

'NONSENSE MY DEAR, this tiger is no threat,
So long it's been since I've seen my pet!'

THE ELF THE TIGER NUZZLED,
Leaving Kariin quite puzzled,

'SAD SHE'S BEEN since losing me,
And now at last, we can be three!'

THE THREE DID travel both far and wide,
The girl, the tiger, and the blind elf side by side,

YOU SEE MY LASS, when one sees dread,
To others, they see only a friend,

YOU SEE MY LASS, when one sees dread,
To others, they see only a friend,

HER VOICE TRAILED off as the seagulls had calmed their caws, as they themselves seemed to be listening in. The waves of the sea grew louder as her voice silenced.

He'd been so enthralled in her voice that he didn't pay much attention to the lyrics, but he heard her singing the word tiger and couldn't help but think of Arken.

"Beautiful." Hydrangea clapped her hands. "You're going to be worth far more than just magic on the long road."

"Yes, you sure got pipes on you, girl," Lucik said, then riding next to Gracelyn. "Interesting song, though. Never heard it before. Is that a northern song?"

"Actually, my great-grandfather wrote it," she said. "It's been in my family many years. He wrote many songs. Most of them spread in the north, yes. He was quite famous in his old age."

"You're not speaking of Harold the Bard?" Lucik asked.

"Great-grandfather Harold Meadowlark," Gracelyn said.

Lucik grinned, nodding. "Quite famous indeed. Explains how you got your voice. He wasn't only known for his songs, but they say he could calm any temper with his voice."

"I don't know if that was true or not," Gracelyn said. "But I vaguely remember his singing, but I was only little. It was the most enchanting thing I'd ever heard."

"How'd he come up with that song?" Hydrangea asked.

"My father told me that while out on the road, a tiger stalked him, and he met an elf that led him to my village, where he met his wife, my great-grandmother, and they had children and lived happy lives. So, he thought the tiger did him a favor by leading him there."

"Interesting," Hydrangea said. "Aren't many tigers around nowadays. The kings cherished their hides too much."

"Pity," Stone said. "With everything after us already, it's a shame there aren't tigers out there too."

"I didn't say there weren't any tigers . . ." Hydrangea said with a sneer.

For hours they rode, making good time down the long coast as Stone could feel the sand in his hair and the rain had finally stopped long enough that all his clothes had dried.

While it was still warm, with the sun high, they'd decided

to take a break and he sat on the sandy beach with Mud at his side, peering up into his eyes. Stone scratched him on the chin, and the dog leaned into it.

"How'd you two meet?" Gracelyn asked him, sitting on his left side. Her hair brushed his shoulder in the sea breeze.

"He actually saved me from a dragon." He laughed. "Bravest thing I've ever met, packed away in a small package."

She smiled, reaching over Stone's knees to pet the dog. "I miss my dog."

"Have you ever been away from home before," he asked, as she drew her hand back. She shook her head. He brushed his long hair back behind his ears. "Your world has been flipped upside down from all this, hasn't it?"

She nodded somberly, as her faced showed a woman who may never see her family again. Her lips quivered, which she tried to cover, but her hand shook too. The new powerful sorceress he'd known almost no time at all, appeared to be another normal person in this world that had been so hard to so many.

Gracelyn dropped her head down to her knees, and Stone was unsure of what to say. But she quickly picked her head back up and looking directly up at the sky she took a deep inhale with closed eyes, and then a deep exhale that came from the depths of her being.

"It's okay," she seemed to tell herself. "I'll see them again someday. You'll see them again."

"You will," Stone said. "After all this, things are going to go back to the way they were."

She turned to him with a cold glare. Her hazel eyes dimmed. A shadow cast over her face . "No, Stone. You're wrong in what you speak. Things will never be the same after this."

He pulled away from her at her darkened demeanor. "I—I didn't mean to . . ."

Her gaze turned back to the sea and the slow roll of the tide crashed into a jutting rock out off the coast. "I—I can't see what's going to happen," she said in a livelier tone. "But I—I don't know how to describe it. I just have these feelings . . . like having a dream about a dream. But I can tell when they are real. I can tell . . ."

"Like when you said I have a father that's still alive," he said. He was fidgeting with his hands so nervously, and his knees bouncing so wildly Gracelyn reached over and put her hand on his hands to slow them. "Yes, exactly like that. I could see as clear as a warm primaver day. There wasn't a doubt in my mind he's alive out there."

She pulled her hand back and dug both of them into the sand at her sides, running her fingers deep into the fine sand, letting it glide through them.

"Is there anything else you can tell me? Anything else . . . about him?"

"Hmm . . ." she muttered, cocking her head to the side. "I can just feel the connection between you two. Like hundreds of strings tying you two together as if you were wooden spools, bonded together, but by over a great distance. That's all I can really feel about him. I'm sorry I don't know more."

"You—you don't know where he is? What he looks like? His name?"

She shook her head.

How am I ever going to be able to look for him after all this is done? And in the end—would he even know who I am? Would he want to know that I somehow survived that coffin I was born out of?

"Do you have a feeling about how all of this war is going to end?" he asked, looking out into the clouds flowing over the sea's edge.

"It's going to end," she said. "Somehow, someday these

lands will know peace again. But which side will win I know not. For sadly, if Arken wins, it will mean peace for his people. All I can feel is that the fighting will end. For everything—one day—ends."

"What're you two goin' on about down there?" Hydrangea asked from up back by the horses.

Stone looked back and saw her and Lucik were leaning against one of the horses, with her arm around the back of Lucik's waist.

Are they together?

"Nothing," Gracelyn said, getting back up to her feet and brushing the sand off the back of her pants. "Just talking about the end of the world." She gave him a sly wink with her long eyelashes.

Mud ran off and pawed at a small red crab scuttling down the beach, huffing barks at it.

I can't believe I have a father, and that he's out there somewhere. I want to know what he looks like. Could he tell me about who I really am?

A deep sadness welled up in him then. He felt it in his bones, down in his thickest core. He felt that crippling sadness of being truly alone. His friends were out there in the wilderness on their own. He was with new friends but that wasn't the same.

I'm all right. Don't think about that right now. There's still much to do. You'll see them again.

Gracelyn seemed to notice his dismay and extended a welcome hand to him, which he grabbed. She hoisted him up to his feet.

"To ye who waiteth and be bold of heart," she said. "True reward cometh to those with diamond-like devotion and courage of stone."

"What did you say?" He raised an eyebrow.

"Stay true," she whispered, as if a person he'd never met

was talking to him then. "Devote your everything to what you must. For the present is urgent, your future laden with rocks, and your past will be all-but a distant dream when this is done. Focus Stone. Your talents are needed here, with me, with them. We have to get to the mountaintop."

Chapter Five

Their horse's hooves splashed through a short ravine, with a narrow creek snaking down along it for miles. The air was crisp and cool, refreshing to their nostrils as the three horses carried them southbound with the foothills of the Worgons to their right. The peaks that grew in the far-off distance in the depths of the range were jagged and jutting, not like the rolling foothills.

In the early morning breeze that filled the valley, tall grasses blew heavily back, bristling to and fro. Corvaire led the way, as he almost always did, with his black cloak's tales falling off both sides of his mighty horse, nearly touching the clear water's surface. Ceres rode Angelix just behind, with her wide hide glistening in the sunlight—wherever it wasn't browned with spattered mud. Ceres had been mostly silent in the two days since they'd split up with the rest of the group.

Adler, however, seemed just as chipper as ever—and Ceres only told him what for after a rant with himself had gone on far too long. Even without Stone to banter with, Adler seemed to have full conversations with himself about the way the moon appeared in different parts of the sky each night, and why it decided to appear in broad daylight sometimes. He talked about it being weird to him that some animals had four legs, some two, and some many. Ceres finally told him to throw himself into the creek, so his mouth would finally be forced shut. Corvaire laughed.

They wove their way down the long ravine for hours, stopping only to let the horses drink and graze. Each time Ceres and Adler would stretch their legs, while Corvaire took the time to climb to the top of the ravine, inspecting the area.

"We've already been on these plains once now." Adler splashed water on his face from below. "What's there to see up there now?"

"You twit." Ceres raised her arms up high over her head, stretching her back out with a loud yawn. "You know exactly what he's doing up there. Is it just part of your nature that you gotta say somethin' dumb about it?"

"I don't know," he said with a twisted face. "I never really thought about it like that. Maybe I'm just trying to impress you with my high-class whit and intelligence."

She spat next to her. "I have a thousand golden tandors if you ever had a lick of either of those two things."

"Give it time." He smirked.

Corvaire walked back down the grassy slope with long strides.

"See anything up there?" Ceres asked.

"No," he said, with a chin full of dark stubble and strands of silver gleaming in his long dark hair.

"That's a good thing," Adler said. "If we keep this luck up, we won't run into anymore blasted dragons or soldiers." He spat then. "I dare say I hate soldiers more than dragons anymore."

"Speaking of dragons," Ceres said, looking back north. "We've had no sign of those two Neferian trapped in Gracelyn's ice. It apparently was strong enough to hold them.

There's some real luck in her knowing how to use that spell like she did."

"I don't know how much *luck* has had to do with us getting this far," Corvaire said in a low voice. "But if it was luck, I hope it lingers around for a bit more. We could use it. We've got a long road ahead of us still."

The horses picked their heads up from the water quickly, each of them glaring southeast out of the valley. Their hides were tensed, yet they remained quiet.

Corvaire inched his way up the grassy hill again, with his knuckles white as they gripped his sword's hilt. Ceres and Adler crawled up after him. Only his hood and veiled eyes peered through the swaying grasses at the top of the ravine. Adler glared through next, and then Ceres. She gasped so loudly her hand shot up to cover her own mouth.

A hundred years out in the plains, Ceres could only see its curling neck with sharp horns swaying up and down in a jerking motion, and she saw its two massive wings looming high. It picked it's head up, with its mouth covered in blood which was only visible on its red-colored scales by the blood dripping from its mouth. It had green eyes that glared out like the predator it was.

"Where'd that come from?" Adler whispered, as the horses in the creek still, trotted back and forth nervously.

"It's a drake," Corvaire said. "It must have just flown in. Killed a bull or boar, or something of the like."

"It's huge," Ceres said, watching its long, muscular tail swing up into the air as its head plunged back down to feast. "Bigger than any dragon we've seen yet."

"Not as big as the Neferian, though," Adler said. "They'd still tower over that drake."

As it spread its wings out wide, they were a charcoal black, and it had lines of white horns from head to tail tip.

"Where'd it come from?" Adler asked.

"Most of them are flying in from the Arr," Corvaire said. "People up on the eastern coast spot them flying in. Not sure where this one came from."

"Seems like they're sproutin' up from the ground," Adler said.

"We'd best get back down." Corvaire lowered his head. "That's the last thing we need right now."

Adler followed, but Ceres curiously stayed. "What're you doing?" he asked.

"In a way," she said, "it's beautiful. Strange that the same gods that made us—made them."

"Now you sound like you're going on one of my rants," Adler said. "Those are for me to use, only. Now get down here, would you?"

The drake let out a loud crackle of a roar—mid-feast. That was enough to send Ceres scurrying back down.

"We just wait it out?" Adler asked Corvaire, who nodded.

A low roar erupted from behind them, sending shivers through Ceres—from fingertip to top of her hairline. They spun, as did the horses who couldn't help but neigh in surprise.

Overhead, casting a dark shadow that basked the empty plains, another dragon was screaming through the sky, soaring toward the red drake.

"Down!" Corvaire said, pressing down Adler by the shoulder. The dragon's roar was so thunderous it echoed through the valley. From underneath, the dragon's gray underbelly was wrapped by scales dark enough to first appear black, but then as the sun caught them—they were revealed to have a cluster of violet. Fire crept out of both sides of its mouth, with thick smoke lining its trajectory behind.

The dragon roared overhead, with the flapping folds in its wings rippling like strong sails in sea wind. It was gliding down at a startling speed. Each of them couldn't help but crawl back up to watch. A fear for her own safety, was quickly replaced in Ceres for that of each of the dragons.

'We're going to need them,' she thought to herself. They shouldn't be killing one another.

The violet dragon with long, curling black horns that shined in the light of the afternoon sun, and with all its huge size landed on the plains gently. It flashed its teeth at the red drake, who snapped back—blood still dripping from its mouth. They both spread their wings wide, snarling and barking at one another.

"Are they fighting over the carcass?" Adler asked.

The snapping of strong jaws and flapping of giant wings slowed, as their tails both lowered.

"I—I think they're talking," Ceres said. Her voice was full of astonishment as her eyes were wide and her hands gripped the grass tightly.

"Ah," Corvaire said, as if he should have gathered it beforehand. "It seems so." He looked back north to where the violet dragon had come. "She may be gathering others."

Adler looked back north too. "Do you think—?"

"They found the two Neferian stuck in the ice—?" Ceres finished.

"Don't know," Corvaire said. "But there's a chance."

"Would they want to break them out?" Adler asked. "Or try to burn them through the ice with lots of dragons' fire?"

"Your guess is as good as mine," Corvaire said, watching as both the dragons flapped their wings once again, turned their heads up north, and lifted from the ground, pushing the grasses around to the dirt.

Each of them lifted off majestically, screeching and hissing.

"I'd be pissed too," Adler said. "If I were a dragon I'd hate those Neferian as much as . . . as well, I do."

The two dragons soared through the air past them, where

not a single animal or insect made a peep or buzz as the two predators flew the skies.

"I hope they kill those two monsters up there," Ceres said with her thin eyebrows angled down. "I hate those things."

※

Mud barked loudly, looking over the foothills to the east.

"What is it?" Gracelyn asked to Stone, who'd quickly leaped to his feet from their resting place by the hot, sandy shore.

"Shh," he calmed the dog. It took him a long moment to see what the dog had been barking at, but as Lucik quickly pointed out—he saw the dragon on the other side of the Worgons.

"Must be a big one," she said. Her lean arm was exposed, but up at the shoulder her tan leather armor with the black straps covered her chest and torso underneath her dark brown cloak. Her silver hair was pulled back, but loose strands whipped behind her.

"It ain't one big one," Hydrangea said. "It's two big ones!" Her tan skin and blue eyes were bathed in reflection of sunlight off the water.

"You're right," Stone said, as Gracelyn got to her feet next to them, and Mud continued to growl. Their horses too were staring at them in the far-off sky. "It's a red one, and the other looks black, or black-violet."

"They're heading for the two Neferian," Gracelyn said. "They're going to try to kill them."

"That means it's a great time for us to get back on our way." Hydrangea pulled her leather vest with bronze rivets up tightly.

"Agreed," Lucik said. "When dragons do battle, the only place safe is far, far away."

Each of them gathered their things and made way to be back upon the horses, but all Stone could think about was one thing: *That's where Ceres and the others would be, just where the dragons are flying past. I hope they made it by without those two seeing them. I hope they're all right . . .*

PART II
HEDGEHORN AND THE MOUNTAIN

Chapter Six

Thirty-five days later.

THERE WAS a familiar chill in the air as the mountain loomed before them. A whimsical fog rolled up it like thin strands of cotton being wound around a spool. Their boots fell heavily into the damp mud as they gazed up at its high peaks.

Boulders formed from eras past of rain were smoothed, yet jagged where they'd been broken off by rumbling earth or the cracks of time. Sheer cliffs rose from the foothills like stone waterfalls, and Stone remembered the first time he'd looked up to the mountain that housed the city of Endo Valaire—the city of the Mystics.

This is where it all happened . . . This was where Arken came and burned the city asunder. This is where Seretha, Gardin, and Vere perished from his Neferian's dragonfire. I never thought there'd be a reason to return . . . I never thought there would be something . . . in the mountain.

To the west, and just down the slopes of the last grassy

patches before the sandy beach, waves crashed onto the tall, sharp stone that resembled a shark's fin with a white stripe painted down its edge. That was the symbol he was told to first look for by Marilyn to locate the city.

Heavy raindrops dropped all around them as the loud sounds of high, breaking waves crashed back onto the dark water. Out on the distant horizon, just over the western edge of the Sacred Sea, the golden aura of the setting sun shimmered just below the dark clouds.

Stone pulled Grave by the reins up onto a grassy knoll between the beach and the mountain's base. Stone's face had sprouted a thin, black beard, which caused his neck to itch, which on more than one occasion Hydrangea had asked him if he'd gotten bugs in there. He even caught her eying his neck once while he'd been getting a brisk shuteye.

"As much as I don't like the sound too much of being holed up in a cave," Hydrangea said, removing her wet boots. "I don't mind the thought of some dry spot to dry these where they won't get wet as soon as we get to walking again."

"How long have these rains been following us?" Lucik asked, tying her horse loosely to a thin, brushy tree next to them. "A week?"

"No, not a week," Hydrangea scoffed. "Just feels that way. It's been four days, no more than that."

Lucik replied, "I miss my soft, dry sheets back in Verren. I miss resting my head on a pillow of cloth and not a cold, damp pack."

"I miss my own bed too," Gracelyn said in a somber, homesick tone as thick raindrops pelted her hood. "I miss waking up to the sound of crowing roosters and wagon wheels trudging by, and the sounds of children playing by the side of the road."

Stone had never known a home, nor a bed he could lay on

for more than a month. The only home he ever knew was beneath the ground, six feet deep—and then wherever his friends were—that was his new home. But they were a thousand miles away then. As Stone and the others assumed, if they'd made good time, they'd be somewhere nearing Salsonere or Hedgehorn. They didn't know if they were planning on going through the Everwood to avoid prying eyes, or go around for haste . . .

"This looks as good a place to camp as any," Stone said, tying Grave up to the same tree as Hydrangea's horse. Mud, soaking wet, shook off yet again, flinging smelly droplets onto each of them. But they all knew they couldn't get any more wet. Stone looked around for some sort of overhang of rock, but there didn't seem to be any that far below in the hills. "I'll go off and gather kindling."

"I'll go look too," Gracelyn said, wiping the rain from her brow and nose with a slick movement of her hand.

Mud ran off after a bushy-tailed rabbit.

Lucik and Hydrangea unpacked the horses and scanned the long plains to the east—looking for any signs of unwanted pests.

To Stone's surprise, he'd not once seen the shadowy creature that loomed with its piercing eyes in the darkness. Yet, that only meant one thing to him . . . that it had gone after the others.

"After we do this," Hydrangea said, with her light blue eyes dimmed by the overcast, still-graying sky. "We need to find Guildmaster Conrad. We must let him know that we've gotten the Majestic Wild back to Endo. We'll need to figure out what to do next to protect her."

Lucik nodded with an aged wisdom on her face. "Yes, we'll need Master Galveston's aid to bring more of us into the war." She leaned in closer to her partner. "As powerful as she is, she's going to need more than a few blades of Masummand Steel and one of the Darakon to protect her from the warring kings."

Stone brought back an armful of twigs under one arm, and hefted larger branches in the other, as Gracelyn came back soon after with even more. Mud killed a pair of rabbits, taking a little for himself and giving the majority up for them to roast on stones by the fire that Hydrangea got going by striking her flint and steel.

Crysinthian may have been watching down on them as the sunlight faded away as the rain slowed, but that didn't do much for the dampness in the wood. But they'd gotten used to getting fires going in those kinds of nights.

They'd gotten to know each other better over the more than a month they'd spent together. Hydrangea Van Heverstrom—as the opposite of her namesake led him to believe—didn't care for flowers or gardening, but she rather loved cooking. Cooking with earthy spices, and lots of garlic.

Lucik Haverfold, who was all-but married to Hydrangea, was as spry as her partner, if not more than two decades older, or at least appeared it just by the folds at the corners of her eyes, and the silver sheen in her hair.

"I've never met a dog that I liked," Hydrangea said, moving the crackling hare with a stick. "And I dare say I like this one quite a lot."

"He's a good boy," Stone said, looking at the dog curled up at his feet, warming himself by the crackling fire.

Gracelyn nudged him with her elbow. "Feel like trying again?"

I don't really want to right now, and I'm tired. But I've got to get my Elessior Magic somehow. I'm just tired of failing.

"I can try." He sighed. "I don't know what's going to make it work this time."

"You've only been practicing since we split with the others," she said. "Give it time but keep on practicing."

She was only a few years older than Stone, but when she spoke to him like that sometimes he felt she was far wiser, with an aura of magnificence about her.

"I don't remember if it took Ceres this long." He rubbed his palms together. "But Corvaire did say it takes most people years to get it, and that's if they start young."

"And your Indiema is difficult to reach," she said with her hazel eyes flickering in the firelight. "Try to focus on that dream you had with your mother that one time and focus on the feeling of your father somewhere out there, thinking of you, wondering where you are. Perhaps he's dreaming about you this very moment."

That was a very warming thought to Stone indeed. He'd often wondered if his father—if he was out there—ever knew if he was still alive. But the thought of his father dreaming about him . . . means that he *remembered* . . .

"You must learn to call the cold," Gracelyn said. "Feel it deep within your bones. Feel its icy breath and embrace it. Say the words now."

He closed his eyes, ignoring the warmth of the fire as best he could, although it was more than welcome to him.

"*Britrelect Infernos Carnum,*" he said.

His eyes widened and he glared at the dancing flamed before him. He could see Lucik and Hydrangea watching the fire intently, as they had so many other times he'd tried the spell.

He said the words again, as both of them lessened their stares.

"Try again," Gracelyn said. "It's okay."

He tried again, but the fire before them burned just as it had before, with the random raindrop every now and then that plopped into it with a *hiss*. "I'm not going to get it . . . again . . ." he said. "It's so frustrating. How am I going to make fire freeze?"

"Well, Stone," Hydrangea said. "If it's any sort of consolation to ya, I'm glad you didn't this night. I'd rather keep a warm fire. I'm going to go off to rest, for we're gonna have a long climb ahead the next few days."

She stirred off to laying on her side on the ground, as Mud perked his head up at her movement, but then laid back down.

Stone had decided to do first watch that night, and Gracelyn let out a loud yawn, and tucked herself away as he stoked the fire.

"*Britrelect Infernos Carnum*," he whispered, holding the stick out into the flames. He tried to think of his mother's voice in the dream he'd had where she visited him in his coffin. He focused on his father, who was somewhere out there—but those flames continued to dance, crackle and pop. There wasn't a lick of frost coming from them.

There's something I'm missing. There's got to be something I'm doing wrong as not to use my magic—if I have any at all . . .

Gracelyn was able to use her magic perhaps before she even knew she had it.

He stood, wrapping his drying blanket over his shoulders. Walking down to the beach he remembered the first time they'd all come to that same beach together, and he couldn't help but miss his friends. It had been a far longer stretch than he'd wanted, and he only hoped that they were safe—wherever they were.

Chapter Seven

They released their steeds, taking down their saddlebags and reins, tucking them away under a wide, flat stone where they'd be hidden from prying eyes, and hopefully stay dry. Stone patted Grave on the back of the neck, as Grave's dark eyes appeared gloomy to him.

"I'll miss you, boy," Stone said. "Thank you for returning to me and getting us all this way. I hope to see you again. But for now, be free."

None of them knew how long they'd be up on the mountain, Gracelyn perhaps would be there quite a long time, so once again, Stone and his friends said their goodbyes to their horses and climbed.

With the sun glowing in the east, over the long prairies, and a moist dew resting on the grass blades and rocks at their feet, they walked up toward the high tip of the mountain. Looking up, Stone couldn't believe he'd already climbed such a high peak.

There wasn't much talking as they strode, one after another up. Stone remembered that part of the climb, but he also remembered how higher up, the sheer cliffs turned into somewhat of a maze—and that they had to find the olive tree. That was the sign of the way up to the city.

"You ever climbed before?" Lucik asked Gracelyn, who was walking in front of her, who walked behind Stone —who led.

"No, I haven't," Gracelyn said, taking precautious steps on the loose stones. "There were some hills just outside of the forest by where I lived. As a young girl we used to go up to them and muck around, pretending they were like mountains."

"Have you ever been outside of your town before this?" Lucik asked.

Gracelyn didn't immediately respond, but eventually piped up. "I've never been far outside of Thistleton. It's my home. Always has been. This is the farthest I've ever been away from them." She sighed. "I miss them."

"I know what you mean." Lucik staggered as a group of loose rocks gave way under her foot, sending round rocks down the slope to their left. "I remember the first time I left home. At first it was exciting, but then I grew quite homesick."

"Where were you from?" Gracelyn asked.

"I was born in a quaint town rather like yours. It's called Pompen, down by the Obsidian Sea. I went off to train in Salsonere, and eventually Verren, which became my home after a time."

"Did you ever go back?" Gracelyn asked.

Lucik paused. "Perhaps after this is all over, then maybe I'll go back again. I write letters, but the only time I went back was when my parents passed. Now, my home is where I make it. But I was quite lonely at first."

"Did you ever have a family of your own?" Gracelyn asked.

"I did." She lowered her head.

Stone looked back at Hydrangea who shook her head in a gloomy manner.

"I'm sorry—I shouldn't have," Gracelyn said with flushed cheeks.

"It's all right," Lucik said, raising her head back up and giving a sigh. "I have a son. We haven't talked in an age."

"He's as bull-headed as a king, and as dimwitted as one too."

"Hydrangea!" Lucik said, glowering back at her.

"Well, it's the truth. Ain't it?" she said.

"We had arguments," Lucik said. "I don't mean to ramble on about myself. If I am, I apologize."

"No, you're not," Gracelyn said. "Please go on."

"His name is Simon, he'd be forty-five as of this year."

"Where is he?" Gracelyn asked.

"In Verren."

"He's there and you haven't seen him? Why?" Gracelyn asked, slightly tilting her head.

"We disagreed on many things, principally the war."

Stone thought he was beginning to understand. *He joined Roderix's war effort, didn't he?*

"What about the boy's—er—man's father?" Gracelyn asked.

Hydrangea interjected, "Perhaps we should change the topic . . ."

"I'm sorry, I should stop asking . . ."

"His father was a soldier too," Lucik said in a low voice. "That was before I killed the *bastard*." The word came out like venom.

She killed her son's father? Why would she do such a thing? What could he have done to deserve such a fate? No wonder her son doesn't speak to her.

"Before you think me evil," she said. "Know that this was while I was still early in my training in Salsonere, and I was only a young nineteen when they came. Verren's men stormed the city, at the behest of Roderix the First—that madman. No real point in it really . . . They sacked the city and didn't stay but for all of a month before they left again. Just the egos of spiteful wrath of kings. But they didn't leave before many of the men took what they wanted."

Stone swallowed heavily.

"I fought them off for a good while," she said. "But one got to me." Hydrangea wiped away tears. "He got what he wanted, but as he did, my fingers scratched their way to my dagger hidden away under a table nearby. I still remember the stench of his breath, like too many nights filled with rum and musty tobacco. I'll never forget that grin he had, pulling off me. He glared into my eyes like I was an empty plate from a quick supper. Those eyes didn't look the same at me when I plunged that dagger into the side of his neck."

"But he impregnated you?" Gracelyn said through her hands clasped over her mouth.

She nodded.

"I'm so sorry," Gracelyn said. "That's horrifying."

"Could've been worse," Lucik said, wiping the cold sweat from her brow at the memories. "He could've gotten away, or he could've stuck me before I stuck him. Too many in those days died horrifically, needlessly at the behest of mad kings."

"They still do!" Hydrangea said with clenched fists. "Nothing's changed! Even a new mad king atop dark dragons hasn't stopped their putrid disregard for life. Nothing's changed."

"Is that why your son doesn't speak to you?" Gracelyn pried softly. "Or is it you who won't speak to him?"

"He holds it against me—killing his father. But I raised him well, or as best I could. When he wanted to join the war because his lads were, I told him he couldn't. He was only thirteen at the time. What kind of child goes off to fight in a war?"

"They sure did sink their claws into the boy," Hydrangea said. "Put cobwebs in his head—they did. They told him all sorts of untruths about his ma. Spiteful and cruel they are to those boys. That won't go unpunished though—not forever, it won't."

There was a hollow silence between them then as the sounds of seagulls overhead was woven with the sounds of the smaller birds chirping in the pine trees scattered across the foothills. The air had grown thick with moisture in the sunny day.

Stone took off his tunic and stuffed it into his pack, the others did the same shortly after. His fingers were dirty from climbing up the boulders of increasing size, all the while he couldn't stop dwelling on his growing hatred of soldiers from Lucik's story.

How could a king know what's happening under the name of their banner and do nothing to stop it? Don't they know that's the defining quality of evil—causing harm intentionally and caring naught of the suffering of others?

They reached a section on the mountain that he vaguely recalled.

"I think it's this way." He pointed right, up a narrow path sloping up.

They walked for the entirety of the day. For as they'd been lucky enough not to be spotted or attacked by man or creature—they assumed the safest place they'd be would be within the protection of the mountain.

As the fading light, turned to dusk, they made camp on a flat bed of rock with a high slab brushing away most of the strong sea wind. As they'd collected kindling on their way up, and gathered cool spring water in their canteens, Mud had been gone the last couple of hours after chasing off after a bushy-tailed fox.

"Want to try again?" Gracelyn asked Stone, as the fire had just been started by Hydrangea.

He sighed. "I can try. But I don't know what to do to make

the spell work. I feel that because I don't have an ancestry, my Indiema may not be . . ."

"We all have ancestry," Lucik said. "All life does. You just need to work harder to get it."

"Have you tried magic?" he asked her and Hydrangea. "Maybe you have the Elessior, but you just don't know it, or haven't tried."

"I've tried," Lucik said. "I tried for years once I learned it existed. But I was already in my forties, and if I ever had it to begin with, it was long gone."

"I tried my luck at it," Hydrangea said. "But I'm fine with a sword in my hand and a dagger in my boot."

"You don't have to," Gracelyn said to Stone. "Or we could try another spell—perhaps *Feral Mongoose or Tusk of the Boar?*"

"Feral Mongoose?" Stone raised an eyebrow.

"Used for fighting of serpents or snakes." As soon as she said that he understood it was a defensive spell.

"If I can't do *Flames that Bind*," he said, "then I can't do those others. No, I'll try *Flames* again."

Mud burst into camp with three more hares in his mouth. His tail wagged eagerly, with his dark eyes staring into Stone's.

"Good boy," he said, as Mud lowered them onto the rocks by the fire.

Hydrangea gutted them and prepped them for cooking while Stone tried again to cast the spell on the flames. He did everything the way he'd heard from Corvaire teaching Ceres, and Gracelyn to him. But he tried six times, even breaking a sweat the fifth and sixth—still with no success.

"You'll get it," Gracelyn said. "Just give it time."

"Maybe you should show him how it's done." Lucik grinned. "Perhaps he needs a little inspiration."

"Not before the hares are cooked," Hydrangea said. "I don't want to have to relight the fire. Especially if she freezes the logs."

"I won't freeze them," Gracelyn said. "The spell only works on direct flames, nothing else."

Hydrangea backed away from the fire as Gracelyn's hazel eyes shimmered in the orange glow of the fire.

"*Britrelect Infernos Carnum*," she said in a commanding voice.

A strong breeze took to the flames as her hands twirled around it.

Stone's jaw went slack as he watched glimmering blue ice crystals creep up from the bottom of the flame. The blue turned clear as the tips of the fire continued to whip and crack while the ice rose slowly, still with Gracelyn's gaze heavily fixed upon it. As the ice froze the tips of the fire, it extinguished with a hiss.

"Amazing," Lucik said. "Simply amazing."

Gracelyn bent down, bending at the knee, grabbing the frozen fire with both hands, picking it up from the wood like plucking a rose from the rosebush. It shimmered in the starlight as she threw it away down the cliffs of the mountain, shattering it into thousands of tiny fragments.

Hydrangea reached in with her blood-covered hands and felt the wood and ash—keeping her hand four inches away.

"Still warm," she said, smiling at Gracelyn. "You were right, this should be a cinch to get her going again.

"You did that so easily," Stone said, rubbing his thighs as his legs were crossed. "How do you know how to do that instinctually?"

"She's a Majestic Wild." Lucik shrugged. "What more to it is there?"

Chapter Eight

✦

This smoke trickled up to the heavens from the small town below. Men wheeled barrows full of hay on its outskirts, dumping them into a large pile at its south end. Women carried large baskets of corn and clothing in tall-woven baskets atop their heads, and the children played merrily—forgetting for the moment that war and dragons roamed the lands freely.

At Hedgehorn's southern tip lay the outer touches of the Everwood Forest. Ceres gulped at the sight of it and its tall pine trees that blew in the breeze. They not only saw the perimeter of the forest, but from their high vantage point on the high hill they were upon, they saw the forest that seemed to reach on forever.

"We should try it out." Adler wiped away a line of drool with the back of his hand.

Ceres didn't like the idea of going into the town, but the smell of fire-cooked meat and fresh bread wafted downwind directly into their nostrils.

"I don't know," Corvaire growled.

"Send Ceres down there alone, maybe," he said, still eying

the town.

"Why me?" she said, twisting her hips and resting her hands on them. She scowled, but there was a tinge of a half-hidden smile rising.

"Because you're a girl," he said. "No one will suspect you're up to anything. But one look at Corvaire and he'll stand out like an albino panther."

"No," Corvaire said. "We're not splitting up, we've come all this way together to get to Marilyn. We're going to stay that way until we get to Atlius."

A small girl with a red ribbon in her hair chased after a handful of pups on the backside of one of the cottages. Watching them was a pair of men in armor with swords in their scabbards as they laughed and smoked their pipes.

"We're so close to a good meal," Adler said, clutching the grass as he leaned over the hill. The three of their horses neighed behind them. "I could die a happy man if I never had to eat squirrel again."

"I wonder what kinda candies they got down there." Ceres licked her lips.

"Want to try?" Adler asked, waiting for a response from Corvaire.

"No," he said. "We'll go through the forest. Wait for the cover of night, and then take the edge of the Everwood down past the ruins of Aderogon, and back to Atlius."

"Sure we can't have her pop in, just for a few minutes to get some supplies? I don't think anyone would object . . . At least not her or I . . ."

"I'll do it," she said. "I'd do anything for some chocolate right about now . . ."

"Let me think about it," Corvaire said. "I don't mind being up north or west like we were. But don't forget that you were with Marilyn when she cast Searing Flesh, burning all those soldiers to death, and destroying that tavern you were staying in. We run into the wrong person down here, and we'll have to worry about more than just lurking eyes."

"I still can't believe she's alive," Ceres said. "We all saw her die. I felt her heartbeat fade away to nothing."

"Something saved her," Adler said. "Bet she's gonna be pretty starry-eyed to see us."

"As long as we're not under lock and key like she is," Corvaire said. "We're going to have to be cunning to get her out of a dungeon cell without knowing where she is in them, and you're going to have to use some of the magic we've been practicing."

Ceres nodded, still staring down at the small town. "I'll do my best."

"I'm going to go find us some food." Corvaire groaned as he pushed himself up off the grass, on the backside of the hill.

The sun had already been hanging low in the sky behind them when they arrived at the hill that overlooked Hedgehorn. They wouldn't have to wait long for the cover of dark so they could creep down the valley into the woods.

While Corvaire was off, Adler and Ceres laid on their backs, looking up at the faint light of stars as the horses grazed.

"What do you think Stone's doing right this moment," Adler asked, with his hands under the back of his head. A dark beard had grown on his chin with a thin-haired mustache bristling his nose.

"I think he's doing the same thing we are." Ceres grinned. "He's up on the mountaintop looking up at the stars come alive. But he's got the sounds and smells of the sea at his side."

"I wonder if Grimdore is still asleep in the ocean?" Adler asked about the teal-colored sea dragon that had helped them fend off Arken's dragon and got them to safety.

"She was hurt in that fight," Ceres said. "And I don't know how long it takes a dragon to heal. As far as I reckon, she's still the only one to ever live through a fight with a Neferian. Let alone Arken's own one."

"I wonder if we're ever going to see one get killed," Adler said. "The dark dragons, that is. You think in our lifetime we'll see that? I don't even know how one could get killed. They're the biggest things I've ever seen with my own eyes."

"I hope so." She picked at her fingernails. "Damned mother of all things. I've got a hangnail. Look at that! I've been so careful, and it finally happened."

Adler laughed, and Ceres scowled at him. "What? We've been on the road over a month now, and if they worst thing you've got is a little ol' hangnail, then I thank Crysinthian for watching over us." She hit him on the shoulder. "I'm not tryin' to be an ass," he said. "It's the truth. I know it's too soon to say this, but I feel like our luck's been changing. Think about it, what has really been hard this whole time since we split with Stone and Gracelyn? Except far too many mangy squirrels and rabbits for our shrinking bellies?"

"You're not wrong," she said. "You're just an insensitive prick who never knows when to keep his mouth shut." She got up and walked away, sitting in another patch of grass by herself, near the horses.

"Prick?" Adler said to himself. "I'm not a prick. I was only speaking the truth."

"Sometimes people don't want to hear the truth sometimes," she said loudly, with her back turned to him still. "Sometimes all someone wants to hear is nothing at all."

"I guess she heard me," he whispered, gauging if his voice was quiet enough that time, which it appeared to be.

Corvaire came back just before the full veil of dusk. He'd gathered a small bag of red and blackberries. There was a small handful of honeysuckles to stave away hunger pangs during the night.

"I've thought about it, and yes, we should go into town to buy what we can for the rest of the journey," Corvaire said. "I'm tired of nights like these too."

"Good, I'll go in," Ceres said. "We're gonna need some coin to buy the things we need."

"No," he said. "I'll go."

"Why would you go?" she asked.

"Because I'm the only one who's not wanted by the Lord Bjorn Daamend of Atlius. People may recognize me, but that's not going to draw attention like an attractive blond girl from the north or a boy with olive skin who spouts on too much from the south."

"Those in power must've heard of what we did in Verren," Adler said. "We saved the king. They'll know we're together."

"Actually, Corvaire saved King Roderix, not us," Ceres said.

"Wish one of the horses could go in for us," Adler said, throwing a pebble out into the dark grass.

"You know," Corvaire said. "That's not your worst idea yet."

"What?" Adler asked with a twisted face.

"You just gave me an idea," he said. "Ceres, you're going to be the one to go in. But you'll have to take what coin we have with you. You're not going to get the chance to do your handy work the way you're going in at first sunlight. Now, let's be on our way down there."

They mounted their horses and galloped down the backside of the hill down toward the tree line, less than a mile down, and once inside they slowed to a trot. The edge of the woods were thinned with trees, but it brought vivid memories to Ceres of fleeing into the woods to run from the Runtue riders on horseback, escaping the confinement by the soldier that drugged Adler, and being led out of the forest by the blessed fairy, Ghost, who'd led them away from the Runtue and back to their horses. She heard the familiar insects chirping in the night, the loud hoots of distant owls, and the howl of coyotes—or wolves.

Once in the forest, and close to the town, they could see the faint glow of candlelight peering out thin tapestry-covered windows. The torches in the street glowed like beacons at sea through the dark trees.

They dismounted next to a large, fallen tree and sat, each of them listening and watching the town.

"So, how's she going to go in there?" Adler asked. "You don't know a spell that's gonna turn her into a horse, do you?"

"No, nothing like that." Corvaire scratched his chin and looked up to the moon above. "We're going to make it so that not only will no one recognize her, they're going to be working to keep their eyes off her. That's when you can go buy all the sweets you desire."

"What're you talking about?" Ceres said. "You're not doing anything to my hair."

"We've got to make it so you're not a blond from the north entering the town, you're a no one from nowhere."

"I don't like the sound of this." She clutched her cloak to her chest. "Can't I just wear a hood over my head?"

"I like Corvaire's plan better." Adler gawked.

"Either of you try to cut my hair and I'll pierce your throat where you stand."

"We're not going to do anything like that," Corvaire said. "And it won't be permanent. But you are going to want a warm bath afterward." He reached down and grabbed a handful of mud by a narrow creek behind them. Bringing it up, he squeezed it, letting it fall in clumps back down the ground. He washed his hand in the cool water after. "We should do it now so it has time to dry before sunrise. Don't want you going in there with wet mud all in your hair and on your face."

She thought he couldn't be serious, but when had she ever know him to not be serious?

Adler snickered to the side.

"I'm going to get you back for this," she said. "I'm going to get you both back for this idea." She took her cloak and hood off, folded it, and placed it neatly at the side.

"You need help with it?" Adler asked.

"You lay one hand close to me and it'll be the last time you see those girly fingers!"

"Girly fingers?" he said to himself, holding them up in front of his face for inspection.

She dove her hand into the mud with her head turned away and a deep frown, and then she smudged it into her long hair.

Chapter Nine

Ceres grimaced from the filth that pasted between her long, normally soft hair. It clumped and itched as Adler chuckled. She walked out of the Everwood in the shimmering sunlight that darted between the trees. She wasn't alone, though.

They'd taken the time to smudge down Angelix, who rather seemed to enjoy the dirt—as to make Ceres look too much like a filthy road rat. She left her Masummand blade back with the others. If the sheen of that sword was seen it would be a dead giveaway there was something more to her than just a simple girl going into town for supplies.

She pulled the reins gently, strolling out of the brush and into the full view of the town of Hedgehorn. The smell of the fresh sweet breads being baked at the center of town was almost too much for her to bear. Her mouth salivated, and her palms grew sweaty. Even the musty aroma of tobacco wafting in the air smelled delicious. They'd been on the road long, after all.

A pair of guards in cracked leather armor and hefting chipped swords at their sides gave her a glare, which quickly turned to a stark uninterest in the girl caked in dirt. They turned away from her with a scoff and laugh between themselves.

Ceres quickly spotted her first destination—straight ahead in the city square, a round cobblestone area with merchants just beginning to place their wares before them. Ten vendors were setting up their tables with spices of vibrant colors and textures, and even an old man selling flowers the likes of which she'd never seen before.

Right in the middle, however, she saw the couple pulling up woven baskets filled with the chocolates she so desperately yearned for. Bread could wait, she told herself. *And it's not as if either of them rubbed mud into their hair to do this.*

"Oh dear," she heard the woman say to the man behind the table at the first sight of Ceres approaching.

"Coin only," the man snapped as she tied up Angelix at a post just on the outside of the cobblestone ring. "We do no bartering."

"I have coin," Ceres said, approaching, and rustling the small pouch at her side that jingled with the muffle of metal rubbing against metal.

"Forgive me' husband," the woman said with a cocked head. "What's happened to ya?" She looked back at Angelix with an obvious curiosity. "What's happened to yer horse?"

"A bit worse for the wear," Ceres said. "T'was a harsh road to get here. And I can't say I'm not chomping at the bit to get some sweets and warm food in me."

"You need a bath is what you need," the man said with a sour glare.

The woman brushed him on the shoulder. "Why don't you go off and smoke your pipe? That's really why yer bein' rude. Ain't it? You heard me. Off with ya!"

The man grumbled and walked off, muttering to himself.

"Now, what can I get ya, dear?"

Ceres eyed the six baskets, hovering over them with a brimming feeling she hadn't felt in months. There was no worry. Only a deep sense of awe. One basket was filled with smooth chocolates, with hopefully something hiding in their center. Another basket had long twists of hardened sugar, two with taffies of assorted colors. One had berries dipped in chocolate, and the last had stiff white cookies with a sweet powder dusted on top.

"One of each. Wait. Two of each. Extra of the chocolates. Better make it a solid dozen o' them."

The woman pulled out a thin linen and picked up each and placed them one by one into it. She looked up at Ceres, who was stuck like a statue, unable to move from the excitement, but her eyes followed each piece as they were dropped onto the linen.

Before dropping the last chocolate into the linen, she paused, and held it out for Ceres. "This one's on me. You do look like you've been hit by these hard times. And I must say, you do have some majestic eyes."

Ceres was startled back alert, and looked up at the woman, but then darted her eyes away. She took the chocolate from her hand and plopped it into her mouth. She smiled as widely as she could as the chocolate dissolved on her tongue. "Thank you," she said, her voice muffled by the gooey candy.

"That'll be two tabers," the woman said, before handing over the linen she'd tied with a piece of twine.

Ceres had almost forgotten where she was, and that she needed to pull up her purse. She startled back to attention, pulling the two silver tabers out and eagerly gave them to the woman, and snatching the bag from her hand. "Thank you," she said, with the final swallow. "It's delicious."

"If you need a good place to wash up, the inn is just right down the road there," the woman said, pointing north. "Old Jim will let you bathe for near-nothin'."

"Thank you."

Ceres bowed her head and walked toward the baker at the other side of the cobblestone circle as more people filled the courtyard, searching for their own items.

Ceres noticed who else had entered into the courtyard. They adorned thick, silver armor and had long swords ready for war. They weren't mere guards of Hedgehorn. Wearing the crest of purple and white on their breastplates, she recognized as soldiers of Atlius.

What are they *doing here? I've got to get out of here, as inconspicuously as possible.*

She pulled her hood up and went to the baker, who gave a warm smile under his thick mustache that still had specks of flour in it.

"How can I help you?" he asked in a boisterous voice that carried out. "Not seen you here before. I would've remembered you by those eyes. Even if you are dressed up like you're going to celebration in a creek bed." He laughed to himself as she rushed up to his table.

"I'll take two of those, four of those and a few of those things over there," she said, looking carefully behind her, looking to make sure the soldiers hadn't noticed her.

The mustached man seemed to notice her unease at the soldiers of Atlius and lowered his voice.

"They're in from the southern road," he whispered to her, leaning onto his elbows on the table. "Nothing to worry about. They'll be gone by the afternoon. They've been around these parts more and more, asking questions about a pack of rats that killed some of them months ago. Lord Bjorn sure knows how to hold a grudge."

"Oh," she said coldly, rustling through the purse. "How much?"

He gave her a twisted face with pursed lips. "Three tabers, one quort."

She handed them to him as he gave her the loaves of bread and couple of pastries, which she tucked into her bag quickly.

"Hey, lass," the man said in a cold tone. "You know what they told me about the three that killed their soldiers and burned down an inn? One of them was a girl with bright green eyes. She had blond hair. There's a reward, a generous one. But I don't know why a girl like that would be around these parts. If you follow my drift."

"Don't know what you're talking about." Ceres turned to leave, but the man grabbed her by the wrist, clamping down with his strong fingers.

"We don't want none of those problems here." His voice was direct, but low. "If one of the kids were to come here, we'd tell 'em to leave. If they were here. You follow?"

She pulled her hand away, as the man's cold expression beamed bright once again as a mother with her two children approached his table.

"How are we enjoying the day?" he asked them, while side-eying Ceres, who walked back to Angelix, keeping her head down.

She noticed one of soldiers strolling over toward her horse.

Keep your mouth shut, Ceres. You don't know nothin' about nothin'. You just fell into a creek in the dark. Your horse misstepped.

"You're new to town," the soldier said, feigning a half-smile. "Where'd you travel from?"

"Salsonere. Came through the forest. That's why I look the way I do."

"Where you headin'?" he asked, his eyes were cold, and his thumbs dug into his belt as he puffed out his chest.

"Nowhere in particular," she said. "Just tryin' to find a safe place where those dark dragons aren't."

"Hmm," he groaned as he inspected her. "Nice horse you got here. Where'd you get it?"

She could taste the bitterness in the back of her mouth. *I hate all you soldiers. Why don't you just let me be on my way? What do I have to do with anything that has to do with your day?*

"My pa gave it to me."

"You're from Salsonere then?" he asked.

"Small town outside of it."

"Which one?" he asked.

She wished she had her sword and could plunge it into him for his smug demeanor.

"Real small," she said. "You wouldn't know it."

"Try me."

She sighed. "It's called Dippleton. Not many know it."

"Dippleton, never heard of it."

"Told ya," she said, trying to contain her snarkiness.

He scratched his temple. Turning, he yelled to his comrades. "Hey, Joseph, you're from Salsonere. Ever heard of a town . . . Dippleton?"

This aroused the others and the one soldiers shook his head. Two of them walked over.

"Hmm," he groaned again. "He ain't ever heard of it, and he's from there. How far outside of the city is it?"

"'Bout a hundred miles and a half."

"Dippleton, you said," one of the soldiers said as he approached. "Never heard of it. Where is it?"

A sharp pain shot up from her stomach to her throat as she watched the soldier's boots step closer and closer. She swallowed hard. There was far too much attention on her, and out of the corner of her eye she could see the reflection of steel from Corvaire and Adler's blades in the woods.

"She said more than a hundred miles," the first soldier said, but then he stirred, cocking his head to the side.

"What is it?" one of the other soldiers said.

"Don't know," he said. "Thought I saw something. You remind me of someone. Sort of, but I don't think we've ever met."

Ceres looked over the soldier's shoulder to see nearly every vendors' eyes upon them—especially the baker's.

"You know her?" the other soldier asked, leaning in to inspect Ceres. "She's about as filthy as a hog in a waterhole."

"Her eyes," the first soldier sneered. "What's yer name, las?"

"Hydrangea," she said out of instinct.

"Hydrangea what?"

"Meadowlark," she said using Gracelyn's surname.

He reached up to touch her hair, but she brushed his hand away. She noticed the whole courtyard had grown deathly silent. His face contorted and he sent his open, strong hand onto her cheek. Her vision was fuzzy, and her eyes watered. But she didn't topple over, and she made damn sure not to cry.

The other soldiers snickered.

"What color is your hair?" he demanded. "Beneath all that shit? Your name's not Hydrangea, is it?"

"None of your rotten business what my name is." She spat on his chest.

An angry red flushed over his face. He drew his hand back to strike her again, and she ducked, looking back to see Corvaire and Adler rushing out of the woods with swords flashing. As his hand was about to strike her, mad jaws with sharp teeth bit down onto his forearm, dragging him to the ground.

The other soldiers rushed to pull their swords from their sheaths, and again—she wished she'd had her sword. She pulled a dagger from her boot and stood defensively in front of her horse.

Ceres thought of all the spells she knew, and how to cast them, but there was no time. The soldiers were only feet from her, and frozen there, she didn't have the time to summon her Indiema. And as Corvaire and Adler ran up to defend her, and the downed soldier cursed and fought to get Mud off him—that's when they heard it . . .

Its roar resounded down onto the town with a thunderous burst and trailing echo as it swooped overhead with its long underbelly gliding over with its snaking tail swaying from side to side. Its enormous, dark wings flapped mightily, which blew Ceres' hood to her back. It flew back up into the air, circling back around, with its venomous eyes piercing down savagely onto the town. The rider upon its back held tightly onto the reins of the dark dragon, whipping them, and causing the Neferian to dive once again.

Panic took the town. Merchants left their wares in a mad rush, and fathers and mothers lifted their children in their arms, desperately running. The soldiers weren't exempt from that, as they staggered back—wide-eyed and unsure of what to do.

"To the trees!" Corvaire yelled out as loud as he could, waving his arms for all to see. "Into the forest. Save yourselves!"

Chapter Ten

Black flames billowed out of the sides of its mouth as its maw opened wide with long teeth like curved swords showing. The rider upon its back had the gold paint on his grim face as his gray cloak's tails rushed behind him as he whipped the reins.

Adler rushed to Ceres' side as she covered her ears from the dragon's roar as it rushed low overhead, flying back up into the sky with a long plume of black smoke trailing behind. Adler helped her back to her feet as the soldiers of Atlius stared up into the sky in a stupor with their swords waving nervously in their hands.

Corvaire ran through them, brushing two of them to the side. "Don't just stand there," he yelled, with his hair blowing over one shoulder and his hazel eyes glaring commandingly into theirs. "Get into the city and get these people out of here. Women and children first! Women and children!"

The soldiers at first looked at one another, unsure as if to listen to his command or not.

He held his sword's sharp tip up to one of their throats.

"We're all going to die unless you get your boots moving,"

Corvaire said. "Now make haste. I'll do my best to stave off the dragon and rider."

"You can't defeat them," one of the soldiers mumbled. "We're all going to die." He ran to the tree line.

"You all going to be cowards too?" Corvaire asked as the mighty dragon swooped around for another pass, this time with the dark flames fully brimming from its mouth. "Women and children. Go!"

They were pleased to see the soldiers finally run off into the village yelling out, 'into the trees.'

Ceres ran to Corvaire's side. "How can I help? What spell can I use?"

"Not you," he snapped. "You get the others out of here with Adler. You're not strong enough yet. I'll do what I can. But you've got to be quick!"

"I can help!" she said as the dragon roared once again, as it was in a fierce dive right toward them. Its eyes were a beaming golden color with fiery reds by its slithery pupils.

"No," Corvaire said, shoving his sword into the ground before him, letting the hilt point up toward the heavens as it swayed back and forth. "Now, go!"

"C'mon." Adler grabbed her by the wrist. "He's right. We don't have time." She followed reluctantly.

Corvaire pressed his palms together with his fingers upward. He closed his eyes as the dragon glided down, screeching wildly.

Dark clouds gathered above Hedgehorn as wind rushed in, bristling thatched roofs and blowing swaths of leaves over the cobblestone. Hundreds ran through the town, many clutching up their young children in their arms as they cried in panic. Ceres and Adler were both leading the people toward the mouth of the Everwood, but Ceres turned back to watch

Corvaire, standing strongly with his legs spread wide. His long tunic's tailed flapped violently behind him.

The clouds in the sky swirled in a layered cone, as the dragon had almost reached the city once again. The rider, with his soulless eyes, pressed his body into the dragon's neck as the black dragon with red wings' webbing that was a dark, vibrant red like blood near the tops of the wings and faded to a pale, red-gray at its bottoms.

"Illietomus Creschiendo!" Corvaire said in a voice that rung out in the whooshing wind.

Wicked dragonfire erupted from the dragon's mouth as the pillar of lightning ripped into it from the eye of the twirling clouds above.

Its mighty head lurched to the side, sending the black fire spewing out onto the northern part of the city. Instantly they could all feel the powerful heat emitting from the inferno.

The bolt of lightning was followed by a booming, crackling thunder as the dragon roared in fury. Its mighty, muscly body landed on the eastern outskirts of the city, a quarter mile from where Corvaire stood.

"Fly back away," Corvaire growled. "Or I'll hit you again."

The dragon's eyes burned with a powerful rage upon him, as the clouds continued to twirl ominously above.

The Neferian lowered its head toward him and flapped its wide wings that were the length of four dozen homes. The rider pulled his gray sword from the sheath at his side, sliding down the side of the dragon and fading out of view behind a string of homes.

"Get it again!" Adler yelled from the forest line. "You hurt it. Do it again!"

Ceres left the forest line with the hundreds of people behind her and ran to Corvaire.

"Illietomus Creschiendo!"

The Neferian flapped its wings quickly, bursting out the

north as the thick, sizzling pillar of lightning went crashing down from the eye. It erupted in a bright explosion of white light, striking into the dragon's tail. Its maw opened wide as it screeched, and it crashed back into the city on its side.

Ceres was soon at Corvaire's side, with her own sword stuck into the ground, she pressed her hands together as he did. Adler ran to his other side, with his sharp sword held out before him.

They then saw the rider emerge from between two stone towers at the far end of the courtyard.

"I'm going to use *Searing Flesh*," she said.

"No," Corvaire said sternly through labored breaths. "You may kill us all."

"We're all dead if we don't kill that thing," Ceres said.

"No, I said!" Craning his neck to glower at her. "Use *Vines that Hold*. That will get us some time."

"*Vinitulas Windum Granum*," she said with her dirty hair blowing in clumps behind her.

In the distance, they could see the vines rising up from the cracks in the stone road, wrapping themselves slowly around the rider's ankles. He pulled his legs away strongly, fighting to break free as more came up, winding around his thighs.

"That's it, keep it up," Corvaire said. "Adler, you ready to test that new steel of yours again?"

"Ready as I'll ever be," he said, shaking the shimmering sword in his hand as the black fires grew high into the sky, sending up huge plumes of smoke that blacked out the sky.

The dragon lifted its head up from the eastern side of the city and growled at Corvaire. That same fire was brimming hot in its long throat.

Corvaire took a deep breath, readying himself to cast the spell again.

"Hurry," Ceres said quickly.

He said the words again, and as the lightning tore into the

dragon, its head buckled to the side, this time sending the hot flames to the southern end of the city, spewing it back toward them as it regained its strength. The bright lightning from the sky, leaving a booming thunder, and many gasps and cheers from the people in the woods.

Corvaire dropped to a knee, sucking in quick breaths, and coughed.

The rider was chopping away at the vines that were winding around his waist, and the mighty Neferian lumbered forward, crushing entire stone homes under its massive weight.

"Corvaire?" Ceres said, kneeling next to him with her hands on his shoulders, looking up at the encroaching dragon. "What do we do now?"

"We need to escape," he said achingly. "We cannot defeat the dragon."

"I can kill the rider," Adler said.

"It's too late," Corvaire said, getting back up to his feet with a groan, as his eyes sparkled and he readied another spell.

"You're too weak," Ceres said. "You can't cast *Bolt of Light* again."

"I'm not," he said. "*Hornrotus Hiven!*"

"What was that?" Adler asked, looking around, as a humming sound filled the air.

"I think it's . . ." Ceres said.

They looked up and found a new cloud forming above them as the funnel cloud with the eye as the center dissipated.

"That's not a cloud," Adler said as the humming turned to a loud buzzing. "Are those . . .?"

"Hornets," Corvaire said. "Very angry ones."

They were looking at a swarm of them that nearly filled the sky as the dragon's fires tore through both tips of the city on either side of them. The heat was building, causing each of them to sweat.

The hornets buzzed and zipped toward the dragon, and

once they got there, the dragon roared loudly, flapping its wings, and brushing its head and neck from side to side in annoyance.

"They won't kill it, or even harm it," Corvaire said. "But they sure pack a wallop of a sting."

"There's thousands of them," Adler said. "That could defeat a platoon of soldiers. Not a pleasant way to die."

"Speaking of," Ceres said, "we should be gettin' out of here while we can."

"What about the rider?" Adler asked.

"I'm afraid this isn't the last time we've seen him," Corvaire said. "Now, to the woods . . ."

They grabbed their swords, turned, and ran back down the hill toward the tree line. Corvaire limped slightly, clutching his abdomen, and taking deep breaths.

Just before they reached the trees, they looked back to the burning city, as the rider slashed away the last bits of leathery vines, glowering at them with his soulless eyes.

The dragon thrashed and roared, spewing down blasts of its black fire through the swarm of buzzing hornets. Its fires crisscrossed through Hedgehorn, sending it ablaze.

"How many were still in there?" Ceres asked softly. "How many didn't make it?"

"We did what we could," Corvaire said. "May Crysinthian send their souls warmly to him."

"Come on," Adler said, turning back around. "There's nothing more we can do."

Corvaire turned and walked into the trees, which Ceres did also after a deep sigh of regret.

Behind them the city of Hedgehorn burned. The sky was painted black by the thick plumes of smoke. The air was filled with the raging roars of another Neferian left undefeated. The rider strode back toward it, waiting for the swarm to be decimated by the hot fires.

Within the woods were the sniffles and cries of those who survived the unprovoked attack. Many of them lost family members or friends whose flesh was being burned from bone within the city. And after such a long journey to get there from where Gracelyn had temporarily defeated two of the Neferians in a block of magical ice—Ceres remembered who the true enemy was—King Arken Shadowborn. As long as he lived, the Worforgon had no chance of knowing any sort of peace.

The monstrous Neferian with the red wings burning the city was only a pawn in the Dark King's game. They had to find a way to defeat him—or the flames that destroyed the city would engulf everything, and there'd be no place to hide from those monsters . . .

Chapter Eleven

❧

"Do you know where we are?" Lucik wiped away the sweat beading on her wrinkled brow.

"It seems . . . familiar." Stone looked up and down the mountain, clutching onto a sharp boulder at his side. His cloak's tails whipped his black hair in the wind behind him.

"It all looks the same," Hydrangea said, gulping down a water from her watersack. "Do you know where to go, Gracelyn? Do you have an instinct for it, or even a gut-feeling?"

"No," Gracelyn said. "At least I don't think so. I've never been here before. Nothing looks familiar."

"We've just got to find that olive tree," he said. "That's what's going to point us up to the trail that will take us up to Endo, and into the mountain."

They'd arrived at a fork in the path they'd taken that split three ways: one that veered off to the left, seemingly going back down, and two others that snaked their way farther up into the mountain that was growing ever steeper. Many steps they took then caused loose rocks at their feet to topple down its slopes.

The air was chill and crisp at that height, as they were perhaps two-thirds of the way up. Stone took a moment to look down on the wide world below, which had much of its plains veiled behind rolling fog that early in the morning. The Lionel Mountains they were in grew ever larger into the horizon to the south, and he could see the distant range of the Worgons to the east, with their snow-capped peaks. The Sacred Sea's waves crashed into the shore on the west as the early morning sun's rays shimmered off it.

"Which way then?" Lucik asked.

"The right one," Stone said, not knowing which one to take, but he figured if they were going up, they were in the right direction. Lucik nodded, and climbed, as Mud darted around her, running up the path nimbly.

As Stone followed her up the trail, gripping onto the rocks at his side with each delicate step up the loose pebbles under his boots, he thought of his friends—as he did so often.

I wonder what they're doing right now?

I still don't know how Marilyn can be alive. I felt her body go limp, but if she is indeed alive, we're going to need her strength in the battle to come. I just miss my friends. I wish they were here with me right now.

"What are you thinking about?" Gracelyn asked, just behind him. "You've been quiet today."

"Nothing really. Just thinking of the others."

"Well," she said in a chipper voice. "They're still alive. I can tell that much."

His head whipped back around to meet her gaze, which startled her. "You can sense that?"

She nodded. Her hazel eyes sparkled in the early morning sun.

A wide grin crossed his face. "Thank you for that. That means a lot to me."

She smiled then, as Stone looked at her soft lips curling up, and noticing the way her smooth skin was warmed by the sunlight. Her eyes were enchanting, and she reached up and grabbed the fingers on his right hand delicately.

"They're going to be all right," she said, each of them looking deeply into each other's eyes. "We've got to focus on ourselves. We're not safe out here in the open. Only in the mountain should we be able to rest our heads without one eye open all the time, or our ears ready to hear the roar of one of them roaming the skies."

"You're right," he said, turning back around to follow Lucik and Mud up the mountain. Mud had found a flat rock up to the right and was panting, looking down at them.

They climbed for the next few hours, having to pick which fork to take—two more times when they got to an area which Stone thought looked vaguely familiar.

"This way," he said, pointing up to an almost hidden trail to the left, that looked like it hadn't been used in years with how narrow and covered in rocks it was.

"You sure?" Lucik asked but seemed pleased enough that he'd made such a quick decision, so she moved that way, and Mud darted up it.

They continued their climb, with Stone glancing up at the high peaks that still seemed far off in the distance, and he was surprised he couldn't see the city of Endo, and the burned away areas that Arken's dragon had decimated.

The city is so hidden, yet so visible when we were there. What a perfect place to hide the Old Mothers. It's just such a damned bastard to find the place!

"Where in the Dark Realm are we?" Stone muttered to himself. He took a moment to look down at the then clear plains that held a vibrant green hue, broken only by scattered lakes that reflected their clear blue. He continued climbing behind Lucik. "It's got to be somewhere close. We're nearing the summit of the mountain."

But then, he caught something out of the corner of his eye. Down on a cliff to their lower right, he saw something prickling out from behind the rocks. There wasn't a path that led down to it, and he'd only seen it by chance because a thorn pricked his right calf muscle—but it appeared to be something he'd seen before.

"Down there." He pointed with his extended arm. Each of them eagerly looked. "I think those are the branches of the olive tree!"

"How do we get down there?" Gracelyn asked.

"I suppose we're going to make our own path," Hydrangea said, after looking up and down the mountain but not seeming to find another way down.

"Mud can't make that," Stone said, looking down at the whimpering dog sitting at his side.

The area between them and the olive tree was a vertical cliff with sharp, gnarled rocks that were only a half-finger deep. If they were to climb, one wrong grip could send that person tumbling down the rocks.

"No, there's got to be another path," Lucik said. "I can hike my way up a mountain with the best of them, but as for climbing, I'm all thumbs. You three go, and I'll take Mud back down to find another path that may lead us there.

"It's like a maze of paths and trails," Hydrangea said. "It could take a full day or two to find the right way up, even when you can see where you want to go! If we ever could . . ."

"Let me try something," Gracelyn said, walking past all of them to stand on the edge of the cliff that overlooked the deep slope between them and the tree. Stone almost immediately noticed the chill in the air.

From behind, he watched as she spread her arms out wide, and then raised them into the air above her head. "Hold on," she said. "It's going to get a bit breezy."

A sharp, cold wind rushed down from the skies above, and

Stone could feel it in his bones. Lucik's teeth chattered as each of them pulled their cloaks to cover their faces. Then the sleet came—wet and thick at first, but then it froze, sticking to the rock's face. While the ice came down, Gracelyn remained with her bare arms exposed in the deluge, with her breath misting out in front of her face.

Her arms lowered toward the chasm, and Stone felt a relief from the cold. The entirety of the storm she'd created concentrated down onto the rocks between them and the tree. As the wind had faded away from them, Stone walked to stand directly behind her. He could see that the icy rain was building up in sheets.

"It's working," he said. "Keep doing it."

For the better part of five minutes, the intense storm pounded tons of ice and snow into the chasm, and as the ice wall rose up to the edge of the cliff they were standing upon, Gracelyn lowered her arms without even a heavy breath taken.

"There," she said, letting her arms sway at her sides. "It's going to be slick. After all it is ice."

"Very impressive," Lucik said, with wide eyes. Hydrangea smiled.

Carving around the mountain, she'd formed an eight-foot-wide path that was sheer on its right side and coated in drifts of snow around four inches thick. Mud ran fearlessly down the ice bridge, with Gracelyn following behind. They walked down the long bank, with the thick snow crunching under their boots, and as they wound the last corner, the flat patch with the olive tree came fully into view.

The tree with its dark green, thin leaves bushed upon its branches as it swayed in the mountain wind. As each of them emerged from the ice wall, kicking the snow from their boots on the rocks, they all quickly found the trail that led up the mountain at the backside of the tree.

"Wish it was a pear tree," Hydrangea said. "My stomach's been growling all day."

"I hope there is something to eat up there," Lucik said. "Or we're going to be relying on Mud going out and hopefully killing some squirrels again for us."

"I'm getting tired of squirrel meat," Gracelyn said. "I miss my mother's baking. I miss the taste of fresh fish from the sea. It's hard to not take for granted going to the market every morning for food. The feeling of being truly hungry is awful."

Stone was all too familiar with the hunger pangs that dug into the inner lining of his stomach. It was never easy out there on the road. It was always easier in town. Up here on the mountain was almost more difficult than the road and forest combined.

"Let's go find out," he said, walking up toward the backside of the flat outcrop which round around the tree at its center. Mud ran along his side as the others followed.

"You remember all this?" Lucik asked him.

"Yes," he said, looking up the mountain path. "All of this I remember as if it were only yesterday. It's not far from here." His boot hit the thin path with large boulders on both of its sides, and his dog rushed up in front of him.

Stone was elated to be this far into their journey after nearly forty days from the northern sea, but he couldn't ignore his stomach. Perhaps something would be left in the burned city of Endo . . .

They climbed silently for ten minutes or so until they came to see the front entrance of the city—a high rock wall with a single slit through it. But his eyes didn't go directly to the front gate, but to where the three charred corpses of the old Majestic Wilds were left like black statues of three women with flesh burned away from dragonfire. But where they would have remained now lay a pile of burned away bones picked clean by vultures. He knelt, lowering his head as a tribute to the great sorceresses. Lucik and Hydrangea stood silently with their arms behind their backs, looking at the morbid remains.

Gracelyn walked over to Stone's side, and asked, "What were their names again? And how long did they live?"

"Seretha Valair, Gardin Herenstead and Vere Drenar. They were Old Mothers as long as Arken has been alive. He was only a man when they were some sort of friends. Thousands of years—they told me. I should have been able to save them somehow."

"He came to kill them," she said with her gaze deep upon the black bones. "He came to erase something he didn't want to resurface."

"What was that?" Hydrangea asked.

"Not completely sure," she replied. "Maybe he hoped to wipe that prophecy away that came into existence the moment he arrived, and Stone woke from that grave. Or perhaps he was just wiping away an old debt now that he was powerful enough. Or maybe it was just pure revenge."

Stone got to his feet and gazed back down the mountain. "The entrance has to be somewhere below—somewhere we passed, because that was where they were running when they were killed. I suggest we look up in the city to see if anything, or anyone, survived."

"Lead the way," Gracelyn told him.

As he walked through the crevasse between the thick rock walls, his hands glided along its smooth edges. Upon the mountain's untold treasure that was Endo, then swayed high grasses in the wind knee-high. He gasped and his hand raised to his chin in disbelief. Out in the fields that had no place being upon a mountain's high reaches were a herd of cattle, more than a dozen with two young calves he could see, a trio of goats were grazing, and that same long-horned steer roamed. The steer's black-eyed gaze quickly met his.

"I can't believe it," he said with his mouth agape. "The animals didn't get burned up in the fires."

While Gracelyn and the others were also in awe of the grazing and calm animals, Stone's attention was next laid upon the center of the city—the great marble tree at the center of the ring of structures—or at least what remained of them.

He took staggering steps forward.

The monumental mound of white marble that wound up into tiny branches that used to stand with glittering gold lights was charred as black as a starless night sky. Twelve structures that used to stand around it were nothing more than blackened, broken rubble.

As he walked toward them, the tip of his boot hit something, and as he looked down to see what it was—it looked like a part of a rock or some narrow piece of petrified wood, and as he reached down, his fingers delicately picked it up, examining the long shaft of it, but then recognizing one end to be a knob of a joint. He dropped it, stepping back quickly.

"What is it?" Lucik asked from behind.

"Bone."

There was a grim silence as Stone knelt to inspect the tall swaying grass before him. Nearly an entire skeleton lay picked clean from carrion as if it had laid there for a hundred years—but in fact was only months ago.

He stood back up, cupping his hands over his mouth.

"Hello?" he called out. His words echoed out with the circular walls of the field. Each of the grazing animals perked up with stiff ears, staring at him. "Hello? Is there anyone out there? Is there anyone who can hear me?" They waited a long moment but didn't hear a reply as the animals went back to grazing with a few of them mooing. "My name is Stone. I'm not here to hurt you. I was friends with the Old Mothers. I'm here to help. Anyone . . .?"

"There's no one left," Gracelyn said, walking up to him

slowly and laying her hand on his shoulder. "There's nothing we can do for the fallen here, or them for us. Come. Let's wet our mouths and be off to find the cave. There's life upon the mountain, but what we truly seek lies deep within it."

PART III
WHAT LIES BENEATH

Chapter Twelve

❧❦❧

The fires roared behind them as the town of Hedgehorn was burned asunder, and the red-winged Neferian was off back into the sky, disappearing behind the plumes of black smoke that billowed up.

Those that had survived within the forest wept hysterically. They called out names of loved ones they couldn't find. Streams of tears fell down their ashen faces. Pain was thick in the air.

Ceres had never seen so much sorrow in all her life. She stood there as people ran past her back up into the burning city. Her mouth was agape, and she dropped her sword to the ground without knowing it.

Loud grunts stirred her back to attention as Corvaire was leading Adler and the soldiers to keep the people in the forest, but from the droves of people many made their way desperately back into the city.

"It's gone!" Corvaire yelled out into the crowds. "The city is lost, there's nothing you can do now. It's dragonfire! You can't go up there. Stop! You will die!"

Ceres watched the frantic people running up the hill, out

of the forest, but she saw most were brushed back from the sheer heat being emitted from the city as the flames rose high.

Her stomach churned and her heart sank from the cries of woe and the sadness of those who'd lost everything. An old man sobbed under a tree behind her, covering his eyes as his lips quivered. Three young children clutched to their mother's apron and they cried. The woman's eyes glazed over at her home ablaze. A young boy ran through the crowds, yelling, "Pa, Ma? Where are you?"

"This is so terrible," Ceres muttered to herself. "They have nothing now."

She thought about all the bad things she'd seen in her life, and especially everything she'd seen since meeting Stone, but the only thing that compared to this tragedy was her own parents' deaths. She'd never imagined she'd watch an entire city go up in flames like that. Even the burning of Endo paled in comparison.

A man rushed past her, brushing her arm with his. He had a bandage over his eye that was stained red with blood, as he called out a woman's name. That startled her enough that she picked up her sword and sheathed it. She ran to Corvaire and Adler, who had held back enough people long enough that they seemed to fall back to reason, and their own sadness.

"What can we do?" Ceres asked him, and he returned a worried gaze.

"There's nothing we can do," he said. "Except to keep more people from dying."

"Remember though," she said, in a tone that showed she even surprised herself with the thought. "I can't be burned. I don't feel the heat. Sonter set magic, remember?"

"No," he said. "It's too dangerous. You don't need heat to kill you. A burning wall could topple onto you. No. You stay here. No excuses."

"It's awful," Adler said with his wet, blue eyes reflecting the orange fires. "We will never be able to forget this day."

"I—I just don't know what to say," she said softly.

"This is too much," he said. "Going after us to kill us is one thing, but Arken's just here to watch everything burn. He didn't even do it himself, the coward. This war has gone on too long, and too far. The kings need to rally to fight him. Why don't they understand?"

"I don't know, Adler. I don't know. None of this makes sense. I wish Stone was here with us," she said.

"Yeah, me too. Me too."

"I suppose we should wish Gracelyn here more than anything." She folded her arms loosely over her chest.

They watched the carnage as the flames whipped high in the air as every building burned. Thatched roofs were long gone, but the dragonfire burned even stone walls.

"She could've stopped that dragon before it did what it did," Ceres said. "Or she could've blown a cold wind through there saving whatever there was left to save." She sighed. "Sometimes it feels like there's no hope left in these parts of the world."

"Don't say that." Adler touched her arm gently. "There's no getting around it that this is awful. Should've never happened. But we can still move forward. We can still win. There's still hope."

"There's just so much pain," she said. "What's really going to change this? How can those things be killed even? If the Majestics can't kill them? How are we ever going to?"

"We're going to have to find a way," Corvaire said. "Because if we can't—who else will." He took long strides up to them.

Another piercing roar echoed down from the sky. The thousands of people shuddered at the terrifying roar.

Corvaire glared up at the sky, firmly gripping the hilt of his sword.

"Hey. Hey, you!" one of the soldiers with the colors of Atlius said, walking up with three soldiers behind him.

"Stay behind me." Corvaire shoved Ceres back.

The four soldiers walked up to them, with the one at front glaring intently into Corvaire's eyes. The three behind shifted uneasily behind him, looking at one another. A crowd quickly formed around them.

"I'll be taking those two back to the keep at our kingdom of Atlius. By order of Lord Bjorn Daamend, they are under arrest for the murder of royal soldiers."

"They're not going anywhere with you," Corvaire growled, still with his sword in its sheath.

The soldier who spoke had beady eyes and trickles of sweat running down his furrowed brow. He had impish ears and a bald head. The soldiers behind him shifted nervously—they surely had on their minds the powerful magic that Corvaire had used to save their lives.

"If you disobey the lord's order, then you will be declared an enemy of the kingdom of Atlius. Stand aside and you won't be harmed."

That's when Ceres poked Adler in the ribs with her elbow. He seemed to get the hint.

"How exactly are you going to harm him?" Adler said walking up to Corvaire's side. His arms were out wide, and he was laughing. The beady eyes of the soldiers squinted and the corners of his mouth curled down.

Ceres knew Corvaire was still weak from the intense amount of magic he'd wrought upon the dragon, sending those searing lightning strikes into it, but even so, he could surely strike down four soldiers if he needed.

"You are under arrest," the beady-eyed man said. Looking

around then at the encroaching crowds around them beginning to tighten.

He drew his sword, but Corvaire was quicker and held his own up before the soldier could react. The other three drew their swords uneasily as the boos started.

Hisses, boos, and yelling surrounded them, as Adler grinned.

"He drove that Neferian off," Adler yelled above the crowd. "If it wasn't for him, none of us would be standing. It's because of him you still have the tiny pecker hanging between your legs."

"Adler . . ." Ceres murmured.

"A royal decree by our lord is our duty to uphold. You will step aside, and we will take those two with us."

"You can tell that to all of them!" Adler steamed. "They've lost almost everything. But they still have their lives. Was it because of you? Did you fight off that dragon? No! So, if you want to try to fight a man that controls lightning itself, go ahead and try!"

"Maybe we should . . ." one of the soldiers behind whispered up to the soldier, still glowering and clenching his sword tightly.

"Think about your next move," Adler said with a wry smile. "We will defend ourselves if that's our only choice."

"There are more important things than a measly arrest warrant," Corvaire said. "These people need to find food and shelter for the foreseeable future. If they're going to rebuild, they could use your help. They'd be grateful, I'm sure."

The soldier's posture relaxed slightly.

"What'll you do?" asked one of the women standing off to the side—her face was caked in ash.

"We ride for Atlius," Corvaire said, making the soldier's face grow pale.

"You ask us to stay here and help these people, who aren't even our own, and you go to ride to our city?"

"Yes," Corvaire said in a stern voice. "We have important business to attend to there. We must free another who wields magic like mine. We're assembling a force to fight off those dragons, so what happened here may never happen again."

"You can't be serious," said the soldier, with spit flinging from his angry lips.

"Deadly."

"Listen," Adler said, putting both palms out again. "We don't need to fight between ourselves. There're more important things to worry about. And besides, you can tell your old lordy we got away when the dragon swooped in. Hell, tell him you fought the thing away."

"Who you after in Atlius with magic—like you say?" the soldier sneered with one eye nearly shut.

"That's none of your concern," Corvaire said.

"I know who you're speaking of," the soldier said. "Nearly died she did."

Ceres felt the hairs on her head tingle, and her heart skip a beat.

"She's the one who burned down Serenity's Tavern, she did. Burned it down with dark magic. A witch she is."

"She's no witch!" Ceres spat. "She's kind and gentle. Saved our lives more than once from gruesome, rat-tailed, runny-nosed soldiers like you!"

"Watch your tongue," the soldier spat back. "We're soldiers of Atlius. You'd be best to not talk to us like that. The lord asked for you to be brought in alive, but I don't mind the other way. You'd be quieter if you were cold."

"Don't speak to her like that!" Adler said, unsheathing his sword with a sharp ringing from the Masummand Steel. "I don't care who you hail from or what colors you bare. Speak of that again and I lop that head clear from your shoulders."

The soldier's beady eye glared at the mirror-like steel in his hand.

"Where'd you get a sword like that?"

"None of your concern," Adler said. "Now, like my friend over here said. We're going to be off. You do whatever you need to do, but we are leaving."

"You will most definitely not," the soldier said. The soldiers behind him were visibly uneasy as the crowds moved slowly toward them.

"Let 'em go!" someone yelled from the crowd. It was quickly followed by others encouraging the same.

"This is business of Lord Daamend," he yelled back at them. "Keep to your own affairs!"

"C'mon," Adler said, turning and beginning to walk away.

The beady-eyed soldier's face reddened, and he lunged for Adler, but to his surprise, he felt strong arms holding him back.

"Sir," one of the soldiers behind said, as all three of them held him back. "Now's not the time. We'll get them later."

"Let me go," he said, fighting their restraint.

But before his eyes, many of the town's folk stepped between him and Adler, Corvaire and Ceres who were walking away in the woods as the city continued to burn on the east side of the trees.

"Let me go! Let me go!"

"We'll need to make haste to beat them to Atlius and free Marilyn before they do," Corvaire said.

"Do you think it was wise to tell them about her?" Adler asked. "If they send a raven, we'll be walking into a trap."

"Ya think those twits know how to send a raven?" Ceres asked.

"Fair point," he said.

"I think they'll make the choice to stay and help these people," Corvaire said. "Once their heads cool."

"I wish we could stay and help," Ceres said.

"Me too," Corvaire said, getting to his horse and digging his boot into the leather stirrup. "But we've got a war to fight, and Marilyn is going to play a large part."

Ceres mounted her horse gingerly, stroking the thick mane of Angelix.

After Adler mounted, he leaned over to her.

"What did you get from the market? I'm as famished as a fish in the dessert."

She opened the bag to reveal the items she'd purchased. He reached in and broke off a piece of bread and ate it ravenously.

"Let's be off," Corvaire said. "We've got days to ride before we reach the city."

They clicked their heels on the horses' sides and rode south at a steady gallop as the dragonfires roared behind them, whipping and crackling in the wind as a stark reminder of what lay for all the lands if they failed in their fight against the Dark King.

Chapter Thirteen

Stone had killed animals before. Hell, he'd even killed men by that point. But looking an innocent cow in the eye, it was never easy for him. Hunger pinged in all their stomachs, and the cow's milk satiated their overwhelming drive to eat. But that cow would make for one of the best meals they'd eaten in over that long month on the road.

The buildings had been burned and broken to piles of ashen rubble, but they found a fire pit with an iron griddle still atop it.

And as the fresh-cut steaks sizzled upon it, Stone found himself licking his lips. Hydrangea had also been lucky enough to find a jar of salt that had been thrown from the attack into a grassy glade.

His hands, even though he'd washed them in the stream, were still stained with the blood from the butchery. And even in the dim last light of the fading sun—he could feel the cows eying him wearily.

In part it was the enticing smells of the fat of the meat falling onto the fire with sharp hisses, and the urgency to put a piece of meat into their mouth that wasn't that of a rodent, but

Stone pulled a sharply cut piece of ribeye from the griddle, sliced it up with his sword with its deep red still inside, and each of them laid it eagerly on their tongues.

Gracelyn had a euphoric look on her face as her eyes rolled up, and she let out a deep moan. Lucik and Hydrangea did the same. Mud sat, with his tail wagging wildly, and as a piece was thrown to him, he jumped, swallowing it in just a few bites. He sat back down quickly, acting as if he'd never gotten the first piece.

Each of them filled their bellies to the point of unease—except Mud, who was still cleaning bones off to the side.

The weather was cool, yet without a blanket over them they found themselves fine to lay on their backs looking up at the countless stars above.

Lucik and Hydrangea were both dozed off, breathing in deep breaths, obviously in deep sleep.

Stone heard Gracelyn stand, gather her blanket, and carry it over next to him. She laid it on top of the grass to his left with a rustle, laid upon it with a lighthearted groan. She lay there for a splendid moment without any talking for one of those rare times where Stone didn't have a care in the world.

"What are you thinking about?" Stone asked.

She sighed. "Nothing. It's nice."

She turned her head to look at him.

"You know, there's something special about you," she said with her knowing eyes.

"About me? There's nothing special about me. You're the one who can stop dragons with your magic."

"No." She waved his response away with a flick of her wrist and looked back up the endless sky. "I'm not talking about the prophecy, or about you maybe being able to wield the power of the Elessior. I can sense something in you. You will do great things . . . at least, that's what I feel."

He didn't know how to respond to her. He just wanted to

wave her off, but there was something about the way she said things sometimes—something that made her feel like some sort of—god.

"You're just saying that because I cooked you supper," he jested. Which made her laugh, with the whites of her teeth lit in the sheen of the moon.

"Do you feel that you know your role in all this now?" he asked. "I mean, I struggle to believe what the Old Mothers told me about my role. Do you feel you are what you are supposed to be?"

"I am what I am." Her face was unchanged as she looked up at the glittering sky.

"But you weren't who you are supposed to be only two months ago. You were just you then, but you were at home with your family. You do realize you're changed now. Right?"

"Yes," she said. "I know I'm different. I'm me from before, and I'm me now. Change is life. I've changed to protect this world. So have you."

"Do you worry at all, that there's no going back after this though?" he asked, scratching his stubbly chin.

"There's no going back for us," she said coldly. "There's nothing for you to go back to anyways." She seemed to sense his withdrawal from her answer and livened her tone. "I have faith. I have faith that we will get out of this alive, you'll be free to discover yourself, and I believe you'll be able to find your father someday."

"I hope so," he said after a deep sigh. He put his hand behind his head and looked up at a bright shining star above. I don't talk about it much. But it's all I think about sometimes. It's really frustrating not knowing who you are and where you came from. I feel worthless sometimes. Especially being away from my friends. I'm told I have purpose, but I can't help but feel deep down inside of myself, that I've got no purpose at all."

She turned and looked at him again, grabbing him by the hand.

"Your time to shine is coming. Like a diamond unearthed, caked in dirt and debris, you'll be cleansed of your doubt, and you will shine in the light of the heavens."

Her eyes were wild, dazzling and piercing. Stone was entranced by them—forgetting everything except their beauty.

She feigned and moved onto her side, facing opposite of him.

"But until then, keep your head on your shoulders," she said. "I'm going to get some shuteye. We're going to enter the mountain tomorrow. Thanks for cooking."

"Goodnight," he said as Mud snuggled up in between his legs. He stayed up for the better part of two hours thinking about what she'd said—about how he'd find his father someday.

Would I be reuniting with him? Or would I be meeting him for the first time? Why can't I remember? Why can't I just remember?

༒

INCHING their way down the cliffs below the entrance of the city, the chilly sea air hit their nostrils with a ting. The rocks were still cool to the touch, even though lit in the early rays of the rising sun. They knew not what they were searching for—other than some sort of entrance into the cave.

Mud meandered around the rocks—mostly looking for food. In each of their packs they'd gathered torch sticks from the town that were strewn around in the grasses.

The four of them had split up, all within eyeshot of one another, and Stone was lower than the rest. His long black hair was down—unusual for him—as it tickled his neck and nose.

Where is it? It's got to be around here somewhere.

"Anything up there?" he hollered up.

"Nothing yet," Hydrangea said. Her tan, bare strong arms glistened out from under the leather armor that clung to her chest and back.

Lucik was nearly out of sight, climbing up and to the left. Gracelyn was standing upon the trail they'd taken up from the olive tree to Endo, gazing up and down the sheer cliffs.

I've been over this path four times now in total, I'm beginning to doubt that we're looking in the right place at all. But the Old Mothers were making their way down in this direction. For the life of me—why isn't it here?

Mud barked from up above, which garnered his attention. Most likely he'd found another squirrel or mountain goat. But, even with the constant barking, Stone couldn't find him.

"Gracelyn," he shouted. "You see him?"

After a moment of gazing, she called down, "No."

"Where'd he go off too?" he muttered to himself, climbing back up the path.

Lucik had climbed back toward him with her gaze curiously upon him.

Stone wound up, with his fingers clenched upon each sharp rock as he climbed. The barking was getting louder—he was getting closer.

He turned a corner around a large boulder, inching along a narrow path with a long drop on one side, leading to jagged rocks at its base far below.

The dog's eyes met his, and he barked twice more at Stone, who made his way onto the ledge that opened into a wider base of rock, covered by a large overhanging stone. Mud sat and wagged his tail.

Stone looked deeper into the base and saw a deep black at the back of it. "Good boy." He petted the dog's scruffy fur at the side of his neck.

. . .

He knew he wouldn't be able to see any of the others from that angle around the rock walls, so he yelled out. "He found it. It's down here!"

They made their way to the cave carefully, and finally when Lucik was the last to enter onto the base of rock—Stone had already gotten his torch alight. They held out their own and he knocked his into theirs.

"Ready?" he asked.

With no response, and only expressions on their faces that showed their determination—for they all knew this was their final destination. This was what they had come all this way for. This was why they split their forces so that their friends were halfway across the continent without them.

Stone walked toward the cave with its entrance a crack in the mountain that rose twelve feet high and snaked up to the right. Once he got there, he found it was wide enough to fit both shoulders through, but not much more than that. Corvaire perhaps would have to turn sideways to squeeze through.

Entering the darkness, the light of torch flickered upon the high walls on both sides of him. Shadows lurked below as his boots found uneasy footing upon the smooth, wet stones. As the cave opened up, giving him more room to walk—he heard trickling water far down below as it echoed up.

Eventually he noticed that the pathway had turned to a staircase of chiseled rock.

This must be it—this has to be the right cave.

Mud ran down the stairs that veered to the left up ahead as the dripping sound of water grew louder.

As the torchlight crept around the bend, it illuminated the two walls on both sides of him, but stopped six feet down, opening into a dark void. Mud barked again, and it rang out within a deep pocket of darkness.

At the bottom of the steps was a drop in the rocks about

four feet down. Stone leaped down carefully, turning to help Gracelyn. He held his hand out for her, and she leaped herself.

"This is it," she spoke softly. "In here is where the Majestic Wilds keep their work."

Stone helped the others down, and Lucik and Hydrangea both walked down opposite sides of the open, dark area. Stone walked behind Gracelyn as she took slow steps into the darkness. From each side behind them the room glowed. Stone looked to see each of them lighting pedestals of stone—each four-sided with intricate carvings on each side, and at their top was a round basin of what looked like copper, and a well of a liquid that burned with a bluish hue.

As they lit those basins, the entire area glowed, as if from below even.

Stone couldn't put into words what had appeared before him, and his mouth hung open and he stopped in his tracks.

Gracelyn continued walking toward it though.

"This is the true city of the Mystics," she said. "This is the real Endo Valaire. We've made it."

Chapter Fourteen

With a glowing blue light tinged with a warming orange hue, the city before them emerged from the shadow. High towers rose to the top of the cave that was at least one hundred feet above their heads. Carefully laid stones of white were polished smoothly upon their round walls.

Before the three towers of equal high was a barbican—a square structure with high walls thirty feet high and corbels on each of its corners with battlements throughout the tops of the wall. A large gate of iron was closed at its center. Finally, he noticed that the streaming water he'd heard before was from a slow trickle of cold water from the left side of the cave, feeding a moat around the barbican.

"It's a fortress," Lucik said with awestruck words.

"It looks like it hasn't aged a day," Hydrangea said. "It appears it was just erected."

"Many thousands of years this place has stood," Gracelyn said in that same hollow wise tone she used when that new knowledge crept into her.

"The gate's closed," Lucik said. "We need to find a way to open it."

Each of them looked to Gracelyn, who strode toward the glowing city of blue. They followed eagerly.

As they approached and the three circular towers which emanated with that same warm blue through their many thin windows that wound up them—the fortress grew ominously higher. The dark moat was eerily still below their feet as they walked across the creaky wooden bridge.

The front gate was thick, black iron which bore an unusual crest that Stone had never seen before. With two delicate hands on either side, they cupped three different spheres that aligned vertically between them. Two were immediately recognizable—the beaming sun with its rays hung highest, and at the bottom was a crescent moon—but the sphere in the middle was like a moon, but held two crescents, one on top and one on its bottom. And in its center was a thin slit that looked almost like . . . an eye.

"Do you recognize that?" Lucik asked Gracelyn warily.

"I'm not sure," Gracelyn said, letting her fingers glide along the hand on the symbols' left side. "It looks somewhat familiar, but I'm not exactly sure what it means."

Hydrangea walked up and pushed on the strong iron doors with her shoulder. It didn't so much as budge, let along creak. Stone had a feeling it was no ordinary gate.

"This one at the top is the sun, and that's the moon," Lucik said. "But what's that one in the center? Stone, you ever seen this before? Up in the city above perhaps?"

He shook his head, glaring at the symbol, trying to recall in fact if he had seen it ever before.

"It's three lines," Lucik said to herself with her fingers on her chin and her lips pursed. "The one in the middle resembles an eye, and I don't know what the other two look like? Eyelids?"

"The eye is a symbol for wisdom," Hydrangea said, stepping back from the unrattled gate.

"Is it a clue?" Stone asked. "Is it a riddle to get in?"

"I don't think so," Gracelyn said. Her thick, dark hair seemed to catch a breeze over her shoulder. "I believe it's a symbol for something. Something very old. Something lost over of the ages. But it feels familiar."

Something ancient but familiar? So, it's something she knows, but is ancient . . . What could that be?

A spark hit him then. "Gracelyn . . . could it be . . . the Elessior?"

She turned and gave a knowing smile at the corner of her mouth. Her hazel eyes caught his with a magical sparkle.

She faced the door once again and pressed her palm against the symbol. Her tan fingers covered all three symbols and were framed by the two hands that cupped hers.

"*Frosce Contacton,*" she muttered.

He heard a crackling sound emit from her hand as a white frost captured the symbols, spreading out from her hand cracking and popping like walking on a frozen stream. The frost spread from her hand, covering the symbol, and each of them watched until the gate was completely covered in a thin layer of white, delicate ice.

"I don't hear anything," Lucik said after a moment.

A low shudder sounded before them, like a thick metal latch being popped on the other side of the door. There was a piercing crack at the center of the door, snapping the ice in two. Gracelyn pulled her hand back and each of them stepped away from the gate.

With a slow, grinding noise, the gate split and opened outwards with a low moan. The two doors opened to reveal a sparkling light peaking between them. As the doors fully opened, the light faded to reveal the interior of a castle, completely free of dust or dirt, with a welcoming feeling, inviting them to enter.

Mud ran into the city, darting into an alley.

"He does that," Stone said playfully.

"It's amazing a place like this has stood as long as it has," Lucik said. "Not interrupted by the rest of the world. I wonder how many know of this place?"

"Not many," Hydrangea guessed.

The three towers shot upward toward the top of the cavern, while below were dozens of buildings and small houses of that same white, polished stone. Each of their walls were cast in the calming blue light, and the first thing Stone wondered was—if there were soft beds in any of those buildings.

Entering into the fortress of Endo, their wet boots hit the smooth stones that paved the roads of the city, even the alleys he saw. Between each of the cracks of the stones the blue aura crept warmly through.

"This place must have cost a mountain of gold to build," Lucik said in awe. "For this to exist without droves of people walking the streets and paying taxes, even a king would have a more than hard time financing something like this."

"You forget it's magical," Gracelyn said with a wave of her hand. "I'm sure any of the kings would love to get their greedy mitts on this place."

"Where do we start first?" Stone asked with a loud yawn he should have tried to muffle, but didn't, with outstretched arms.

"You may go find a place to rest if you wish," Gracelyn said. "It should be safe here. I feel as if the Elessior is flowing through this place like blood through veins. She watches over us. That's why we had to use its own magic to enter."

Stone looked back and was startled by what he saw.

"The gate," he murmured with a hard swallow. "It's closed. I didn't hear even a whisper from it."

"Yes," Lucik said. "I believe we will be safe here. Now I'm going to heed Stone's battle cry and find a bed of my own for these aged bones."

"You're not aged." Hydrangea smiled. "But I'm going to go off with Gracelyn. Don't think I could close my eyes for a second I'm so anxious to see what this place holds."

"I think we'll start over there," Gracelyn said, pointing to an octagonal building at the base of the center tower. It had cathedral-like windows that rose to stiff points and had ornamentally woven brass throughout them. The glass reflected that warm blue. Above the building rose a high spire that buttressed down with a golden metal piece at its peak that resembled a leaf to Stone.

"We'll head over there after I've gotten some shuteye," Stone said. Him and Lucik walked to a homely looking structure to the right, with two stories, had an angled roof of tile, and an awning with wooden rocking chairs underneath.

They split up, and as they popped the latch and entered the building there was a musty smell of old air. Fresh air whooshed throughout its walls from the outside and they found a kitchen with dustless counters, a basin of fresh-smelling water and a pantry with dried beans, rice, coffee beans and tea leaves.

Stone's mouth dropped. "I'm never leaving this place."

An hour later after he had a belly full of rice and warm tea, he laid in a bed that looked freshly made in a room off to the corner of the house. Once he removed his clothes, laid his head back on the pillow, Mud came prancing into the room. He laid next to Stone.

Stone dropped his hand over the side of the bed and brushed the back of his neck. He hadn't laid in a bed for as long as he could remember. It felt like he was lying in a cloud. The way the soft sheets brushed up against the skin on his legs prickled the back of his neck and he grinned wildly.

He drifted quickly off to sleep.

There were many strange things about the city within the mountain, and as Stone rose, wiping the sleep from his eyes he realized he had no idea what time of day or night it was. He could have slept three hours or three days. Mud was still asleep at his side—so it most likely wasn't the latter.

Not knowing what room Lucik had ducked into to rest, he got up and made himself some coffee before going off to find Gracelyn. Walking through the streets, he felt that unfamiliar feeling of safety, which he reminded himself was only an illusion. No matter where he went, he knew the Dark King was plotting and waiting.

He remembered the offer Salus Greyhorn, the Vile King, had made to him. If Stone wanted to know the truth about Arken and how to kill him, he'd have to offer Gracelyn allegiance to him. *No way that is happening while I still draw breath.*

It was nearly a half mile to the building with the cathedral windows and spire, and it felt good to stretch his legs out again. Mud trotted along next to him, sniffing and peeing on the corners of nearly every building they passed.

He found the large wooden doors to the building were opened wide and entered the eight-sided room that was completely without inner walls. It had a second story that wrapped around the outer walls with dozens of white columns supporting it.

Hydrangea was immediately visible at the center of the building with her head drooped onto a table surrounded by a half dozen thick books opened. On both levels of the building were perhaps hundreds of shelves of books, packed to the brim.

"It's a library," Stone muttered. "Can you even fathom how much knowledge is shelved here?" He couldn't tell if he was talking to Mud or himself.

He walked over to a spiral staircase in one of the corners of the room to make his way up to the second floor. He was looking for Gracelyn. Meandering through the aisles of shelves, half-looking for her, half-marveling at the ancient texts with pristine spines—as if they'd never been touched.

She came around a corner as he was running his fingers down a book titled, *Twelve Ways to Kill an Ogre.*

"Ogres are real?" he whispered to himself.

As she turned the corner into the aisle, he turned to look at her as her chin was pressed into a pile of books she was carrying.

"You've been busy," he said.

"Take these," she said, pushing the pile toward his chest. "These are for you to read first."

"Oh, thanks," he said. "What are these for?"

"These are things you'll need to study up on if you're going to become powerful enough to defeat Arken."

Holding the pile, he glanced at a few of the titles: *The Habits of Dragons, The Arts of the Elessior Volume I,* and . . . *Cooking Delicacies of the Road.*

He raised an eyebrow at her on the last one.

"If we're going to be going to war," she said with a wink. "It doesn't mean we have to eat poorly."

Chapter Fifteen

※

They'd ridden for eight days to finally get to the hill that loomed over the city of ruins that used to be the capital of the Worforgon. It would only be two or three more days ride to reach the city of Atlius to the south.

Their horses grazed as the three of them looked down upon the castle that looked like nothing could live there except the ghosts of the fallen. Piles of heavy stones lay in rubble beneath what used to be a towering palace. Overgrown grass and weeds overtook what used to be the hundreds of dwellings and homes surrounding the castle.

Ceres remembered the first time they saw the Dark King upon his Neferian. She remembered the first time she heard the horrible shriek of the beast. They'd witnessed his dark dragon devouring the head of another dragon in a terribly gory battle. She swallowed hard.

"We'll ride down in the morning," Corvaire said, bringing down his pipe from his lips and letting out a bellow of pungent smoke.

Above the ruins of Aderogon, dark clouds loomed low while the sun was shining its last rays to the west.

"Let's make camp for the night." He scratched the dark hairs on his angled chin.

"You don't want to try to find shelter down there?" Adler asked, after taking down big gulps from his canteen.

"You ever been down there?" Ceres asked him. He shook his head. "It's no place for the living. That's where I found Stone when I was scavenging for anything worthwhile to sell. Didn't find nothin' but broken stones and damned dragons."

"Aye," Corvaire said. "I've heard nothing but bad tales about the city after its destruction."

"Another war taken too far," Adler said coldly. "How many died in the siege on the palace? Thousands? Tens of thousands?"

"Will these lands never know peace?" Ceres scratched her thigh as a cool wind whipped through, blowing the grass at her ankles.

"If we succeed," Corvaire said. "Then we will have a chance for it." He turned and took down the saddle from his black mare. Ceres did the same to Angelix, and Adler went to making a fire. They ate bread, cheese, and smoky dried meat again, and Ceres was first for the nightly lookout.

Those nights, after so many hours on horseback, the others would be quickly off to slumber.

As the clouds blew by quickly overhead, and the sheen of starlight sparkled, Ceres prodded the fire with a long stick. She glared, nearly in a trance, at the smoldering wood crumbling as it popped and crackled. The horses neighed while they dreamt.

While she stared into the flames, she thought of the last time she'd been in the city. Ceres remembered the muffled sound of the screams and cries she'd heard beneath the ground in that graveyard below. She wanted to run away, after all, what good could come from digging up a grave? But there was something inside of her telling her that she *needed* to dig it up. She *needed* to free whatever was below. That was the first time she'd met Ghost too, she was the one who helped her free Stone.

Hedron's head perked up and the horse gazed north.

Ceres jumped to her feet, looking out in the darkness. Clouds concealed the moon's rays, but as she scanned out in the tall grass, the clouds parted to let the bright moon shine down.

Hedron was still laying but looking north. Not startled enough to rise, his dark eyes were unblinking.

Ceres still saw nothing and wasn't alarmed enough to wake the others behind her. But then, she saw something move about thirty feet out. It was well hidden, but in the swaying grass, it only sat like a rock. She'd seen it before. At its crown, two faint reflections on dark glass gleamed in the moonlight.

She took a deep breath. With a wide stance, and her hands held out before her, she gathered her Indiema, thinking of her parents and the beautiful—and tragic—memories she had of them. Her head swelled with emotion and her heart raced. She let out a long exhale.

"*Vinitulas Windum Granum,*" she whispered in an enchanting voice.

Concentrating hard on the words, she extended her fingers out in the direction of what had startled Hedron awake. Feeling the magic flowing through her fingertips, she focused on the object that looked like no more than a rock.

Then she felt it connect like thread wrapping around a needle's eye.

The rock jolted, shifting to the right, then shaking its head to the left. It tried to spring into the air but snapped back to the ground quickly.

That's when the shrieking started.

Adler and Corvaire were both startled awake, each snatching their swords in their hands.

The shrieking and crying spilled through the air as Ceres

continued to keep her fingers and gaze fixed toward the shadow creature that was desperately trying to jump away—but found itself being trapped.

"What? What's going on?" Adler asked in a rushed voice. "Are we under attack?"

"No," she said in a strained voice. "But if you want to know what's been following us all this time, I suggest you go find out while I still hold it."

Corvaire and Adler ran toward the creature that was howling in a high pitch, letting its voice crack as it wailed.

A white glow flowed up Corvaire's left arm as he readied a surge of lightning if he commanded it.

They were halfway to the creature as it tried to spring free as it gave out a high-pitched squeal and moan. Ceres took slow steps forward but focused her Indiema deep within herself.

Adler huffed and puffed as they ran at full speed through the tall grass and sprang over boulders in the night.

The creature saw them, and with dark, wide eyes full of dread it dug at the vines that wrapped tightly around its legs and torso. It howled as it clawed at them, but as the sharp tips of their swords were thrust at its neck—only stopping just before they pierced its thick flesh, the creature's eyes rolled back, and it let out a faint sob.

"Free me," it moaned in a raspy, yet articulated voice.

The two of them looked at the creature as it sobbed, with the vines still growing to wrap around its chest and shoulders.

"She's going to be so disappointed in me. So disappointed . . ." it cried to itself.

"What is it?" Adler asked with a raised eyebrow.

"It may be," Corvaire said. "*Who* is it?"

Ceres made her way over to the patch of grass, and she instantly felt a lump in her throat as the sound of the whimpering creature, sobbing to itself.

Looking at the knobby-shouldered creature as it rocked in a

cradled ball with its hairy arms clutching onto its shins—it almost looked *human* to her . . . almost.

"What are you?" Corvaire said in a stern voice, letting the cold, flat edge of his sword press onto the creature's back. "Your crying will not make us free you. You've stalked us how long under the starry skies?"

It continued to sob, sniffly sobs. "She's going to be upset with me. So upset. You don't understand."

"Who is she?" Ceres asked, still not letting the vines release it from her grasp. She'd seen how quickly the creature could bound off into the dark fields under the cover of night.

". . . So upset with me . . ."

Adler lifted his boot and kicked it in the knobby shoulder—not hard, but hard enough to make it turn its head and let out a loud hiss at him. Adler and Ceres took abrupt steps back.

The eyes of the creature were as black as tar. They were wide and bulbous. It was bald with a pointed head and had a thin, bird beak nose. Its mouth was wide with thin lips and its skin was thick, wrapped on its thin frame. Its arms were proportional to its torso—like that of a man, but they could see its legs—and even though they were bound in the thick vines, they were thin and long. It was wearing pants, tattered and stained, that covered its very long, reptilian legs.

"What are you?" Adler gasped.

The creature snapped at him again, hissing with its thin teeth showing.

"We're not gonna let ya' go until you tell us who you are and why you're following us," Ceres said. "We don't want to hurt you, unless ya' give us reason ta'."

"You tried to kill me!" it groaned. "That one!" It pointed at Corvaire. "Tried to sear me alive! Like a shrimp in hot oil!"

"We have no idea of your intentions," Corvaire said. "You know what's going on in these lands. Why would we not think you were doing harm, slinking in the shadows like you do."

"Because the light burns my eyes," it said softly.

"Who are you?" Ceres asked. "You must have a name."

It tried one last time to leap away, but Ceres tightened the vine's grip on him, pulling it down farther toward the dirt.

"M—Mogel. My name is Mogel . . . There! Happy?"

"Where do you come from Mogel?" Corvaire commanded. "And who was the *she* you were talking about?"

"Free me," Mogel said in a raspy voice. "Free me of these plants and I'll tell you."

"Not a chance," Adler said. "You'd be leaping off before that last vine even left your frog legs."

"They aren't frog legs you twit!" it barked. "Do I look like a frog to you?"

"Well . . ." Adler said in a snarky voice.

"I'm a Skell. You've never heard of Skells?" His eyes were narrow, showing a more refined side to the creature as he let a smirk cross his face.

"A Skell?" Adler asked himself.

"Aye," Corvaire said. "That makes sense now. Though I've never seen one of your kind before."

"Corvaire?" Ceres asked. "You know what he is?"

"Not exactly," he said. "Not until this moment. They're a people from the far east. But they live on an island in the middle of the sea, isn't that right? How are you here?"

Mogel's grin widened. "I'm sure you'd love to know the answer to that . . . Wouldn't you?"

"Tell us," Adler steamed.

"I—I can't," Mogel said, letting his smile fade.

Adler and the Skell were locked in a heated glare.

Ceres went over and knelt by the creature.

"Ceres, don't," Corvaire said. "We still don't know his intentions."

"Or he could be a liar," Adler said.

"Mogel, I promise I will release you if you answer a few of our questions."

"I know I could trust you, Ceres," Mogel said. "But I don't like that one." Looking at Adler. "Not one bit."

"He's an . . . acquired taste," she said. "Now, tell us, who is *she*? Is she the one you work for?"

"I've been following you," Mogel sighed, "because she wants me to watch you, keep you safe. She wants to know what the Mystics wanted with you, and with Stone."

"You know his name?" she asked, taking a slow step back.

"I know all of your names," he said. "As do all of the kings and queens. You've got a reputation. Arken trying to kill you hasn't gone unnoticed."

Ceres stirred back to her feet. "Well, you seem to know about us, and you've followed us far enough. Do you know where we are goin' and why then?"

"You believe your friend is held in Atlius."

"I'm confused." Adler shook his head. "How could you know that?"

Mogel raised his hand to point to his pointed ear.

"He knows too much," Adler said. "We can't let him talk about what's he heard."

"This isn't good for you," Corvaire said. "If you've been spying to leak information. You need to tell us who you work for. Was it Salus? Was it the Vile King?"

"Salus," Mogel spat. "I'd never side with that worm."

"Then who?" Ceres asked, raising her hand, and letting her magical fire glow.

"It's." He sneered. "And it's not those bumbling kings either." He let out a deep sigh. "It was . . . the Queen. Queen Tritus."

"Queen Tritus?" Corvaire gasped. "Why would the queen send out her own spy? You've come all the way from Dranne to follow us?"

"Why would the queen send out her own spy?" Ceres asked. "Surely the king has plenty."

Mogel smiled again. "The queen is not after the same prospects as her husband. While they focus on their skirmish with their war. Queen Angelica knows what the true war is—and the real war that must be won."

"So you feed information back to her?" Adler said. "There's no way you could make it to Dranne and back. You must be sending ravens."

Mogel nodded with thick wrinkles in his forehead.

"What have you told her?" Adler said, flashing the moonlight off a twist of his sword.

"I've told her everything I know," Mogel said. "But don't worry, she's not telling the king anything. He wouldn't listen if she tried."

"How do we know what you're telling to be truthful?" Adler asked. "What proof do you have?"

They all eagerly awaited his answer.

"You do see," Mogel said, still wrapped in the vines, "I didn't come here simply to spy on you. The queen has sent me to aid you. The Skells have abilities that humans don't."

"Aid us?" Adler sneered. "Why would we want your help?"

"I've also been watching over you while you camp at night in the wilderness. I covered your tracks in the forest when the Runtue riders sought you out. I helped the Assassin's Guild find you when the Runtue finally caught up with you. I've hidden your tracks more times than I can count."

"Liar," Adler said. "You didn't do those things."

"How would he know about them?" Ceres asked.

"Because he's been listening to every word we've said."

"And . . ." Mogel said. "Because if your friend is indeed alive, I'm going to help you get her out so you can get back to the real war. You need to get back to Stone and Gracelyn. You're going to have to find the other new Majestics when they are born. I'll show you the safest way to get into the city of Atlius. If you didn't notice from just a few soldiers back there that spotted you quickly—word has spread of you. Everyone in Atlius knows of the bounty on your heads."

"So, if we release you," Ceres asked. "You're not going to run away? You're going to help us save Marilyn? Do you promise this?"

"I cannot help you under that bastard sun," he said, "but under shade of night. I will help you. If you must save her so you may continue the fight, then I will assist you in her rescue."

Chapter Sixteen

❧

"You know we can't trust him, right?" Adler sipped on a hot mug of tea while the cool dew clung to grass blades that tickled his ankles in the early morning light.

"He didn't pounce off when I undid the spell that bound him," Ceres said, brushing her hair with a coarse brush. "Mogel stayed and talked freely to us. I don't know if I trust him, but he kept his word about that. And he may help us to free her."

Corvaire was off at a nearby stream cleaning himself, as the horses grazed in a circle around the smoldering last breaths of the fire.

"He said it himself," Adler steamed. "He's a spy!"

"For the queen, not the kings."

"Same thing!"

"Maybe," she said. "At least he's not working for Arken, though—or Salus."

"He could be sending a raven at this very moment to send a legion down to kill us," Adler said, spitting on the ground next to him.

"Are you mad . . . at me for this?" she asked with a raised eyebrow.

He swallowed hard. "Well . . . no. I'm just, um . . ."

"We all agreed to let him go," she said, getting up to her feet to loom over him. He shifted back. "If you need to take this out on someone, why don't you take it out on him!" She pointed to Corvaire as he bathed. "Or take it out on yerself! You coulda lopped his head off if ya wanted!" She leaned into him with her finger extended not even an inch from her face. "I don't trust him—not yet. But I'm getting sick of you taking your tantrums out on others. You need to grow up, Adler. Act like a man, not a little boy takin' his problems out on others."

Adler's face paled, and his eyes darted around, trying to collect what to say to her, but no words formed.

She leaned back on her log by the fire, warming her hands. "I wish I had some sweets to go with this bland tea."

An hour later they were back on their horses heading south toward the city they'd never wished to see again—the city that took Marilyn from them.

"Two more days ride," Adler said later in the afternoon, almost speaking to himself. "Mogel said he'd come back to us under the night sky and tell us more about how he was going to get us in to rescue her. We'll see if he does or not."

"We'll see," Ceres said in a flat tone.

"What do you think about all this?" Adler asked Corvaire, whose black hair whipped over his shoulder in the wind and his freshly shaven face revealed the tan his face had received after so many days out on the road, by the pale skin that had been hidden under his beard. "What do you know about the Skell?"

"I assumed he is telling the truth that he is working for someone," he said. "For a Skell to sail across the sea to get here, there must have been one of the mightiest ships of the fleet of Dranne to get him here. I've never heard a tale of a Skell that liked the water—let alone sailing. Someone paid a lot of coin to enlist his service. I only wish that service wasn't following us. The queen would have the fortune to do that if she wished. But there are others too that could pay that amount of coin. For the life of me though, I don't know why a Skell would need such a fortune. Didn't even know they knew a taber from a marble."

"This whole thing stinks to me," Adler said, throwing his hood back and wiping his forehead with a kerchief.

"He didn't really care for you either," Ceres laughed.

"What if we just found our own way into the city?" Adler asked. "Wasn't that the whole plan all along?"

"Yes," Corvaire said, "and no."

"What do you mean?" Adler asked.

"I didn't know the extent to which Lord Bjorn wanted you still. And with your more recent celebrities, getting into the city would be a fool's errand. Now, with your sighting at the burning of Hedgehorn and my battle with the Neferian, word must've spread that you were near Atlius. Bjorn will undoubtedly be sending out scouts."

"But we saved so many people up there," Adler said. "That must count for something. He should let us go!"

Corvaire gave a rare laugh. "Seems you know little of the scorn of kings."

෴

THAT EVENING, as the darkness of night flooded the sky, their fire rose dancing sparks up toward the Golden Realm above. A nervousness sat in Ceres' stomach as each of them were as curious as a starving mouse to see if Mogel would hold to his word and show up again willingly.

Hours passed, and eventually Adler gave up and turned to his side to sleep.

They'd found a large bluff that day they'd decided to camp

by, and they were then hidden behind a large stone that shielded them from the southeast to the southwest—even someone to the east would have trouble spotting them, except the thin trail of smoke that rose in the overcast, dark sky. They knew that would be their last fire until Marilyn was rescued, and they were far away back north or in the Everwood once again.

In the middle of the night, each of the horses lifted their heads to gaze into the darkness, and Angelix let out a soft neigh. Ceres and Corvaire wiped away their tiredness and rose.

"Mogel?" she asked.

The Skell man sprang high into the air, landing with a soft *putt* on the dirt just outside the ring of light that the fire cast out.

"We didn't know if you were gonna show," she said.

"I said I would come, and here I am," Mogel said. He was just lit enough for them to see him in his true, free form for the first time. He was squatting, with his forearms laying over his thighs as he bobbed slightly. His legs stretched out nearly four feet to both his sides, and that was only to the peak of his knees. Standing up, Ceres thought, *he must be ten feet tall!*

"What's your plan?" Corvaire said, as Adler stirred awake behind them. "How are you going to get us into the castle? And how do you know where she is?"

"If she's there and alive, she'll be in the dungeon of the keep," he said. "That's why I've only gotten here. A raven was sent from the messenger of the queen after I sent one last night after our talk."

"What did it say?" Corvaire asked urgently.

"There's no word of her being alive. Word traveled that she died just the way you said she did."

"But Gracelyn said—" Adler said.

"Gracelyn is a Majestic Wild," Mogel said. "I don't doubt her words. And there is a way to sneak into the castle and get to the dungeon. But I am no locksmith. I know not how to open a cell door's lock."

"Leave that to me," Adler said. "Or her?" He pointed to Ceres, who nodded.

"Meet me at a stone at the back entrance of the outer walls of the city when the moon is at its highest. The stone is two hundred yards and hidden in patches of trees and thick brush. The stone is waist high and has a black circle painted on it."

"How do we get into the castle?" Corvaire asked. "What is your safe passage? I insist you tell us."

Mogel whispered, "There's a tunnel. It's used as an escape in case of a siege. But it can be opened by the outside if you know where it is." His black eyes widened. "And *I* know where it is. It will lead us into the dungeons beneath the keep. That is how we will free your friend." He grinned wide with his thin lips under his beak of a nose.

Alder folded his arms over his chest and tightened his mouth.

"If you don't trust me, you don't have to follow me," the Skell said. "You can just walk through the front gate with your hoods over your heads and hope for the best. Again, I'm helping you because the queen wants you back with your friends. You need to be preparing for the war. You need to get to Endo Valaire so you can form the army you'll need for your fight with Arken."

Ceres let out a deep exhale. "If you are helping . . . thank you. It seems we don't really have another option. We're nearly there now. And unless there's a spell to change each of us into snakes so that we can sliver down into the lowest parts of the castle . . ."

Adler cringed, with a sharp shiver running up his spine.

"Oh, yeah, sorry," she said with a short laugh. "Forgot you hate them."

"Nasty little things," he said.

"The rock with the black painted circle," Mogel said. "When the moon is at its highest point. Don't forget."

With a spring of his wiry legs he shot off back, fifteen feet into the air, quicker than any of them would have had the reflex to draw their swords if they needed, and he disappeared out of sight.

"So," Ceres said. "I guess there's our plan."

"I suppose it is," Corvaire said. "And if he's right, it's not a bad one."

". . .If he's right," Adler said.

Adler stayed awake for lookout while the others gathered what sleep they could before their last ride for the city. He prodded the fire, looking around every once in a while for the black eyes of the Skell, but didn't find them once.

The following morning, they found themselves clinging to the side of the bluff to keep themselves out of the heavy rain. The sky thundered as lightning crashed into a field below. A dark sky hung over with thick, rolling clouds and the rain pounded into puddles, splashing their boots.

They saddled the horses and readied their last push to the city. Knowing they'd have to stay off the main roads, they'd slink their way through the edge of the forest, and then ride through the beginning of the night with hoods over their heads to the spot Mogel told them they'd meet at.

As early twilight approached, and each of them were completely soaked from the heavy raindrops falling from tree branches above, Ceres' stomach churned as the smoke of hundreds of fires from chimneys that rose above the city came into view.

The matte-gray stone of the castle shown as its windows glowed from flickering, warm candlelight. The city wasn't nearly as impressive as that of the kingdom of Verren, but it may have stood just as long, she thought. She remembered the ancient-looking roads and old awnings over aged, cracked rocks that many of the buildings were erected from.

Rising like a dagger from the city's heart, the main palace stood high above all else, fifty feet it rose, again—nowhere near Verren's keep—but a lord resided here, no king. Torches flickered around the outer walls of the city, as guards stood at each tower—watching.

"We wait here until the full cover of nightfall," Corvaire said. "Rest as best you can until then."

"Corvaire," Adler said. "There's something been bothering me today, one thing I noticed."

"There's no one on the road," Corvaire said, with his hand over his brow, shielding the rain as he scanned the city."

"Well, yeah. You noticed too?"

"It has been a gloomy day," Ceres said. "Bad for riding."

"Yes," Adler said. "But still . . ."

"Well, perhaps that's our answer," Corvaire said, looking out past the city to the far eastern sky.

"Which is it?" Ceres asked, squinting. "I can't see from here."

"I don't see a rider," Adler said. "I think it's just a dragon."

A lone, wide-winged dragon with a long tail was flying through the clouds—far past the city. But it was surely frightening enough to deter any man with a speck of brain to go out into the open plains—save for the three of them.

They waited two hours after nightfall, and then they mounted their horses yet again and strode out of the forest under the cover of night, riding on the backside of a hill to snake around the city to its backside.

It took them a half hour to find the patch of trees that Mogel must have been eluding too. Thunder rumbled through the air as the faint screech of a dragon roared behind. They'd reached the end of the hill and drove their heels into their horses' sides.

Sprinting through the darkness, tall grasses rushed past. They were nearly there, they were almost back into the trees, when a crack of lightning sparked to the east, illuminating the fields with a bellowing snap of thunder, followed by a low grumble.

"Faster," Corvaire called out, with each of them driving their heels into the horses, snapping the reins.

Moments later they flew into the trees, slowing their steeds, and instantly scanning for the stone.

"There," Ceres said. "Over there." She was pointing to a waist-high stone near the closest edge of the forest to the castle.

They rode over, inspecting it. Corvaire dropped down, tying his horse to a tree. He wiped some brush away from it, showing the faint black circle painted on its flat base side.

"Aye," he said. "This is it." He looked up at the overcast sky. Tough to tell when the moon is going to be at its . . ."

Mogel bounded in from deep inside the forest all the sudden.

"Talk about perfect timing . . ." Adler said.

"No time to waste," Mogel said with quick words. "We must find the entrance, quickly. If there's one thing I hate more than anything about your lands . . . it's dragons…"

Adler and Ceres tied their horses to trees also, and she whispered to Angelix to stay calm and to wait for them.

They followed Mogel as he walked along the forest line away from the rock. He walked in a manner that made him to have bob from side to side like a man who'd indulged in too many sweetcakes, but this was because of the length of his bent legs.

"Not far," he said. "Should be just up here. Yes, yes, here it is."

He was brushing away twigs and fallen leaves off a patch of sparse grass and mud that looked nothing out of the ordinary to any of them.

"Don't see nothin' there," Ceres said.

"Not to the unknowing eye, no," he said, as he dug two of his knobby fingers on his left hand into the mud. They slid down easily, and the stringy muscles in his arm tensed as he pulled.

Each of them eyed him curiously, and eagerly awaited to see if he'd found anything. A pop sounded from within the earth, and a line in the mud revealed itself from his two fingers as they pulled up.

A square door wide enough for a man to fit through opened slowly, as it was nearly two inches thick of iron.

"Thank Queen Tritus for this," Corvaire said.

"You weren't lying," Ceres said. "It's here."

"I told you," Mogel said.

Adler still eyed him, glaring. But quickly enough, he'd gathered his torch from under his cloak he'd been trying his best to keep dry.

The door fully opened, revealing the deep darkness below. A hinge kept it open without slamming back to the ground.

"You first," Adler said to Mogel.

"I'm not going in there," he snapped.

"What do you mean?" Adler said with his eyebrows lowered. "You said you were going to help us free her."

"I'm not going into the passageway. I never said I was going to. It leads to the dungeon. You have swords and lock picks, don't you? Skells aren't good with swords. Skells are good at sneaking in the dark. Now hurry, free her and get back here before daylight and they find she is missing. Go!"

"We have no choice now," Corvaire said. "I don't feel completely good about this either, Adler, but what choice do we have?"

"We can leave Ceres behind," Adler said. "If anything happens to us, she can ride for Endo and tell the others."

"No, I'm going," she snapped.

Corvaire was left in contemplation as he walked over to the hole.

"Light the torch," he said, "Let's get down there. We've come this far together. Let her make her own decision, but something tells me she isn't going to want to not be part of this."

She crossed her arms and stuck her tongue out at Alder.

"Fine, let's get on with this," he said.

Adler lit the torch, handed it to Corvaire, who found the wooden ladder that led down into the passage and climbed down into a low-hanging ceilings hallway held up by braces of thick wood. Ceres went down next and the Adler behind her, looking up at Mogel.

"You better be right about this," he said as he couldn't tell if the hurried expression on the creature's face was sincere or not.

Soon, they were each crouching as they hurried their way down the long, straight tunnel.

"If we run into trouble," Corvaire said. "Ceres, you cast *Juniper's Red Haze* to hide us. I'll cast *Webs that Wind*, to bind them. Remember, any sole down here wearing the colors of Atlius is our enemy. Don't hesitate, for they won't."

For another couple hundred yards they traveled underground, eventually getting to a thick section of rectangular rocks overhead.

"This must be the outer wall of the keep," Corvaire said. "We are close."

Another couple hundred yards in, and the passageway led to a dead end. Corvaire quickly began searching for a way out as Ceres' heart pounded in her chest.

"This is it," Adler said to her, grabbing her hand nervously.

Above him, Corvaire pushed the top of the passageway, which was a single, gray rock. As he shoved the rock it squeaked open. He handed the torch back to Ceres and told her to keep the light away from the opening as best she could, which she did.

Corvaire pushed the rock open enough for him to squint through. A low glow slipped through the seam in the opening.

"Drop the torch back there," Adler told her as she placed it on the ground.

Corvaire gently opened the rock door enough for Adler to hoist him up out of the passageway. He delicately laid the back of the stone door onto the ground and grabbed Adler's hand to help him up—all the while looking around.

Once Adler was up, Corvaire drew his sword and Adler turned to help Ceres up. They were all soon standing in a dark corner of the dungeon, with empty cage-like cells along both walls. There was a single, open door before them with soft candlelight on the other side.

"Ready?" Corvaire whispered. They both nodded. "Be ready for anything, and don't make a sound."

They pulled their Masummand Steel blades and followed behind him as he crept toward the door, carefully, for their footsteps to not make a sound. Ceres felt as if she could barely breathe her heart was pounding so hard in her chest. Her palms were sweaty, the humidity of the caverns made beads of sweat trickle down her brow.

Corvaire inspected the room beyond and motioned for them to follow. He entered the room, and she nervously followed behind Adler. As they made their way into the wide room, and they crept behind another empty cage in the shadows, the door behind them smashed closed, with thick locks clicking into place.

"Mogel," Adler said with full disdain. "That fucking devil! I'll kill him for this."

Corvaire was looking between the cage bars as men in armor strode into the middle of the room where a large torch lit the cavern.

"Stick together," he said to them. "Remember, show no mercy, for they will show you none."

One of the soldiers spoke strongly in a voice that rang off the cavern walls and made Ceres' heart skip a beat.

"By order of Lord Bjorn Daamend, first of his name, you are all under arrest for the murder of soldiers of the crown. Surrender your weapons and your lives may be spared."

"This guy obviously doesn't know us very well," said Adler with a sneer.

Chapter Seventeen

❧❦❧

The half dozen soldiers that had flooded into the round room wore dark gray armor with many notches and cuts from sword and spears strewn across them. Each of them wore an angular helmet that shimmered much newer in the torchlight than the rest of their armor.

Four of them brandished swords and shields and two carried long spears with barbed points and wore their swords on their hips—ready to slide from their sheathes when needed.

"Only six?" Adler sneered. "For a trap that's not bad."

Ceres turned to Corvaire to ask what spell they should ready but saw he was concentrating and moving his hand to cast a spell. He opened his mouth to speak the words, but then his eyes widened.

"Something is wrong here," he said in quick words. "Draw your sword, Adler. Ceres—your bow."

Another figure moved into the room—he was dressed the same as the others except with a red plume of feathers down the top of his helmet. He stood with a wide stance, and his fists on his hips, glaring at them behind the metal bars of the one of the empty cages.

"Your magic won't help you here," he snapped.

"What's going on?" Adler asked Corvaire. "What does he mean?"

"I can't use my Elessior," he said. "It's not coming to me when I call it. I don't know how he's doing that though."

"Is he a mage?" Ceres asked, but Corvaire just shook his head.

"I know why you're here," the captain of the soldiers said. "You came for the bitch that burned up some of my men—some of my friends."

"Where is she?" Corvaire called out.

The soldier turned his head back and whistled loudly, letting it ring down the corridor behind him.

From the dim tunnel walked a frail woman with her head drooped low. Her hands were bound behind her and her tattered dress rustled at her knees. Her feet were caked in dirt and her skin was ashen.

"Marilyn?" Corvaire murmured. "What have they done to you?"

"Go ahead," the captain of the soldiers sneered. "Say hello, why don't ya?"

The woman raised her head weakly as he said that.

A frightful well of pain lurched in Ceres' stomach at the sight of her friend.

Moving her head from side to side, Marilyn's eyes were covered in a dirty blindfold, her head was recently shaven, and as she opened her mouth and tried to speak, they could see her tongue had been removed.

"You monsters," Ceres gasped.

"You think we keep witches with spells that can destroy an entire building without taking from them that which could kill us all with a single word?" The soldier laughed. "The only reason she's alive was we'd hoped you'd be foolish enough to come back so that you may be punished for your treason."

"And Mogel," Adler snapped, through near-clenched teeth. "He works for you?"

"No," the soldier said. "He only just came to us hours ago."

"What's he talking about?" Ceres whispered to Adler.

"He sold us out," Adler said.

"The creature heard about the bounty on your heads," the captain said, lowering his hand to the pommel of his sword. "Seems gold is in his heart."

"He said he worked for the queen though," Ceres said.

"I'm gonna skewer that lyin' rat's heart for this," Adler said.

It wasn't until that moment that Ceres saw who was holding the binds of Marilyn.

"Look," she whispered. "Behind her. You see that light?"

"I see," Corvaire said. "That's the mage. That's the one keeping our magic from us."

"How's he doing it?" Adler asked.

"I don't know yet," Corvaire said with a growl.

A full light emitted from behind Marilyn's hand. The cloaked figure whose face was hidden in the shadows' hands were glowing from some sort of spell that was being concealed from them.

"How are you keeping my magic from me?" Corvaire shouted to the mage behind Marilyn, startling her frail form from the volume of his voice. "Tell me and I may spare you."

The mage then crept backward back into the shadows of the corridor behind them, pulling Marilyn in with him.

"You don't seem to understand," the captain said. "You will die down here in this prison if you don't surrender your weapons. Your carcasses will be strewn into ditches, and we'll piss on your rotting flesh. Or you live, if our lord deems it so." His eyes squinted and his teeth showed behind a raised upper lip. "Or—you could not lower your weapons. I'd personally prefer that way."

He drew his sword with a crisp ring of metal.

Corvaire stood out from behind the cage and held his sword out at the captain as the other six soldiers shifted their stances, readying themselves for combat.

Ceres could tell from their eyes that they were fearless, hardened soldiers. She stood and ducked behind the cage to the left, pulling an arrow back in the bowstring, aiming it at one of the soldiers with the spears.

Adler stood next to her, framed by the two cages, also holding his Masummand Steel sword out, as it glowed in the torchlight.

"Get out of my way," Corvaire said to the captain. "It doesn't need to come to this. You don't have to die, you can tell them we snuck in before Mogel got to you. But know this—I'm not leaving without my kin."

"Oh," he said. "So, the bitch is your kin, eh? A cousin you married? I get so sick of your lower kind thinking you have any blood worth anything but refuse." He spat thickly on the ground.

"You know what, Corvaire?" Adler asked. "I don't think there's any reason not to cut this guy down just so we can shut him up."

"I'm beginning to agree with you," Corvaire growled, and then whispered to him. "Aim for the openings in their armor. It is strong plate. Go for the neck, groin and underneath the shoulder."

Adler nodded.

"Well?" the captain asked. "How you want to do this? Seven against one and two kids doesn't exactly spell a good gamble."

"Last chance," Ceres said to all in the room, and after a long pause, she murmured. "Fine . . ."

The bowstring of Ceres' bow snapped, and an arrow whistled through the air, plunging into the side of her target's neck with a *thuck*. He clutched it with both hands as his spear fell to the rock floor with a *clang*, and immediately all the men with swords stormed into the middle of the cavern.

Corvaire and the captain were the first to meet with both of their swords clashing in the center of the room, and Ceres let another arrow fly at the other soldier with the spear. It ricocheted off the armor on his shoulder, but she quickly restrung and sent another which slid through the gap next to where the last one shot off, and it plunged into his neck, causing him to fall to the ground in agony.

Adler was met by two soldiers with swords as one of the others had joined the captain to flank Corvaire. Ceres drew her sword and made her way to help him, but found the beady, bloodshot eyes of a man rushing at her with his sword drawn.

Ceres gulped deeply, and then held up her sword to parry away the strong arching blow by the soldier. His sword didn't brush away like she expected, but instead, it bounced off her sword and his sword vibrated so strongly in his hand he had to grasp it in both of his hands as his eyes opened wide, staring at the jostling blade.

She was so surprised by the action, she was just as entranced as he was by the unusual turn of events. Ceres quickly shook off the surprise, and just before the man came to his senses, she thrust her sword through the direct center of his chest plate. With no gap in the armor there, and with the steel armor at its thickest there, the sword should have stuck, or done no more damage than leaving a dent. But the sword's tip slid through, and she felt it tear through his flesh, diving deep into him.

As the chaos of battle rang and echoed throughout the cavern, the soldier before her mouthed something inaudible, and his eyes grew wide again in fury and shock. Feeling his weight on her blade as his strength quickly slipped away, she slid her sword from him as he fell to the ground with a loud series of clanks from his armor. He weakly clutched at his chest as he scuttled away to a corner of the room—gasping for breath.

Corvaire was holding his own, swashbuckling back and forth, inching his way to the side of the room, where he'd be able to narrow his opponents together, so he'd be able to fight both of them in front of him. They didn't speak but grunted as they lay slash after slash upon one another—as their swords rang out with each metallic collision of their blades.

Ceres heard an unfamiliar sound of battle over with Adler, she turned to look, and just as she did so, she saw the flicker of the thin piece of metal a foot-long fall to the cavern floor and bounce with a clatter as it shimmered in the firelight of the torch. Above it, the soldier stared with bewilderment at the sword he was holding out before him, with it cut nearly in half.

Adler stood in a sort of shock too, staring at the soldier's blade, and then his own, which had sliced it in half. Gathering himself back in the moment, he went to send a lethal blow into the soldier, but the larger soldier with the bulky frame and strong shoulders dove at him. Before Adler had time to react, the soldier's helmet burst into Adler's face. He gripped him by the shoulders and fell on top of Adler.

He fought to get the man off him, and Ceres' heart pounded as she watched the blood gushing from Adler's nose. The soldier reached to his back where she saw a dagger sheathed. Adler continued to struggle, but it looked like he could barely even keep his eyes open from the blood that was stinging into them.

"Ceres," he said through clenched teeth.

She was over ten feet away and had not even a moment to hesitate. Wishing more than anything, she wished she had her magic at that moment.

Instead, she dove to her left, rolling shoulder over shoulder on the rocky ground, sliding her fingers around the middle of her bow, and while tumbling end over end one last time, drew an arrow from her quiver. She landed in kneeling position, desperately getting the arrow strung.

The soldier pulled the dagger from his back and was holding it high over Adler, ready to sink into him.

"Shoot him!" Corvaire yelled from the other side of the cavern, still embattled in a wicked flurry of thrusts and parries.

"Only one shot," she whispered to herself as she brought the arrow's nock back into the bowstring as it tightened with a sharp squeal.

The dagger loomed over Adler as his hand flew up to hold the soldier's arm and the dagger at bay, but the soldier proved far stronger than him, and the dagger was driven down farther and farther.

"Help," Adler said in horror as the dagger was mere inches from his face.

"One shot," she whispered again to herself. The bowstring snapped and the arrow whistled toward the soldier, who heard the snap and turned his head toward her. The movement caused the gap in armor to shift, and when the arrow landed, it pierced the thin part of his armor at his collar, plunging into him. Yet in his berserking, killer rage, he turned back toward Adler, pushing the dagger farther toward him.

She quickly pulled another arrow and strung it. For a moment, she thanked the gods her hands remained calm and steady.

"Kill him!" Corvaire yelled.

She aimed at the same spot she'd aimed at before, gulping deeply.

Still holding the dagger at bay, and with drool falling from the soldier's mouth with clenched teeth, Adler took his hand not holding the dagger away, and grabbed the bottom of his helmet, flinging it over his head. The soldier was so entranced with sending that dagger into Adler's face, that he didn't seem to care about his helmet rolling away, until the arrow entered into his ear.

The soldier's head cocked toward Ceres, as one eye drooped, and then turned back to Adler, weakly trying to drive the dagger into him one more time. Another arrow struck his head, and he fell limply onto Adler, who groaned from the weight of the fully armored large man.

She wanted to help get him off Adler, but quickly turned her attention to Corvaire, and to one of the soldiers with spears who'd gotten back to his feet, but the front of his armor was covered in dark blood and dirt. He staggered toward her, and she sent an arrow into his eye, sending him back down one last time.

Stringing another arrow, of which she only had one left, she aimed it at the captain.

"No," Corvaire groaned. "Go after Marilyn. They can't take her from the cells. We've only got one chance. Run!"

She hesitated a moment. *I can do both, I can kill the captain, we can help Adler to his feet and then—*

"I said run!" he yelled at her.

She loosened her bowstring and ran out of the cavern as quickly as her legs could carry her.

As soon as she turned the corner, she could see there were many passageways down the long stone and mortar hall. Torches hung upon both of its sides, burning low, and each of the passageways on the sides held that same glow from deep within.

Boney fingers clasped around iron prison bars and she could see the whites of the dozens of prisoner's eyes leering inquisitively at her.

"Which way did they take her?" she asked between quick

breaths. Gaunt men with wiry beards only stared back in what she thought was fear. "Which way?"

One of the men finally stuck his dirty hand out of his cell and pointed directly down the hall. With no hesitation she made her way as quickly forward as she could.

She believed Corvaire to be right. If that mage made it out of the prison and locked the door behind them, they'd have almost no way—or the time—to save their friend.

Sprinting down the long hallway, it turned to the right and she ran down another long hall, at the end of which was a figure standing in its middle, bathed in shadow.

"Stop!" she said, not knowing to draw her sword or string her bow.

The figure lurched around, and she instantly saw Marilyn still in the clutches of the dark-cloaked figure. Again, Ceres wished she had her magic.

The dark figure's eyes glared at her from under its dark hood, and with a rattle of keys, it turned back. It was trying to flee.

Many eyes lay upon them from the dozens of cells down the long, torchlit hall. But as Ceres ran, their frail fingers pulled back from the iron bars.

"Let her go!"

The figure didn't turn back around, as it was struggling to get the key into the keyhole. That's when Marilyn's arms flailed. She was weak, but she must've known that was her only chance for escape. And she still had her ears.

"Marilyn, fight! I'm coming for you!"

The cloaked figure had to turn back around to keep hold of Marilyn's bindings. She was indeed weakened, but she was putting up a hell of a fight. The mage jerked her back and tried to get the gate to open so it could flee, but as Marilyn pulled away another time, it turned and faced Ceres squarely as she ran at it.

It brushed its hood back, revealing the pale skin and beady eyes of an elderly bald man with a solid-black tattoo striped on the top of his head. He held Marilyn firmly in one hand, and in the other a pale golden light appeared.

Magic . . . I can't use it, but he's going to use it on me!

A startling realization hit her like a punch to the chest then—she was not going to make it to her in time.

She flung her bow from her back and took her single remaining arrow, putting its nock to the bowstring as quickly as she could. All the while the mage was muttering his spell as his hand glowed brighter.

Pulling the arrow back, she gave herself time to aim that was only a flutter of a hummingbird's wings—and she loosed the arrow. It flew straight and true at the mages head, but time slowed, and Ceres found herself unable to move. Her bowstring was paused in a wavy vibration, and her hands were held in place. The arrow even—stopped halfway to its target, and a deep dread filled her as the mage pulled the dagger from its sheath. He had a sinister smile creeping along his face.

I was too late.

The mage took a single step forward, as Ceres' mind ran to what she could do to fight back. What could she—?

The mage's eyes shot open and the smile wiped from his face as Marilyn drove her heel as hard as she could blindly onto his thin boot. She spun and drove her knee into his groin then, and Ceres found herself instantly able to use her hands and move again.

She went to draw her sword, but as the arrow resumed its flight and ran its way in between the mages' eyes, she instead found herself running to Marilyn.

As the mage dropped to its knees, and then onto its chest, Ceres wrapped her arms around Marilyn in tears.

"You're alive! I can't believe it! You're really alive!"

She pulled away and brushed the blindfold back, revealing

her blackish-gray eyes like dark, shaded oak. Her eyes had lost none of their luster even in her weakened state.

Marilyn couldn't speak, but her eyes told her she was happy to see Ceres too as streaks of tears flowed.

Ceres untied her hands as Corvaire and Adler turned their corner to see the two of them. They ran down the hall and Corvaire hugged Marilyn and then inspected her wounds. It was then she collapsed, and he and Ceres caught her fall.

"We've got to get her out of here," he said. "We can heal her, but more soldiers are sure to come soon. Marilyn, we've got you, sister. You're safe now. You're with family now."

PART IV
TWO RAVENS

Chapter Eighteen

❦

Corvaire heaved the door upward, letting it collapse onto the soft grass behind it with a dull thud. Adler and Ceres both helped lift Marilyn's limp body up the ladder, and Corvaire took her in his strong arms and pulled her up, laying her on her back delicately.

Adler ran up the ladder after, holding his nose as the blood covered his mouth and hands. Ceres followed up behind, closing the heavy door back into the ground where it was nearly completely hidden again.

"Are you okay?" she asked Adler as he groaned in pain. His eyes were a dark shade of red, and the bruising was already taking color on his face.

"That goat lover broke my nose!" he said with a slight squeal in his voice.

"It'll heal," she said as she rushed over to Marilyn's side. "At least you're alive. Thank the heavens we're all alive."

"She's still out," Corvaire said, holding his hand over her mouth to check her breathing. He stood then and gave a great sigh to see the horses were still tied up to the trees.

"I see Mogel didn't totally screw us," Ceres said. "S'pose he didn't think we'd be coming back out."

"How much did they pay him to betray us?" Adler groaned. "How much do you need coin for?"

"We can ask him next time we see him," Corvaire said, leaning down and picking Marilyn up. "For now though, let us ride as far away from here as we can. They'll surely be after us soon."

They ran over to the horses.

"Adler," Corvaire said, "you take the lead and I'll take Marilyn with me. I'm heaviest, but I'll have to hold her up until she comes to."

After he and Adler helped place her atop Corvaire's horse, Corvaire gave him a cold look.

"What? It looks that bad?" Adler asked with a raised eyebrow.

"Hold still, this is going to hurt." Corvaire brushed his hands away from his nose, and gripping it between his fingers, Adler's eyes grew wide.

"Wait, no, no!"

With a twist of his hand there was a swift *crack* and *pop*, and Adler fell to his knees, gripping his face in agony.

"You'll thank me later," Corvaire said as he helped him back to his feet. "Now, get on your steed. We ride, now!"

They got up on the horses and Adler wiped his tears away. He kicked Hedron's sides and they were off the thick sound of heavy hooves hitting solid dirt, back northwest toward the Everwood. They knew that would be the only way to avoid the many lurking eyes that would be after them for an unimaginable bounty on their heads then.

Not only had they killed soldiers before and fled, but then they'd killed even more, and took the lord's most prized prisoner, Ceres thought.

The horses ran as fast as they could with them upon their

backs. Ceres' heart pounded in her chest as she dared not look away from where the horse was carrying her at the speed they were traveling, and she worried what she'd find if she looked back.

They rode for over twenty minutes until they heard the first alarm. A loud trio of horn blows rose from the city in the hours just before the first light of day. A shrill shiver ran through her as she feared for the droves of soldiers that were sure to stream out of the castle like ants leaving the anthill for a fresh morsel of food.

The dense Everwood was before them, but Ceres hadn't the faintest idea how they'd be able to avoid an army looking for them. They'd burn the forest to the ground this time in order to find them. She tried to imagine the red-faced fury Lord Bjorn held as he spat his orders to find them.

Riding as quickly as they were, and with the real worry each of them held, they didn't yell out to one another as they rode in a single line toward the forest. Ceres had been so preoccupied with the rescue that she'd spent almost no time considering how they'd be able to escape the clutches of the army of Atlius.

"I hope to never see you again," she muttered to herself.

She swallowed hard and looked back to see Marilyn bobbing on the horse behind her with Corvaire looking over her shoulder. They weren't keeping the pace of Hedron and her horse, but they also weren't terribly behind. And in the early morning hours of the still dark night, she saw the riders parading out of the front gate of the city with the lord's fury at their backs like a strong wind.

They were making haste toward the forest, which was three hundred yards away.

"We're going to make it," she said, "but what will we do once we get there?"

Again, she looked back and saw the endless line of the

soldiers on horseback flowing from the gate. Hopefully they hadn't seen them riding toward the forest in the low light, as they were riding off in different directions, with other horses leaving from the back of the city toward where they'd entered and left the tunnel.

Once they hit the forest line, they dashed in carefully as the branches whipped by and loosened the reins of their steeds. Ceres and Adler dismounted quickly after they were in the trees and waited for Corvaire to catch up. After he rode into the forest five minutes later, they helped bring Marilyn down, who was finally stirring awake.

Helping to sit her down so her back was up to a thick tree, her eyes opened.

"Yes," Ceres said. "That's it. Here, drink, eat. Regain yer strength."

Marilyn took the canteen and gulped down the water to the point of choking on it.

Ceres looked back over her shoulder at Corvaire who was glaring down upon the hundreds of soldiers on the plains. "What're we ta do?" she asked. "They're gonna find us here. And she's not strong enough yet to hardly walk even."

He didn't respond.

"You, Corvaire," Adler said with reddened eyes. "There's got to be a spell for this. You can fight the Neferian, surely you can stop them!"

"I'm not as powerful as Gracelyn or Seretha was," he groaned and looked deeply into Marilyn's eyes. "I can hold them off for minutes, perhaps twenty. But I'm no sorcerer, and even if it means our lives, I can't kill thousands of men because they hail to a banner. Even if I did, it'd mean that many more would be after us until we all drew our last breath." He sighed and lowered his head. "We're already in a war, I'm not about to create a new one with thousands of innocents. We're going to have to ride. Ride hard, ride swift. Hurry, mount your steeds and prepare for . . ."

Marilyn raised her right arm and laid her hand on Corvaire's. She feigned a weak, yet soft smile. She motioned for him to help her up with a nod of her head. He gently did so as Ceres helped by raising her from the ground by holding up her other arm.

Once up to her feet, she brushed them away, looking up at the trees whose leaves gusted in the early morning wind.

Ceres watched her eagerly, but knowing she couldn't speak, watched the flicker of his eyelashes, the way her fingers moved in the breeze above her and way her dim eyes seemed to grow a vibrant, glossy charcoal hue.

A raven cawed from one of the trees, gazing down upon them. It cawed three shrill times before leaping from its branch and gliding down to perch upon her left forearm. In her right hand, a blue light burst from her palm, startling Ceres. It erupted like a pane of glass breaking to shards, and as the light quickly faded, a curled roll of papyrus lay in the small of her hand.

She held it out to the raven, who cawed once more and with the flapping of its black wings, flew from her arm and back off into the sky—but not before plucking the blue-glowing scroll into its claw.

Adler's mouth was agape and even Corvaire seemed to be trying to put the pieces together of what he'd just seen.

"It's flying west," Ceres said. "You—you sent a raven to . . . Endo?"

Marilyn nodded.

"Great, now Stone and Gracelyn will know we are alive, and that Marilyn is too!" Ceres said.

"Alive," Adler added, "for now."

As the hordes of soldiers on horseback and foot flooded out of the castle and out into the plains before the forest like water gushing out from a broken dam, Marilyn waved for them to follow her.

She staggered as she did so, and Ceres helped her back up and placed Marilyn's arm over to her to assist. Corvaire and Adler pulled the horses behind.

"Where's she leading us?" Adler asked him.

"I don't know, but I trust her."

They followed behind as Ceres assisted her deeper into the woods. The ground grew shadier as the trees thickened above. Silence fell over the forest as the sounds of yelling soldiers grew behind. Marilyn led them to a shallow stream that was clear and cool.

Pulling Ceres with her, they walked into the stream as it nipped at Ceres' ankles. Corvaire and Adler led the horses in behind. The shouting grew louder behind—the soldiers had penetrated the forest.

"Hope she knows where she's taking us," Adler said.

"As I said, I trust her," Corvaire said.

"I do too," Adler said. "But if something doesn't happen soon then we'll have to figure out something else." He gripped the hilt of his sword.

Corvaire growled. "Give her a little more time. If we break out into a fight, the whole kingdom will know where we are."

Marilyn pulled at Ceres as she seemed stronger than her then, dashing through the stream to a bend where a tall hill lay upon its right side. The cliff was covered in lush, green vines. She pointed to the vines.

"I'm not sure what you mean," Ceres said. "I—"

Marilyn pointed again at them, and then at Ceres' lips.

"Gather your Indiema," Corvaire said to her sharply. "You're going to have to cast a spell to save us."

Ceres hesitated only a moment no longer than the time it takes to draw a quick breath.

"I'm ready," she said.

"You have to call upon the vines to invite us in," Corvaire said. "Like a key, you're going to create a key for us."

Ceres nodded.

"The casting words are . . . *Terranas Invictum Abiertus* . . ."

Ceres concentrated to focus her Elessior's magic upon those thick vines before them, and she spoke the words clearly. She gazed at them as nothing appeared to change, and the hollering and stampeding of the soldiers behind made her heart race.

"Again," Corvaire said. "Focus."

Ceres looked deeply into the knowing eyes of Marilyn, a friend who'd saved her many times, and Ceres knew then that it was time again to save her friend.

"*Terranas Invictum Abiertus,*" she said in a powerful voice. Again, nothing seemed to happen to the vines . . . until . . .

A rustling sound appeared behind them, like snakes slithering in the brush. Then the vines curled back slowly, peeling back like the rind of an orange. Behind them was a thick shadow, deep and hollow.

Marilyn urged them through, pulling on Ceres' hand then. The opening was wide—wide enough for the horses and they were soon within the deep, cool dark. Behind the vines curled back over like layers of thick tapestry covering a bright window, and once fully closed, not a ray of sunshine poked through.

Marilyn once again pulled Ceres by the hand, deeper into the cave.

From just behind the vines they could hear the splashing of soldiers' boots and the calls of frustrated soldiers with anger thick on their tongues.

The ground of the cave was dry and smooth, as Ceres was worried about stumbling over large rocks and rolling her ankle. Sparks flared up from behind where Adler stood, and he lit a torch which lit the cavern in a golden hue.

Marilyn reached down and grabbed piece of dried wood

the thickness of a rope by her feet and carried it over to Adler. She held one end of the stick over the flame as he held it up patiently for her.

Once the tip was fully in flame, she blew it out, letting its smoke rise to the top of the tunnel. She turned to the wall of the cave and stuck it into it, dragging it in a curving pattern. She lifted it and drug in a few straight lines. All eyes watched eagerly until she had finished and stepped back away from the wall.

Ceres could see the writing clearly and gave a deep sigh of relief.

Upon the wall, she had written the words *Safe Here* in ash.

"Thank you," Ceres said to her friend. "You're incredible." Marilyn bowed to her with tears in her eyes. "You're safe now too. We'll take care of *you* now."

Marilyn burst into tears and fell with her back to the wall weeping. Corvaire went to her side, laying his arm over her. "We're going to take you home."

Chapter Nineteen

He turned the page slowly with his fingers, his cheek resting flush on the palm of his other hand. Mud snored easily next to him on the stone floor. Sitting at the main table of the dining hall in the city that lay beneath the dragonfire ravaged mountain town of Endo Valaire—Stone's eyelids felt heavy.

The book he was half-reading, half-skimming was titled *The History of the Great City of Valeren in the Modern Age*. The table he sat at the head of was a thick, white marble slab—warm to the touch, with piles of books before him with bookmarks scattered throughout each. Mud stirred awake next to him, looking with keen eyes up at the front entrance to the hall that was framed by two thin, blue drapes each with the symbol of the Mystics on them—the Artican.

"Find anything worthwhile?" Gracelyn asked as she approached with another stack of five books held in her arms. She wore a white linen shirt and tan pants that buttoned up on the sides and dark leather boots nearly up to her knees. Her long brown hair swooped behind her as she made her way to the table, laying the books next to him gently.

"King Rivermark, Queen Basteral, Prince John Pricip the fifth who died a noble death of being poisoned by his jealous cousin." He groaned. "How's anything of this going to help? It's been almost two weeks since the others rode for Atlius. They're out there in the wilds. They're fighting, helping to win this war for us while I trade in my pillow for stacks of papyrus."

She sat next to him and gave him a serious look with kind eyes. "Are you still upset about this morning's spell work?"

"I just feel like I'm better served to wielding a sword than in here reading. There's a war going on out there," he said.

"The clues to win this war are hidden somewhere in here," Gracelyn said, placing her hand on his forearm. "Why don't you go get some rest in your room? You've been in here for days now. You may not enjoy it, but you've been reading as though the war did depend on it. Honorable really!"

Her sighed again, relaxing his shoulders. "Maybe you're right. I think it's getting to me—not being able to use any magic I might have efficiently. I don't know how Ceres was able to use her Elessior so quickly, and so well."

"I believe your greatest hurdle to overcome is the strength of your Indiema. You don't know your parents, your ancestors. But like all things, it takes practice. But we'll find it for you. Its buried inside you, and just like you were, it will become unearthed in time."

"I hope so," he said running the fingernail from his index finger down the leather-bound cover of a book. "I don't think I can defeat Arken with just a sword . . ."

A glint sparked in Gracelyn's eyes and she stood abruptly. "C'mon, let's get you out of here, you're dwelling. You need a break." He stood, and she grabbed his hand pulling toward the entrance to the hall, and back out into the fortress walls. She released his hand and galloped toward the main gate of the inner fortress. "Let's grab a bottle of something nice and pretend that there's no war going on, no king to kill, and no magic other than everyday little sparks that fly."

They went through the main gate with its bars suspended above and as he walked with Mud at his side, she galloped as if she were dancing through tall grass under golden sunshine.

Within the castle they stopped into the cool, stone cellar and grabbed a bottle of a light, rosy colored wine and grabbed two glasses. She grabbed some walnuts and apples too.

He was never sure how the castle was stocked with food and drink, but that wasn't the only secret the castle held . . . *Where do the blue lights come from? How has no one ever entered from the outside except the Mystics? How was it immaculately clean after standing for so long? Perhaps the answer is in one of those books?*

They made their way to the main throne room which had two thrones, both built from a dark, richly grained wood and a purple upholstery. There were more of the delicate blue drapes with the Artican on them, running along both sides of the room with low-burning torches scattered between. Behind the two thrones was a great hearth where a small fire smoldered, ready to be stoked with large logs.

Up the stairs they went to one of the tallest spires of the kingdom, which was a round room with three tables and sets of chairs, a rack with bows and quivers full of arrows, and a splendid view of the fortress below.

Layer by layer the castle and fortress flowed down lower until it reached its outer walls, and the cave and stream beyond. Gracelyn uncorked the bottle and poured two glasses for them. She held hers out for a clink. "To what?" she asked.

"To friends, and family."

The glasses met with the *clink*, and they sipped. She let out a relieved sigh.

"That's nice," she said, taking another sip with puckered lips.

He swirled his, staring into it.

"Can I ask you something, Gracelyn? How do you seem so strong all the time? You must miss your family, yet you hardly talk about them. I miss my friends, although I'm profusely happy with our friendship. How do you do it?"

Glaring down at the city below, she said as calmly as if she were talking about the weather, "I weep at night—every night."

He didn't know what to say, and a guilt sank in his stomach for broaching the question. "I didn't mean to . . ."

"No, it's quite all right," she said. "I suppose I should act more casual during the day about it, but I've always tried to stay strong for my siblings and family—it's just something I've always sort of done."

"Oh—I didn't . . ."

She turned to face him. "It's only natural that we miss those we care about while we're cooped up here. I know it's safest for my family that I'm not with them, and I know that it was wise for you to come here to gain your strength for the battles to come with the others off to free Marilyn. Sometimes the most difficult things in life are those that we must do, even though they feel completely the opposite of what our hearts tell us."

There was a long pause, and Stone didn't quite know what to say to that.

"How old are you?" he asked with a laugh.

"You know that's the question you're never supposed to ask a lady," she replied with a wry smile.

"I only mean because you seem so wise for your age." He scratched his face.

"I'm probably younger than you," she said. "If we're going by years. But . . . ever since I *awoke* to become one of the

Majestic Wilds, I'll admit there are times my head seems to go to war with itself. My heart battles my mind, and sometimes that voice inside of me whispers and sometimes it screams at the top of its lungs, like when I battled those two Neferian. Instinct is powerful. Stone, I'll never tell you to not listen to your heart, as your instinct has led you to where you are right now, but we also have to trust. *Trust* that they will find their way without you. They are strong."

"I know they are. Thank you for saying that. I feel worry often . . . After all, she was the one who dug me up, and let me breathe in air. If something happens to her when I'm not there . . . I don't know if I could forgive myself."

"Adler is with her, and Corvaire too, they'll protect her. I wouldn't be surprised if she's been the one doing the saving even . . ."

"I wouldn't be surprised either," he laughed, "that girl was made from brimstone and grit."

Mud barked and growled out the window.

Stone's attention stirred to life and he placed his glass on the table next to the tall window whose both sides met at a sharp peek at its top.

"What's he barking at?" Gracelyn asked.

"Not sure, don't see anything. But you want to talk about trusting instinct? Of anyone I know, his gut I trust the most."

Below, they both spotted Hydrangea and Lucik running out into the main courtyard, looking up at the tall tower from where Mud was barking.

"What is it?" Lucik yelled from below.

"Don't know," Gracelyn said down to them.

"You see anything?" Stone asked her, and she shook her head.

Mud reared up and put his front paws on the windowsill, barking down to the darkest part of the cave. Spit was flying out from his mouth as his teeth showed.

Stone went to place his hand on the hilt of his sword, but his eyes widened as they looked down at his hip where a belt and scabbard should have been, but realized they were resting next to the chair in the main room by the long, marble table.

"Salt in slash, damn," he said.

Gracelyn looked down and saw him try to grab the empty spot on his hip.

"What a fool I am," he said. "We've got to make it back down there!"

"Wait," she said in a cool voice.

"Wait? Wait for what?"

He saw her looking down at the darkest part of the cave, the main entrance from the outside that led to the mountain of Elderon.

Mud stopped barking and whimpered, looking down at the same place she was. Stone walked over the window and glared down from behind the dog.

From within the darkness, a speck of blue light appeared.

"What do you see?" Lucik asked from the other side of the city walls, unable to see what they saw."

"Not sure," Gracelyn said. "It's a glowing light of some kind. It's blue and coming closer."

Then, as the light rose toward where they were in the spire, Stone heard a familiar sound and knew at once what it was. It cawed twice before he could see its black wings flap and it landed on the windowsill as Mud let his paws rest once again upon the stone floor.

The raven cawed again. It was sleek with glossy black eyes and cuffed in its claws was a small scroll glowing in a light, blue hue.

"Who sent it?" Stone asked, inspecting the scroll. "And why's it glowing blue?"

Gracelyn knelt and touched it delicately. "The blue light is the Elessior, and I think that only those who wield its magic can take and read it." She placed her fingers on the scroll and plucked it from the raven, who cawed once, released it from its grasp and glided back down into the darkness.

She unrolled it, and her eyes grew wide as she read.

"What's it say?" he asked urgently.

"It's from a friend," she said, turning it to him and pointing at the signature at the bottom."

He couldn't believe his eyes. "M—Marilyn?"

Chapter Twenty

※※※

They must have seen the raven clearly, or they just saw something fly up to the tower they were in, but as the thoughts of Marilyn being alive swelled within Stone, he heard footsteps running up the staircase.

Hydrangea burst into the room first with her sword drawn, but with a dismissive wave of Gracelyn's hand, her posture relaxed. Lucik ran in after but seeing only Stone holding the tiny scroll in his hand, she sheathed her sword.

"What is it?" Hydrangea asked, with her blue eyes peering at the scroll.

"It's from Marilyn," Gracelyn said.

"What's it say?" Lucik asked impatiently, she brushed her silver hair back from her face to reveal the burn mark on her cheek and temple.

"It says . . ." Stone read aloud to them.

STONE,

. . .

This scroll is being inscribed by a spell *I* learned in the cells of Atlius.

We have escaped and are making our way into a hidden pathway through the forest.

The others are well, albeit Adler got a bit bloodied and the others have bruises to show for our battle beneath the castle.

I have been maimed, and was nearly starved in my imprisonment, but I met an ally in the darkness down there. He taught me ways to use my magic still, without the use of my tongue.

We are on our way back to you and the others now.

I hope this finds you well, for there's oh so much to do still.

Sincerely,
Marilyn Corvaire — The Conjurer

Stone let the scroll fall to his side, still cupped in his hand.

"They're all alive, and they're coming here," he said with his mouth left agape.

"I told you they'd be all right," Gracelyn said, wrapping her arms around him, and holding him tightly.

"I always forget that Corvaire's first name is Drâon," Hydrangea said, scratching her cheek and smiling.

"What kind of way of using magic was she speaking of?" Lucik asked. "Words must be spoken to cast spells with the Elessior? Is that not true?"

"To the best of my knowledge that is true," Gracelyn said, stepping back away from Stone who still seemed to be in a state of disbelief. "The name of the incantation must be said at least once to initiate the spell."

"Is there a spell to write a scroll and send it with a raven?" Lucik asked.

Gracelyn shook her head and her shoulders raised. "She is

of the Sonter set. She's also Marilyn the Conjurer, possibly the most powerful wielded of that set of magic in all the Worforgon. She would know more spells than any. I've been studying the set while we've been here. Why are you so curious? We should be happy they're all alive and well."

"I am," Lucik said. "I've just never heard of it before, with the Elessior specifically."

"These are trying times," Hydrangea said. "Many do what is needed to survive."

"Lucik," Stone muttered. "How long will it take them to get back?"

"Depends on if they are on horseback or not. With horses they could be here in three weeks if they use a good trail through the Worgons. If they're going to be on foot, we may not see them for quite a while . . ."

"Three weeks, eh?" Gracelyn said, rubbing her chin. "That's too long."

"We don't know what happened exactly down in Atlius," Hydrangea said. "But we can be assured the lord there isn't going to want them escaping again from his city."

"Corvaire is smart," Lucik said. "He'll lead them as best he can in the shadows and remain hidden from prying eyes."

"Three weeks can hold a lot of prying eyes," Gracelyn said.

"If Arken finds out they're out there alone," Stone said. "He could send out his dark dragons after them. We've got to go get them."

"What were we just talking about?" Gracelyn said with a scowl. "Your place is here for now, with your nose in books and learning your magic. They've made it this far alone. You can trust them."

"I'll hail the guild," Lucik said. "Those that are able will find them and protect them on their journey back."

"I'm not sure that's the best idea," Hydrangea said with a corner of her mouth puckered. "Do we want dozens of people leaving their cities all at once and heading in the same direction. That would be sure to draw Arken's—and the warring kings' eyes."

"They will do best to be on their own," Gracelyn said. "Trust in Corvaire. He led them that far."

※

LATER THAT EVENING as Stone finished washing up, looking into a musty mirror in his room as he shaved the dark whiskers of his pale face, he muttered to himself, "I still can't believe Gracelyn was right about Marilyn being alive. How did she know?"

He walked down the curving road on the inner side of the exterior wall of the city with thin streaks of blue light shining up between the cobblestones that it was paved with. Mud trotted along next to him.

Two streets down he turned and stepped up three steps to Lucik and Hydrangea's place where he knocked twice and then walked in. Hydrangea and Gracelyn were both in the kitchen, finishing a roast leg of lamb that smelled heavily of rosemary and mint.

They greeted him as he entered and went back to mashing potatoes and finishing dusting a loaf of bread with flour before placing it in the oven. He went and sat down next to Lucik.

The place they'd chosen had the kitchen tucked off to the right of the front door, with a long table separating it from the main area of the home. A small fire burned in the fireplace where a bearskin rug lay on the stone beneath for chairs turned to face one another. Through the windows on the three sides of the house opposite from the staircase, dull lights beamed in from the city.

"She's putting too much garlic in the potatoes," Lucik said

to him, with her gaze peering into the crackling fire. "I can smell it from here."

"I like garlic," Stone said.

"Well I do too, but I don't want to walk around all day smelling like I bathed in it." She sipped a glass of crisp, white wine.

He laughed.

"Did you get yourself a drink?" she asked him, looking up at him with her forest-green eyes.

"I'm all right, I think I'll wait for the food."

"Quite the thing," she said, looking back at the fire. "Someone surviving that kind of cell."

"It's still difficult for me to believe," he said.

"Killing soldiers in the city, known as a sorceress, being mutilated like she was, and able to escape? She really does live up to her reputation."

"She saved our lives," he said. "I suppose now it's time for us to save hers."

Lucik smiled widely at him, showing her teeth and patting him on the thigh. "Good lad. You're a good lad."

"I only wish I could do more. I feel terrible being here. You know that?"

She nodded. "I can see it in your eyes. The way you walk even."

"It's just not the way things should be." He sighed. "We're here drinking and eating until we get tired and lay in our goose feather beds. But they're out there—in the mud, in the cold, having to hunt for their own dinner every night."

"You miss it, don't you?" she asked.

"I don't know if I miss it, or I just miss them . . ."

"Try to enjoy it, Stone. For now, try to enjoy this place. We won't be here forever you know. The war wouldn't let us if we tried. You're going to play a role in Arken's destiny—whatever that entails. You want to be out there, and they'd give their little finger to be here to have what we have."

"All right, bread's in," Gracelyn said from the kitchen cheerfully, clapping her hands together as the flour puffed in the air. "I think I finally figured out the right temperature for this oven!"

She poured three glasses of ale on the kitchen table and took one over to Stone.

"I guess I'm ready for my first drink now," Stone said with a laugh. Lucik leaned in to clink their glasses as Gracelyn tossed over a small chunk of lamb to Mud, who ate it in nearly a single bite and swallow and trotted over to the kitchen, begging at her side with a wide grin.

"Time for a toast," Gracelyn said. "And this time I don't think we need to ask what for!"

They all stood and toasted to their friends and their safe passage home.

"Endo Valaire is growing more powerful every day now," Lucik said. "Soon two of the Darakon will reside here once again, and with Crysinthian's blessing, we may find the other two Majestic Wilds when they awaken. We will have a fighting chance against the evil shadow growing in this world."

"Hear hear!" they all said.

Mud growled in the kitchen. He ran to the door and barked wildly, seemingly from nowhere. But Stone knew better than to not trust his friend—and this time he didn't forget his sword.

Each of them grabbed their swords and went back out into the city. From within the city you could not tell whether it was morning or night, and the lights always burned the same brightness. There was no lack of visibility ever, no fog, no cover of night.

They saw nothing out of the ordinary as Mud barked and growled.

But then Mud stopped barking, sat on his hind legs and scratched the side of his face.

"What was that all about, boy?" Stone asked.

"He must've heard a . . ." Gracelyn began, but then her sight snapped to over the outer wall, toward the dark entrance of the city.

Stone noticed her gaze, and he quickly saw what she saw.

Its wings flapped quietly as it descended from over the wall with its black eyes and sharp claws.

"Is that . . ." Lucik asked, ". . .the same raven?"

It was flying toward Stone. He held his forearm out and it landed on it, perched upon it, cawing and inspecting the area with its black eyes.

"A new scroll," he muttered.

"Go on," Gracelyn said. "Grab it."

He untied it from its leg, and the raven flapped its wings, flying back off over the wall and out of view quickly. The scroll was sealed with a small wax stamped with a symbol he didn't recognize—three stars around a flower.

"Is it from Marilyn?" Hydrangea asked.

"Don't think so," he said.

Each of them walked over to inspect the small scroll.

"That's most certainly not from Marilyn," Lucik said. "It's not from anyone we should expect a scroll from."

"Lucik, do you recognize the symbol on the seal?" he asked.

She eyed it with a squint. "That symbol is from the city of Dranne."

"It's from King Tritus?" he asked with an upturned eyebrow. "Why would he reach out to us?"

"It's not the symbol of the king," Lucik said. "It's the symbol of the queen."

Chapter Twenty-One

He read the words aloud, still unable to grasp the queen of Dranne had sent a raven just after Marilyn's scroll appeared. It reminded him that things were still happening out in their world while they read old books, ate warm food, and slept in clean, dry beds.

STONE *and the new Majestic Wild,*

I HOPE this scroll finds you well.
  I'd hoped to not intervene directly in this war, but there are things that have come to light you should be aware of.
  Your life is in danger more than you know.
  One of my employed, the one I entrusted to watch over your friends has betrayed me and attempted to have them captured in their rescue of Marilyn the Conjurer. The only news I have of that thus far is that they have not been recaptured yet.
  It is with regret that I tell you that a Neferian attacked the city of Hedgehorn, and while Drâon Corvaire was somehow able to drive the

beast off, it left the city in ruin, and many lives were lost. This is the future I fear for all the cities of the Worforgon if King Arken is not defeated.

That brings me to Arken—my sources tell me he is in the southeast. He's gathering forces to him, and I believe he is planning something much larger than his previous attacks.

My husband, the king, is obsessed with conquering his war before beginning this new one, I fear many more will die before the warring kings end their rivalry. Arken knows this, and he knows of your prophesied destiny to hurt him. He has not forgotten your first encounter and I would assume if he moves to attack again, you may be involved in his plans to strike.

Not many know of where you are, but Arken is not mad, like many suggest. He remembers his past. Although he may be driven by his anger, it has not blinded him. I believe he may know where you are.

I put much of my own position on the line with this raven. I trust you will keep this information to yourself.

I believe the time may arrive soon for you to put those Masummand Steel weapons to use.

The Worforgon needs a true leader to save itself from the Dark King, and whether or not that is you, is yet for us to know. But the time will come when your strength will be tested, and in those moments, I believe you will be strong enough to prevail.

MAY CRYSINTHIAN WATCH OVER YOU, and all of us,
    Queen Angelica Tritus.

HE LET the scroll spring back into a lose cylinder.

"He knows where we are?" he said to himself with wide eyes. "He knows about the castle under the mountain?"

"I suppose he does," Lucik said. "I'm not sure why the queen would have any reason to lie to us. She seems genuine in her worry. And she has a reputation for being the wise one within the warring cities."

There was a long pause between them.

Hydrangea finally broke the silence. "Do we leave?"

There was another pause then.

"If he's in the southeast," Lucik said, scratching her cheek. "Even in flight it would take days to reach us. So, we at least have some time to think it over."

"If he's coming himself," Hydrangea said, brushing her hair back from her face.

"I'm not running and hiding any longer," Stone said. "If he wants a fight, I'll give him one."

"Stone, did you hear what the queen said about your weapons?" Gracelyn asked.

"That it would be time to use them?"

"Yes. She named the *steel*," Gracelyn said, leaning in slightly.

"Are you saying . . . ?"

"It seems so," Gracelyn muttered.

". . . She was the one who funded our weapons? Was she the one who made the deal with Seretha and the other passed Old Mothers?"

"Doesn't it sound like it?" Gracelyn said. "Without actually saying it? How many know of those weapons? And who would have the amount of wealth to purchase such sought after steel?"

"We may have another ally in this fight," Lucik said with a smile. "We could use all the help we can get."

"What if we draw allies to us here?" Hydrangea asked. "We are in a fortress after all, and the cave would limit the numbers that could invade. The Dark Realm knows if the dragons could even enter the caves."

"They may not," Gracelyn said. "But Arken and his

Runtue could. The queen made it sound as if he is growing his army."

"You could defeat them all with your magic," Hydrangea said. "I've seen what you can do."

"My Elessior won't work on him," Gracelyn said with a stern gaze. "Nor his against me. We are both of the Wendren Set."

"It's the same with me," Stone groaned. "Even if I were able to use any magic I have. I'm only as good as my sword arm and this steel I wield."

"Perhaps that will be enough," Lucik said. "Should we call upon the guild to join us here? Many will come, and they will rally others."

"I wish Corvaire was here," Stone said. "He'd know what to do."

"But he's not, Stone," Gracelyn said sharply. "We are. We'll have to decide if we defend the city or go back out into the wilds. We can't do both."

"Let's give ourselves the night to sleep on it," Stone said. "In the morning we can resume this discussion. Does that sound fine to everyone?"

Each of them nodded.

They returned to their dinner within the warm house and tried to dabble in conversations, while it was evident they were mostly mulling over the new information that had entered into their lives that night.

After supper, Gracelyn and Stone left together while Mud trotted at his side.

As they walked next to each other, Stone felt a warm, calming aura about her that made his shoulders relax and his stomach soothe.

Once they approached her home, a round, single-story dwelling with orange tapestries covering the interior, arched windows they said their goodbyes and she walked toward the front door.

"Hey, Gracelyn," he said when a fresh idea popped into his head.

"Yes . . ."

"I—I want to show you something," he said as he waved for her to follow him.

With one of her eyebrows raised, but quickly lowered and a smile crossing her lips, she followed.

"What is it?" she asked as they walked toward the front gate of the fortress.

"Just come," he said. "You'll see."

He grabbed one of the torches that rested upon the stone walls as they exited the city through the wide gate. She grabbed one too. The blue light of the city faded as they found the cave that initially led them to find the city, and it glowed a warm fiery-orange and smelled crisp and cool.

She followed him, as Mud ran ahead, eventually they left the mouth of the cave and a gust of forceful mountain air rushed past, blowing both of their dark hairs over their shoulders, and Gracelyn's into her face, which she brushed aside.

"This way," he said, walking up a steep cliff to the right. "Be careful on this part." Once he was halfway up and Mud was panting up at the top of the twelve-foot incline, Stone reached back and let her grab his hand and he helped her up the narrow path.

They were soon upon a flat stretch of rock with mists hanging below—obscuring the cliffs below, but the pinpricked sky of millions of stars shimmered as the full moon nearly bathed in the sea, low on the horizon.

"It's just over here," he said, walking another forty paces and turning around the backside of the large boulder. He disappeared behind it, and Gracelyn followed, and as she turned the corner, he looked to watch the expression upon her face.

Trickling down the side of the mountain into a small clear pond at their feet, a gleaming waterfall poured down from above. Stone had always liked the sound of it since he'd found that place only a week prior, but it was the view that he always found spectacular.

From their vantage point they would look down and see the sea breaching onto the high rocks below. The harsh mountain winds were blown away by the mountain that cradled them on both sides, leaving only cool sea air filtering in. The Sacred Sea waved on endlessly, until that far off spot where it met the sky with nearly the same hue of dark blue.

"It's beautiful," she said. "Your own little spot."

"Mud and I come here when I can't sleep. Only found it recently. I suppose this may be one of our last nights to come."

"You never know," she said. "But . . . you really shouldn't be out here alone. Lucik wouldn't agree."

"I'm not alone," he petted the scruff on Mud's neck. "There's something else you've got to see . . ."

He led her to the waterfall's edge, and with the torch held out, he brushed to the side some hanging vines. Gracelyn leaned in, holding her own torch up to see what lay behind the green vines.

"What is it?" she asked, cocking her head.

"I was hoping you could tell me," Stone said.

Behind the vines, dancing in warm torchlight, was a carving in the mountain's rock wall. It was a woman's face, although aged by the years of water and weather. Her nose was broken off, and it appeared at one point her arms were both held out, but both were broken at the elbow.

The woman's eyes were wide and pupil-less, yet gentle and wise. A hood covered her hair and her mouth was flat, almost frowned down. She had a necklace that fell down her chest, but whatever was there at one point was weathered down to a small bump.

"Hmm," Gracelyn said as she leaned in. She peered hard into the carving's eyes. "Looks . . . familiar . . . somehow."

"Found her two nights ago," he said. "Strange place to find a statue like this."

"Yes . . . Curious."

Gracelyn knelt and inspected the ground beneath the carving.

Stone clapped his head, not realizing to look below for anything that may have fallen from it. He knelt with his torch low too.

They were both pawing at the ground as Mud lapped the water from the clear pond.

Gracelyn walked to the other side of Stone and sifted through the rocks behind him, slowly inching toward the pond.

"Find anything?" she asked.

"No." But then something caught his eye, it was a small sparkle in the rock and debris. At first it looked like nothing more than a grain of sand, but as he pushed away the fine rocks, he picked it up and wiped it with his thumb, leaving smudgy streaks.

"What is it?" Gracelyn asked as she got to her feet and walked over.

"Not sure." He walked over to the waterfall and let the gleaming water wash off the untold years of grime from its face. As he washed the many sides of the small stone, something happened to Stone.

The majestic white and clear blues of the waterfall faded to a pink hue. Everything he saw, while his eyes were focused on the stone then turned a deep red—the same color of blood. It was so intense, and he was fearful that he was falling unconscious that the red stone fumbled from his shaky hands, falling to the stream below that flowed down to the pond.

But slender fingers slyly snatched it before it could fall into the stream.

"Careful," Gracelyn said, opening her hand to show the red stone shimmering off its many, cut sides. The stone was small, no more than the size of a thimble, but it was trance-like and hard to look away from. "This is no ordinary gem. Don't want to lose it."

"Do you . . . Do you know what it is?" He leaned in closely to look at it.

"If it's what I think it may be," she said looking back over her shoulder. "We need to hide it, and quickly."

"What do you mean?" he asked, perking back up with his hands out. "We just found it."

"No, Stone. This isn't just some rare treasure." Gracelyn handed it back to him quickly. "Keep it close but hidden."

"What? There's no other people around here . . ."

"We need not only hide that from people," she whispered. "Any eyes that lay upon that gem . . . I need to get back to the library within the fortress. Come now."

He followed her hesitantly, unsure of what she meant. Although he trusted her, he simply wanted an answer, but she appeared to have none—only a vague hunch.

They'd made it back to the steep slope, and Gracelyn hurried down first. Stone placed his boot on the first rock down, but then felt something. He reeled back around, glancing up into the dark, star-filled sky. Not seeing anything, he looked to Mud, who was scratching the side of his muzzle carelessly.

"Stone, c'mon now!" she urged him from the mouth of the cave.

Suddenly he felt something drive into the side of his neck, like a red-hot dagger piercing his skin and cutting into his veins. He swatted it, feeling the course hair upon whatever had caused the pain. Mud barked loudly next to him. Another crippling pain roared into him in the small of his back and he groaned in anguish.

"Stone!"

He shoved something into his pocket, looked down at his footing on the rocks, as they swayed and rippled as if they were under rushing water.

"Gracelyn . . . I . . . I . . . need help . . ."

Chapter Twenty-Two

Ink jars shattered, letting their ink stain the stone floor in long streaks like blood spatters. Papers flew from the tabletop as Hydrangea shoved them from the table in a mad rush as Gracelyn and Lucik laid down Stone on his back, as he moaned with heavy sweat pouring profusely from his brow.

"Spit and fire! What in the Dark Realm happened to him?" Lucik asked as she felt his forehead with her palm. "He's burning up!"

"I—I don't know," Gracelyn said with a shaky voice. "One minute he was fine, and the next he said he needed help and almost fell down the mountain. I—I ran and caught him as he fell and dragged him here . . . I—"

Lucik tore the front of his shirt with a dagger as her eyes darted around nervously. "Was he poisoned?"

"Look." Hydrangea reached over and pulled down his collar to reveal a large, swollen red bulge on the back of his neck.

They both turned him on his side, as his body was nearly limp and with shock.

"Stone," Gracelyn said, cupping his head in her hands with her nose only inches from his. "Stone, wake up. Wake up!"

"Here's another one," Lucik said, cutting the shirt from his back.

"What are they?" Hydrangea asked as Mud whimpered next to the table, looking up at Stone's sullen eyes.

"They look like—insect bites," Lucik said. "Did you see what bit him? Gracelyn!" Her voice was direct to get her attention. "Did you see what bit him?"

"I didn't see anything."

"It's not a bite," Hydrangea said, inspecting the bump on his back. She had the tip of her dagger pointed at it, and as she delicately used her fingernail to wedge something out of it with the tip of the dagger, she held it up for them to see. It wriggled and writhed—a single black curved stinger—nearly two full inches long and covered in puss and blood.

"It's a stinger," Lucik said. "But I've never seen one like that—or with such potent venom."

"Do you know any spells for this?" Hydrangea asked Gracelyn, whose looked around the room, trying to think if she somehow knew a spell that would cure him.

"I don't know." She shook her head. "I don't think so."

"We need to concoct a potion to cure him, and quickly," Lucik said.

"How do we do it?" Gracelyn asked.

"Well, we need the recipe, and more of the venom," she said in a dry tone. "Or we need a miracle."

"I'll go search for the body of the insect that did this," Hydrangea said. "There may be more venom."

Lucik nodded.

"If you understand me at all," Hydrangea said to the dog, "come help me find it will you?"

She left the room and Mud ran with her.

"What do I need to do?" Gracelyn asked.

"You know that library better than us, go find some sort of book on potions for advanced hornet stings or something like that. I'll watch over him. I have a few tricks to slow the spread and keep him with us. Go!"

Gracelyn knelt back down to meet his eyes, and tears streamed down her face as her lips quivered—fearing that may be the last time she would see him. "Stay with me. Don't you dare go anywhere." She kissed his cheek as she closed her eyes. "I'll be right back. Hang on . . ."

She ran out of the small house as though a strong wind was at her back. Through her mind she was already trying to figure out what stacks to search. Running into the main hall of the library she ran up the right staircase, past the section on old knights and their deeds, past the section on unknown species and their locations, nearing the area at the center back section on potions.

Not knowing the potions books well then, she ran her fingers down the spines of many at eye level first.

"*Intermediate Potion Making of the Larlets*. No, probably not. *Exotic Animals of the West*. No. *Potions to Ward off Enchantments of Arcanica*. No, probably useful later though . . . Where is one?"

She hurried down stacks, trying to find any sense of organization for the books.

"*Potions from Scrolls of the Sea Kings*. No."

Reaching the end of the row on her right, she turned and looked to the row on her left.

"*Greater Healing of a Fire-Bitten Man*. Closer perhaps." She looked at the row beneath. "*Healing Moderate Insect Bites*. Ah hah." Snatching it quickly, she looked at the surrounding books. They all seemed to have the words *Insect*, *Venom*, and one even had the word *Hornet* on it.

Rushing back down the stairs she almost lost her footing carrying all the books but grabbed the railing quickly as three from the piles fell over the bannister and down onto the floor below. She scooped them up and added them back to the pile before heading back toward the small house at the entrance of the fortress.

She burst back through the door, throwing the pile onto a small table next to them as they fell into a loose pile.

"How is he?" she asked in a labored breath.

Stone lay on the table on his back, pale as snow and shivering as if he was filled with it too. His eyes were distant and sweat continued to flow down his face and neck. He muttered incoherently as if in a dark, distant nightmare.

"Not well. I don't know if he'll last the night . . ." She threw her hands back. "I've never seen anything like this."

"Hydrangea? Has she not returned yet?"

Lucik shook her head. "Get to reading, girl."

"What am I looking for? A hornet's stinger? A spider's fang?"

"Just look for both those things. I just don't get it. The size of that black stinger . . . It's just not natural. It's as if . . ."

Gracelyn was already brushing pages back, searching through the first book when both of their eyes locked.

"Queen Alexandria . . . she did just warn us . . ." Gracelyn said.

"Arken?" Lucik said. "If it was him . . . who knows what did this to Stone." She backed away slowly. "He didn't send a wasp or hornet . . . this is something far more deadly."

Gracelyn stomach sank and twisted. "What good is a potion going to be?"

"We'll try anyway," Lucik said. "Throw me a book. With any luck Hydrangea will find the thing that did this. Even if it is like looking for gold in the desert sands."

Gracelyn was about to throw a book to her, when she realized she'd been so worried for her friends' life she'd forgotten the red stone he'd found just before.

"Hand me the book," Lucik said in a puzzled tone.

Gracelyn went over and handed it to her, which she took but seemed more interested in watching Gracelyn than opening the book. Gracelyn pulled the blanket off his body and moved her hand slowly down his hip. She couldn't see what was in the pocket, but she saw there was something in it, and felt it through the cotton that covered it.

"There's something in there," Gracelyn said. "Something strange." Pulling the lip of the pocket back, they both peered in to see what was there when Hydrangea ran back into the room.

"I couldn't find anything . . . I'll go back out . . . He's still looking . . . I—"

"Shh," Lucik quieted her.

With her slender fingers Gracelyn pulled from the pocket a curled, dead black body of an insect they'd never seen before.

"What is it?" Hydrangea asked.

"He had enough within him to give us what we needed before he passed out," Gracelyn said. "Stone." She smiled at him. "That a guy."

Lucik laid it on the table next to the books and held a candle close to it.

In the candlelight, the insect was nearly doubled to where its thorax met its abdomen. Its body held a deep, black sheen to it but with sharp bristles of fur on its back. One of its wings had fallen off but three remained, and they reflected white in the light of the candle. Most peculiar though was its size, as it was three inches long, but stretched out it would be nearly six. Unlike a hornet, it had two rows of four small eyes, and eight legs like a spider's.

"I've never seen anything like it," Hydrangea said, with her hands over her mouth.

"I think that's because it's not from here," Lucik said.

Stone coughed a deep, hoarse cough, murmuring something frantically with wide eyes staring blankly up at the top of the room.

"Gracelyn," Lucik said. "We need to look for something about curing exotic venom from insects to the lands to the west."

"I saw one! At least it might be one . . . *Exotic Animals of the West*, I think it was. It might at the least tell us what this is!"

"Hurry, child!" Lucik said, turning her head to look at Stone dying and placing her hand on his sweaty brow. "He doesn't have much longer left."

Gracelyn was back minutes later, after plucking that book and couple of others from the stacks. Stone was on the table, mumbling in a gasping voice, which made her heart beat thickly in her neck. She opened the book on the side table and scrambled through the pages. Hydrangea took another from the ones she'd brought and thumbed through it. Meanwhile Mud had his front legs up on part of the table that the black insect lay dead upon, and he gave it a low growl.

"What are we looking for exactly?" Hydrangea asked. "This one has no drawings. It could take hours to read through."

"Take another," Gracelyn said, handing her another book while staring down the one she was reading which had anatomical illustrations scattered throughout. "The first step is finding out what this thing is and where it came from."

"Hurry," Lucik said, while wrapping Stone's body tightly in the blanket. "He's still sweating and ice cold to the touch."

Gracelyn feverishly brushed through the old, browning pages. There were drawings of animals the likes she'd never seen or imagined. She almost never imagined she'd seen a real dragon until she did—and then she wished she'd never see one again.

There were pages of massive tigers with horns upon their heads, lizards with three heads, and even a picture of something that slightly resembled Ghost with her fairy wings, but this picture was much more . . . evil looking with course fur, tiny horns, and sharp teeth. Those drawings made her want to go back through at another time and read about these supposedly real creatures.

Toward the later third of the book she found the animals got smaller, and after turning the page with a rat with nine tails, she shrieked, "Here it is!" They all rushed over.

"*Vespe Nor Morten*," Gracelyn said, running her finger along the name. "Also called . . ."

"The black death hornet," Lucik said.

"You've heard of it?" Hydrangea asked.

"I've heard the name over my years, mostly long ago, but never saw one, so never took much mind to if they were real."

"They're real," Gracelyn said, glaring at the curled up giant insect with its stinger missing.

"What's it say?" Lucik asked.

"It says they went extinct in the Worforgon ages ago, around two and a half thousand years ago. It says they lived on an island to the west. One called Crestrun."

"That," Lucik said, "was one of the Bright Isles that fell off into the sea when the earth shook hard enough to once that it sent many of them drifting off into the Obsidian Sea."

"Here's an interesting bit," Gracelyn said. "It says they only grow to two to three inches. This one is nearly double that."

"Had to have been Arken," Lucik said, glowering. "What about the venom?"

"The venom is what they deem a class five venom, and causes fire in the brain, ice in the body, and causes the black to creep in quickly." She turned to look at Lucik. "I don't know what class five means yet, but I don't think it's going to be a good number." She read more, and as she did Stone convulsed on the table, and Hydrangea went over to try to soothe him as Mud whimpered next to him.

"We're losing him," Hydrangea said. "The light in his eyes are fading."

"All right, here's something," Gracelyn said. "Because of the fire, ice, and black elements of the venom, and based on the amount of venom injected into the specimen, survival is rare. It's been shown that a trio of potions has been known to work. They must be mixed individually, and all cooled to the same temperature before they can be mixed, or they may break."

"Let's get to concocting then," Hydrangea said.

"Are you any good at it?" Gracelyn asked.

"No, are you?"

"I—I've never tried," Gracelyn said, shaking her head, but then perked up with a wide smile, "but I've been surprising myself quite a lot lately with what I don't know that I know!"

"Three potions then," Lucik said. "Which ones?"

"It doesn't say," Gracelyn said, even turning the page to see another strange insect drawing. "But we'll need a potion to cure Ice Venom, Fire Venom, and Black Venom. Hand me that book over there." She pointed to one next to Hydrangea.

Thumbing through the book, her eyes narrowed as she studied. "I believe I'll find them, but it will take me a little time to find ones that say may be mixed, or at least not break when combined."

The next hour drug on painfully as Stone grew paler and his murmurs turned to screams that made each of their hearts ache. Gracelyn had drops of sweat beating onto the pages of the book as she turned pages back and forth, wildly scribbling notes on several sheets of fresh papyrus at her side. Lucik had joined in with another book on potions, while Hydrangea took care of Stone—the best she could, trying to give him water or cooling him when he heated, and warming him when he chilled.

Finally, in an exasperated sigh, flinging her head back from the pages.

"I don't know if this will work," she said, wiping her brow her sleeve. "But we've got to get making some potions soon, or it might be too late."

Chapter Twenty-Three

～❀～

Below the fortress, walking into the deep dark gloom where no blue lights shaped their way through the rocks, Lucik sparked a torch to life as she and Gracelyn made their way down a jutting stairway into the dark.

The underbelly of the fortress smelled of old iron and pools of water found in caves. They'd found the laboratory in the first few days of discovering the fortress under Endo Valaire, and didn't expect to be using the long, rectangular room filled with flasks of all shapes, vials in cupboards of wooden shelves with glass windows—some of which were labeled in old languages even Lucik had never seen before.

Lighting the torches along the walls of the laboratory, Gracelyn went to opening the long rows of eye level cabinets searching for the order in which the ingredients had been shelved.

"Well, they're not in alphabetical order," Gracelyn sighed to herself. "Of course it's not going to be that easy . . ."

Lucik ran over after hanging her original torch in the far

corner of the room under an odd-looking pair of white, brittle antlers.

"Let's be careful of using fire anywhere but where those torch holders rest," Gracelyn said. "No knowing which of these vials like flame."

"What are we looking for?" Lucik asked.

Tearing a corner of her scribbled sheet off, she handed it to Lucik.

"Need to find these six ingredients," Gracelyn said.

Lucik opened a cabinet to the side, glancing down at the torn page and fingering the vials behind the glass door.

"*Thelum root? Silver eel roe? Powder of ogre tooth*? Do we know they are all here?" she asked.

"Just keep looking," Gracelyn said, and then plucked a vile from the cabinet with a grin. "*Thistleberry*! Excellent."

They hustled as they opened many of the cabinets lining the south wall of the room as the torchlight flickered, causing shadows to dance within them. Nearly every glass door of the wall was opened as one by one, slowly they shortened the list of remaining ingredients. The drawers beneath were pulled open—that's where Lucik found a jar of what resembled a fine sand but was indeed labeled Powder of ogre tooth. She gave an excited shout of glee.

Gracelyn nervously, yet frantically searched out the remaining four ingredients—all the while hoping with all her heart that Stone was still alive, or at least not to the point of no return.

For another twenty minutes they searched until there was only one remaining—*Saliva of the Tangier.*

"You keep looking for that, Lucik. I'm going to start brewing the potions." With that Gracelyn ran over to one of the tables on the north wall of the room where bare spots of table were surrounded by neatly organized collections of glass bottles, mortars and pestle, and so many things Gracelyn didn't recognize she felt an overwhelming nervousness creep up her back.

"You've got this," she said to herself, taking a deep breath. Tacking the sheet up to the wall above the desk, she one by one laid the ingredients in rows for their recipes. "One at a time. Fire Venom first . . . two fine pinches of *Sand of the Arr*, three *Hairs of the Iox*, and five *Silver eel roe*."

She read the recipe carefully, three times fully before beginning. The water needed to be heated slowly as to not overheat, as not to kill the roe, and the sand could only be dissolved by an orange viscous liquid on the table that needed to be added at just the right temperature, and right before the hairs were added so it wouldn't dissolve them.

Gracelyn's chin nearly touched the surface of the wood table as she eyed the ingredients carefully as she added each one, with beads of sweat streaming down her face. She was pleased to find that her nervousness at it not only the first time making a potion—and the grave importance of their perfection—her hands didn't shake as she concocted them.

"Found it!" Lucik said, nearly causing Gracelyn to add one too many roe to the potion, who turned and cocked her head with wide eyes. "Oh, sorry . . ."

For the next several hours Gracelyn carefully created the three potions, letting all three of them simmer on their three fires, while Lucik paced the room behind her, and Gracelyn only took her eye off the three of them to wipe the sweat from her brow. At one point Lucik returned with water for her, even though Gracelyn hadn't noticed she'd even left.

"How much longer?" Lucik asked, with her leg bobbing as she sat in the chair next to her.

"Almost done, just waiting on the Black Venom potion to reach two more degrees. Here, take these other two up Stone, where they can start to cool."

Lucik took both from their iron arching handles with dry

towels, but Gracelyn stopped her with a delicate touch on her forearm.

"Careful. Don't spill a single drop now."

Lucik nodded and went off, carefully eyeing each step as she exited the laboratory.

Ten minutes later, the Black Venom potion hit the desired temperature and she without any excitement she was off quickly with it, and a bowl of glass and a thin copper stirring rod.

With rushed, short steps she made her way to the room with Stone without spilling a drop, and where she met eyes with Hydrangea, who looked nearly as pale as Stone.

"Is it ready?" she asked, with both hands clasped on her cheeks.

"Almost. Lucik, we must stir and blow on each of them to get their temperatures down. You do those two, and I'll do this one. Remember, when you see the line on that stick drop to fifty-eight, we need to add one-third of each to the glass bowl, which should keep it from dropping or rising. No higher though, and no lower."

Stone had gone past his murmurs and shrieks, as he then lay motionless on the table with his arms and hands hanging limply off. Yet he remained sweating, and his chest only moving rarely as his breathing slowed. His face was beginning to turn a blue hue.

Several minutes later, Lucik had dropped the Ice Venom potion to fifty-eight and poured in one-third into the bowl, and a couple minutes later poured the Fire Venom into it. Her hands shook as she did so, and Gracelyn and Hydrangea watched nervously hoping she wouldn't spill any or add too much.

Another long fifteen minutes later, Gracelyn stopped stirring and blowing. "There," she said, looking at the brink of exhaustion, but adrenaline was pumping through her veins.

Pouring the Black Venom in quickly, and being careful to add the perfect amount, she stirred it with the rod. "Don't have to worry about spilling now." She dunked a mug into the trio of potions and ran over to Stone with it. "Help me hold his mouth open. He's going to have to swallow it."

Hydrangea held his chin down as Gracelyn poured it into his mouth.

Gracelyn pulled his chin up, covered his mouth and pinched his nose shut.

Hydrangea and Lucik both stood back, holding one another.

"Please let this work," Lucik said. "Please, Crysinthian. Please."

"I just hope his body's alive enough to choke it down," Hydrangea said.

Gracelyn was pressing with all her strength down onto his mouth and nose, and finally his body started to convulse. With his mouth full of the potion and not able to breathe, bits of the amber liquid beaded up between her fingers, and she pressed down harder. Tears came to Hydrangea and Lucik's eyes.

Gracelyn saw that a gulp went down Stone's neck, and she quickly removed her hands as his body gasped for air. Opening his mouth wide she saw the potion was swallowed, and she staggered back and collapsed into the chair behind her with a deep sigh.

Gracelyn wept. It was the kind of deep sob that left her struggling to breathe between the sighs of exhaustion and grief. She had nothing left to give, nothing left to do, all she could do was cry and moan as if she'd lost a loved one.

"What do we do now?" Hydrangea asked, watching the motionless body of Stone next to the inconsolable girl.

"We wait," Lucik said. "Now it's Stone's turn to fight."

FEELING out in the bleak darkness, he reached out for his fingertips to run against something . . . anything . . . He felt nothing beneath him or above, and that sent a stark throng of panic shivering up his back. Stone could feel himself sweating in the blackness, but when he reached up to his forehead . . . he felt nothing.

Is this . . . death? I don't remember how I got here. Or is this just a dream . . .?

But then his fingers scratched against something on both sides of him. They were rugged and felt like torn wood under his fingernails.

It can't be . . . I can't be back . . . in that coffin . . . That's impossible.

"Gracelyn!" he called out into the crisp air. "Gracelyn, can you hear me? I don't know where I am. Ceres!"

He remembered the roar of the dragon above his coffin when he first awoke in that nightmare. The vivid memory of Ceres diving that shovel into the dirt came rushing back to him.

"Ceres! Someone. Anyone. Please help. I'm scared."

He could feel his eyes were open as he pawed at the top of the coffin futilely—as he could feel the heavy dirt piled on top of it. Banging his fists, he hoped for some chance it would budge, but the dirt fell onto his face and got into his mouth, as he spit it out to his side.

"Gracelyn! Help me, I'm stuck. I need help! Anyone? Please!"

Then, beyond the top of the top of the coffin, still bathed in shadow, he saw a dim white glow. It was small enough, and faint enough that he couldn't make out what it was, but it was slowly bobbing toward him, and he became sure of one thing . . .

"I'm not in a coffin . . . I'm in a dream."

He swallowed hard as the white object came toward him, and he felt sturdy ground beneath his feet.

A harsh voice grew out of the darkness, he realized the white that was inching toward him was reddening, and then he saw the dark pupil within it.

"This is no dream . . ." the voice said, and Stone's voice seized. He was frozen in disbelief.

"This is a place between dreams and where you live your idle life . . ."

Stone took a deep breath as the figure emerged from the shadows, and he found both of them standing under the light of a shimmering, bright moon above. All else was bathed in that same utter blackness.

". . .Arken . . ."

The Dark King towered over him, with his one eye glaring down upon him. He wore the same curled, horned helmet that made him look like some form of demon. His heavy, gray armor marked with thousands of nicks and scrapes shown like a sign of his achievements. That leathery cape fell motionlessly behind him.

There was no wind, no sound beside the almost humming of the shining moon down upon them. He felt utterly alone.

"Finally, we get this chance to talk." the corner of Arken's mouth curled upon his ashen face. He pulled his helmet down, holding it at his side, opposite the thick sword he held in his other hand. His hair was slick and black, and fell below his shoulders. At the crest of his forehead was the widow's peak not entirely unlike Stone's.

"What do I have to say to you?" Stone said through clenched teeth. "I heard your riders burned Hedgehorn to the ground."

"Yes, they did."

Both of Stone's fists balled up.

"I'll burn it *all* to the ground if I must . . ."

"Why? Because you were tortured and sent off to sea? Because you felt the Old Mothers betrayed you?"

"Yes. And more. So much more . . ." Arken growled. "You're young, far, far younger than I. The Majestic Wilds threw you into my war that has naught to do with you, but here you are . . ."

"But here I am . . ."

Where am I? And why has this bastard come to me again? How is he able to do this to me?

"Last we spoke," Arken said, turning to the side and slowly pacing, staring at the dark ground below his boots. "I made you an offer. Not only for you, but for your dear friends."

"I'd never barter a deal with you." *The thought of that still resonates with me. It makes me feel sick to my stomach he would even offer . . .*

"I was . . . disappointed you didn't send me to her. What's her name—? Gracelyn?"

"You don't say her name!" Stone burst forth, with his fist readied to bury into Arken's sinewy face, and as he lunged forward, he hit as hard as he could into the Dark King's temple, but it passed through it with only a faint wisp of smoke. Arken turned and smiled.

"Don't you remember how these things work?" Arken said, touching his cheek with a drawn-out slide of his strong, yet wrinkled fingers. "In this place, we can do no harm to one another. This is our . . . round table, if you will."

Stone drew back and pointed an angry finger at him. "You wanted me to give her to you? To *you*? I'd rather pitch myself from this mountain and fall all the way down before death's grip before I'd give any of my friends to you. You're evil. You're nothing but evil and death."

Arken turned about and paced to the right with his head still down.

"There was a reason I wanted you to tell me where the

Majestic Wilds are. That's the thing you are blind to. You are blind to so many things. I don't want to kill. I don't want to be the evil you proclaim me to be. I want to save. I bring justice. If only you'd introduced me to Gracelyn, and all her power, I wouldn't have had to burn Hedgehorn. This all could have been averted."

"Don't you dare tell me you killed all of those people because of me!"

"It wasn't just you, Stone. We both did it. We both killed those people by our decisions. King Tritus and young, naive King Roderix II are to blame. Salus too, that rotten sorcerer. And the kings before them, and Queen Velecitor of Valeren even." He laughed briefly as a thick line of black saliva fell down his chin. "It's all of us. These wars will never end until all those responsible are given retribution."

"Retribution?" Stone said shaking his head with fists still clenched, wishing he had his sword and the Dark King was actually in front of him. "What do I need retribution for? You say I'm involved in all this bloodshed? All I'm trying to do is protect me friends."

"—Is that all you're responsible for?" Arken said, glancing over at him slightly and then continuing his slow back and forth pace, with his thick gray sword dragging along the black ground.

"All right, I'll listen. What am I responsible for? Helping to kill a few of your people who attacked us? Trying to kill your Neferian for attacking us? For being this foreseen one to assist in your death?"

"Everyone thinks they're innocent until their dark tapestries are drawn back for all to see in the bright sunlight. I offered you the chance for your friends to have their lost parents back to them. They could've lived with their most loved again."

"Don't you say that, Arken. Liar!"

"I offered to give you the one *true* family that you have, back to you . . ." He gave that same sinister, sneering smirk.

"You shut your fucking lying mouth. I warn you!"

"I could give you everything you've ever desired, and still you despise me. You and me, Stone. We are meant to become something . . . something that will change everything!" His voice roared and echoed in the darkness.

"I don't want to change everything!" Stone's teeth clenched and he felt the blood pumping thickly and hot in his veins. "There are good—great—things in this world. I just want to end the misery. I want to end the pain. Help those who need it. I've seen people die. So many people have died. Tell me, Arken, why have you come here now? A new offer?"

"No. You've decided," Arken snarled, with more black ooze drooling down his chin and neck. "I know I can't tempt you with my future. That's why I tried to kill you. But Gracelyn is a Majestic Wild after all . . ."

Stone remembered that horrendous pain in his neck, and stumbling down the steep rock face, but that was the last of his memories.

"Don't underestimate her," Stone said. "She could be the end of you."

"Hmpf," Arken said. "That remains to be seen. I don't fear her." He shot a wicked glare at him then. "And don't forget . . . there are going to be two more of them awakening."

Stone swallowed hard. He'd seemed to have forgotten that there would be two more Majestic Wilds.

"They'll kill you," Stone said in a raspy voice. "They'll never join you."

"Stone," Arken laughed a low, growling laugh. "You don't even remember your own name . . ."

Stone took two steps back without realizing he had. He tried to speak, but only gasped.

"That's right . . . I know who you are. I know who your

father is. I know about your past. I know . . . about your mother . . ."

Stone gasped. "You . . . you lie!"

Arken coughed, sending dark spit flinging from his lips, and then smiled, wiping it from his narrow lips. "Do I? Do you really believe that? Feel deep within yourself, I think you know the truth. I could tell you all you want to know. If you wanted. I could tell you where you were raised, if you had a brother, sister, lover . . . But you don't want to know. You don't want to give in to the *evil* in this war."

"No! I'd rather die than be your ally!"

Stone's heart was racing so hard he thought he was going to collapse, his arms and shoulders throbbed with hot blood, and his mind was racing so quickly he didn't know to run or try to fight.

"It's all right, we have time," Arken said darkly. "I have a new fight. You didn't fully succumb to my pet's sting. But now that I see you again, I'm glad you didn't. I enjoy you. I marvel at the man you're becoming. You remind me of myself as a young man. Yes, Stone, I believe we're going to have many, many fun times ahead for the both of us . . . But for now, I must go. Many things to do, many things . . ."

Arken turned and walked away with his leather cape brushing behind him in the dimming moonlight.

"Arken! Tell me where my father is! You tried to kill me twice. Just tell me where he is, who he is! I need to know . . . I need to know . . ."

Stone fell to his knees in exhaustion, finally unclenching his fists and staring down at his reddened palms.

"Father . . . Father . . . I need you . . . Please if you're out there somewhere. Please . . ."

PART V
ARMIES OF STEEL AND MAGIC

Chapter Twenty-Four

With the final whisper of peach-colored sunlight flowing through the thinning trees like streaks of stretched, soft silk, they placed each boot step carefully on the crisp leaves beneath them. They slunk their heads low as they inched their way—finally—to the outskirts of the forest.

Their faces were tarnished with dirt, their hair thick with dried mud from resting their weary heads on the ground at night. Horses gently neighed as they pulled their reins behind them.

The sounds of the forest made their ears perk to attention with any strange sound as they were making their way toward the plains that seemed to roll on endlessly past the trees. Chirping insects, the cawing of birds high above and the ebbing cascade of the sounds of cicadas filled the woods from canopy to forest floor. A sound of something splashing in shallow water broke to their right, and each of them stopped and looked over, but once they thought it was nothing more than a frog slipping under the water's edge—they pressed on.

"Do you see it?" Adler said in a soft tone to Ceres who was just in front of him.

Ceres brushed her hair back behind an ear and looked to where he was pointing. Through the trees it was so faint it almost resembled another thinning cloud to her, but then she realized it was trails of smoke winding up to the heavens.

"Is that . . ." she whispered back to him, her voice was more raspy than normal from her parched throat. "What would that be? Salsonere?"

"No," Corvaire said from the lead. He didn't turn his head back but scratched his horse on the side of the neck as he peered out into the gloomy twilight spreading throughout the plains. "Salsonere is farther north. One hundred and half miles or so."

"You think they're out there, hunting?" Adler asked with a deep gulp.

"Hunting for us mos' likely," Ceres said.

Marilyn nodded solemnly from atop the horse Corvaire pulled along next to him. Looking at her, Ceres was pleased that even out in the deep Everwood Marilyn looked thicker and color had returned to her face. Squirrel meat and fresh water had done wonders to her compared to whatever drivel she was fed down in dungeons beneath Atlius.

"We will make camp here tonight," Corvaire said.

"Here?" Adler asked with a sigh. "There's nothing here. Let's head into the plains through the night. I'm not tired, and I think it might be a warm enough night to sleep without a fire."

"Would you rather have one fire tonight? Or not one at all?" said Corvaire. "Here, within the trees we could have one last fire before we cross out into the Argoth Plains. The worst place for us to be is right on the outskirts of these trees. They'll surely be waiting for us out there."

"Isn't it safer to pass through there at night?" Adler asked, swatting a mosquito buzzing in his ear.

"Of course, it is." Corvaire stroked his black. "My question was—do you want to rest one last time and have a fire, or do we want to go out there this night?"

"I think we should go," Adler said, brushing his tan, greasy hair that hung below his nose then. "We've come this far, why wait?"

"'Cause we could get one more good night's rest," Ceres said, flicking him in the forehead.

"But what about Stone? Gracelyn? We need to get back to them. They might need us," Adler said after brushing her hand away.

Ceres laughed. "One night isn't gonna make that much of a difference—"

Adler's voice rose. "One night could make all the difference." His eyes were piercing, even past the dreariness in them from someone living in the woods for nearly a week and a half. "Who knows what they're doing. They may need us tonight."

"Well, if they need us tonight, then—" Ceres began again but was cut short by Adler's passionate words again.

"I don't care what it takes, I'll sleep three hours a night. We need to get back to them. We've been gone far too long."

"We came down here for a reason," Ceres said, motioning to Marilyn, who was listening intently on their conversation, nearly motionlessly atop the horse. "Listen, Adler . . ." she walked over to face him as his tan face was reddened and Hedron neighed next to him. "We all want to be together again. We're stronger together. But Stone is strong, he can take care of himself for now. He's with Lucik and Hydrangea too. And you saw what Gracelyn did to those two Neferian. And we got her! He's gonna be some happy to see her again when we get her back to Endo. We just need a little rest. One last night . . ."

Adler's shoulders relaxed and he took a deep breath. "I suppose you're right. I just miss them. You're right too, Ceres, we are all stronger togeth—"

A piercing roar finally shuttered through the gray, cloudy sky above, sending each of them ducking low to the ground, looking up with wide eyes. It rang out for miles as the forest quieted to nearly a chirp. The cicadas retreated, the wind slowed and even the running water of a nearby stream seemed to silence.

"It's distant," Corvaire said. "But can't mistake that tail end of the roar that sounds like shattering glass. It's one of them all right. Arken's sent one out."

"Who's it after?" Adler asked. "Us . . . or them?"

"Could be both," Ceres said. "He makes no mind for who he kills."

"With the shade of night coming," Ceres said. "This may be a blessing."

"What do you mean?" Corvaire asked, as if beguiled by the pretense of a dark dragon being something fortunate.

Marilyn tapped Corvaire on the shoulder, and she wrote upon the skinny slab of stone that had become her voice to them over the days. With a piece of charcoal from a fire, she wrote on the smudged piece of gray slate—

'If there are hidden watchers out there, then they might be . . .'

"Then they might be the ones the Neferian attacks," Adler said with a wide smile.

"Too dangerous," Corvaire said. "Safer in here."

She wiped the slate clean again with a tarnished cloth, and they all watched as she wrote. *'Woods burn brighter than grass.'*

"We're better at sneaking than they are," Adler said. "We can hide in the shadows and creep past those creeps while they're all disoriented by the Neferian and the riders! And she's right. It could burn down the forest all around us."

Corvaire groaned. "I don't know . . ." He looked to Ceres who was the last one to give their opinion.

She looked at each of them as the Neferian let out another distant screech that sent a shiver down her back and make her neck feel a chill.

"Am I the one to decide?" she asked nervously.

"Well—?" Adler flicked her back in her forehead. "What do you think?"

She sent a strong finger toward the middle of his eyes. "You do that one more time and you won't have a finger to flick! I'll cut it off while ya' sleep, throw it into the fire and let the worms crawl up the bone til there ain't nothin' left."

"Whoa, whoa," Adler said with his hands up. "I was just gettin' you back. You don't have to threaten me with hand castration."

Ceres took a long, slow stride toward him, looking him square in the eyes. "Of all the people I'm stuck with in this world, why did Crysinthian curse me with a child dressed in a man's clothes?"

She groaned a deep, low groan and turned back to the others.

"But I believe them right," Ceres said. "We should hurry into the night while they scurry on about the dark dragon."

"Then we will go," Corvaire said, looking up at his sister then. "Are you sure you're up for this ride? We will ride fast, ride hard."

Her dark eyes peered into his as she postured up upon the horse's back. She gave a slow, calculated nod, without breaking their gaze.

"I suppose that's it then," Adler said. "We ride fast and hard."

Ceres moaned, rolling her eyes. "Why does everything have to be like that with you?"

"What're you talking about? I was trying to be inspiring like him."

"You just—"

The roar pierced the air once again. It was so loud each of them covered their ears and Ceres' skin crawled. "We should move . . ."

From the roar, it sounded as if the Neferian was to the north.

"With any luck," Adler said. "It'll take out those hunters and their camp."

"How do you know those are hunters hunting us?" Corvaire asked, still gazing out the plains as they continued their walk out of the trees.

Adler didn't seem to know what to say.

They stepped out into the moonlight. The sun had slipped away. The endless stars filled the sky like a kingdom's horde of sparkling diamonds, and the faint light of scant fires glowed out on the plains.

"There are those out there," Ceres said. "So many more than I've ever seen."

"This is the night," Corvaire said with narrow eyes, seeing all of the encampments. "This is our night."

They mounted their steeds, breathing in the fresh, crisp air of the plains as a strong breeze blew past, sending large patches of grass rolling like fresh sheets about to be strewn on a bed.

Corvaire sat behind his sister, and for the first time since they'd all been reunited, and after all the conversations they'd had in the forest, Ceres looked at the two family members together again, and she felt sadness. It'd been so long since she'd been with her own family who was lost to her, and it'd been over a month since she'd last seen Stone—she didn't want to lose it all then to a dragon of Arken, but what choice did they have, she thought. This was their best.

They galloped off out of the forest, and as another resounding roar bellowed from the north, she could finally see the monster. It sped down from the sky like a hawk, finally slowing above the camp whose fires Adler had spotted earlier in the daylight. It flapped its wings over the camp with its black body hovering vertically over, nearly invisible in the dusk. But she knew as soon as she saw that first speck of white in its mouth, that someone was going to die.

Riding on, Corvaire yelled, "Onward! Ride!"

But her and Adler couldn't look away. They knew what that nighttime white fire meant. They'd seen it before, and far too up close. The dark dragon cast raging white fire down upon that encampment as though it was a city that had stood against it for centuries.

The wrath of dragons had never ceased to amaze Ceres. Each time she saw one it took something from her: some innocence, some naivety. And now that she'd seen the Neferian and their wrath in full, she didn't know if she was too scared to fight, or couldn't do anything but fight.

"They're lost," Corvaire said as his horse galloped on. "Probably would've tied us up like swine and taken us back to the castle."

Their horses continued west, while Ceres turned her head back and watched the plains burn in a white haze from the flame.

"The stars are dimming," she said to herself.

Chapter Twenty-Five

In the middle of the night, the sounds of chirping insects and rolling of thin streams were drowned out by the sounds of their horses galloping upon the hard trail that led them west. For hours they'd ridden under the dark, cloudy sky hoping—praying—the rain would stay away. If a downpour were to come, it would surely impede their haste to leave the plains that surrounded the forest behind them.

The white flames of the Neferian still left a faint haze to the east, but at least its roars had gone, Ceres thought. *At least maybe it's flown back to where it'd come from . . .*

Corvaire's horse slowed, with him sitting behind Marilyn as her horse heaved heavy breaths. He'd stopped next to a stream to the right side of the path. He dismounted, and helped his sister down, easing her delicately down to her feet.

"What's the matter?" Adler asked, leaping down as well, with the grip of his sword firmly in his hand.

Ceres watched both of them from Angelix's back.

"Marilyn needs to rest for a moment," he said. "The horses too. Gather water. We'll be back on our way shortly."

Adler looked like he wanted to press on by the thin wrinkles in his forehead, but after a moment of clear thought, he went and helped Marilyn down the bank to the water's edge to wash their faces and fill their canteens.

Dropping down from Angelix, Ceres could see an uneasy gaze from Corvaire as he scanned the plains for any sign of something that might cause them . . . trouble.

"What are you looking for?" Ceres asked. "Of all the things that hunt us, what is it that worries you most?"

"What worries you most?" he quickly responded, still scanning all around them as a cool wind blew through. Lightning glowed in the clouds to the far south with a faint rumble of thunder rolling down after it.

"I—I don't know. Arken I suppose," she said.

He groaned. "Yes, indeed. He is the true enemy. But I would say part of me would like to set my sight upon that betraying shadow Skell. Wrap my hands around its neck and send the power of the gods surging through its spine."

"Did Mogel need coin that 'a much?" Ceres asked, scratching her itchy scalp. "It just doesn't make sense one way or the other to me . . . Betray a queen for a lord? Risk reprisal for a small mound of riches?"

"If I have my way . . ." Corvaire lay his stone-cold eyes to her. "There won't be no use or time even of asking him one single thing . . ."

"She can ride with me," Adler said, helping Marilyn up the grassy hill as the three horses grazed and drank.

Corvaire's head cocked.

"I'm lighter," he said. "We'll ride faster if we both take Hedron."

"How far is it until we are safe enough to make camp?" Ceres asked. "Or at least rest our heads somewhere? I know me must make haste, but we haven't had a wink of shuteye in over a day and a half, and we've still got a long ways ta' go."

Corvaire looked concerned, scratching his beard with his head looking out again at the plains.

"Marilyn," Ceres said softly. "You knew about that hidden entrance to get us away from Atlius. You got any more of those surprises hiding in ya'?"

For a fleeting moment, Marilyn looked as if she was about to grab her charred stick to write something, but then shook her head with her eyes closed.

"We'll ride until we find a cave or someplace that could shelter us long enough for a reprieve from wandering eyes," Corvaire said.

Another crack of thunder flickered in the southern sky.

"At least it's down there," Adler said. "With the way the wind is blowing, if we see that where we're heading, might be a better time to find that cave sooner rather than later."

"Ceres, do you need water?" Corvaire asked, and she shook her head. "All right, Marilyn will ride with you for a while, Adler. Let's be off."

Hours later, as the night darkened and the rumbling of angry clouds boomed overhead, the scattered droplets turned to hard drops on their hoods. The horses' hooves hit damp dirt, and their pace slowed.

"We need to find some shelter," Adler called up to Corvaire. "Marilyn is shivering."

Each of them looked around, and the lightning that crackled in the clouds above lit the area around them. Mostly small trees were strewn about, and a large mound was to the north, and few smaller ones to the south. Up ahead seemed to be more grass.

Corvaire spun his horse, unsure where they would find what they sought.

Through the rumbling thunder a familiar sound grew from behind.

"Horses," Ceres said. "There!" She pointed behind them and to the north, off another trail.

"Dozens of them!" Adler said, with his hand over his eyes to shield them from the rain.

"They're coming for us," Corvaire said. "They're in armor under their cloaks."

"Do we fight?" Ceres asked. "There are so many of them."

"No," Corvaire said. "I fight."

"No," Adler snapped, spinning toward him.

"Swords won't win against so many soldiers, only the Elessior can."

"We will stay and fight," Ceres said. "We don't leave each other behind."

"There's no time," Corvaire said. "There's no time. Ride!"

Then, they heard the other noise growing from the north.

"Over there!" Ceres said. "More of them, riding through the grass. We can't outrun all of them!"

"Ride!" Corvaire yelled. "There won't be any of them to chase after you if they try to take my sister again from me."

Then, as Ceres panicked for what to do, jostling the reins and drawing her sword—she saw an unusual sight. "What is that?"

"It's a banner," Adler said. "No wait, it's no banner." His mouth gaped. "It's a white flag . . ."

"Who are they?" Ceres asked. "I don't see a banner."

But as Corvaire seemed to turn from anger to curiosity, and as the riders approached closer, he saw the colors with which they rode.

"They're soldiers of Verren," Corvaire said. "You can see the red and yellow on their cloaks now."

"Do we put our weapons away?" Adler asked him.

"No way in the Dark Realm do you drop your sword," Corvaire said.

Adler nearly remarked that they were friends of King Roderix II, after all they had saved him from an assassination attempt, but he held it in as the two sets of riders reared up to meet them.

"Knight Drâon Corvaire?" the lead soldier asked, with a long, silver spear in his hand and a sheath of fine black leather on his hip. His eyes were a deep blue and wet blond hair stuck to his strong cheeks.

Corvaire nodded. "You ride from Verren. We are friends of your king. We mean no harm to your king or your home."

"You ride with Ceres Rand and Adler Caulderon, but who is the woman who rides with you?"

"What does that matter to you?" Corvaire growled. "What business do you have with us. We are making haste and not trying to let every thief within ten miles know where we are . . ."

"The *king* sent us to find you," the soldier said, leaning forward in his saddle with a furrowed brow.

"Now, now, now," a voice said from far back in the first line that came from the trail behind them. Ceres knew the voice but didn't recognize it at first until she saw the man in a silky cloak dyed violet that rolled rain off effortlessly. And then she saw the beady blue eyes of the chancellor gazing at them from under the hood. "No need to make harsh words with one another. We are all on the same path, we are all in this together, after all . . ." He smiled and many thin wrinkles formed on his face.

"Chancellor Kellen," Adler said. "What are you doing all the way out here? You came here to find us?"

"Yes," he said with that sneering smile. "All the way out here." He put his pale palms out and up at his sides to let the rain splash on them. "What are we doing out here? Isn't it obvious?" He raised an eyebrow.

"You're not taking us to the king," Corvaire said. "We don't have time to travel north. It's west we seek."

"We're not here to take you with us," Kellen laughed. "No. We came for you to take *us* with *you*."

"What riddles do you speak?" Corvaire asked. "Tell me true, why are you here?"

"His majesty King Roderix II sees the importance of your mission. And while we have our own war to wage. He has sent me to lend you what aid I can. We are here to make sure you get to where you need to go. And I suspect that is . . . Endo Valaire on the mountain Elderon?"

Ceres' heart sank.

Adler swallowed hard.

"We don't need your help," Corvaire said. "We ride better on our own."

"You'd decline the help of forty of Verren's finest?"

"Yes."

"I dare disagree with you on that," Kellen said with a short laugh. "Just from where you left the Everwood, we spotted six groups of spies searching for you, not to mention another that was burned out by Neferian fire."

"We've gotten this far without ya," Adler said.

Kellen sneered at him.

"Don't think your forty would help much against a dark dragon," Ceres said. "You ever put one down? You even ever seen one in person? So far as I know, we're the only ones who've fended one off and lived to tell about it."

"Yeah," Adler said. "Suppose you just want our help to get to the west coast."

"We regretfully decline your offer," Corvaire said.

Kellen sighed with a high pitch as many of the soldiers grew uneasy at their answer.

"Well, all right," Kellen laughed. "This is *not* an invitation. This is too important, and we have come too far to not follow our king's orders."

"Orders?" Adler asked. "What are the other orders?"

"To find you and do what we can to assist you in killing Arken Shadowborn, of course."

Ceres turned and whispered in Adler's ear. "I don't trust him, but I don't mind the king so much. Maybe it wouldn't hurt for the night so that we can get some rest?"

"I don't trust him either," Adler said, glaring at the man as the rain waned.

"You may accompany us for two days," Corvaire said. "That will give us time to speak over food and fire. That is my only promise to you at this moment. We are friends of Verren."

Kellen bowed his head. Corvaire strode over to him as the other soldiers seemed oddly entertained by Kellen's uneasiness as the legendary knight approached him.

"Men with honor hold their promises," Corvaire said, stopping short of Kellen's horse, and held out his hand. "Do you promise upon your king and the Great Crysinthian above you speak the truth?"

Kellen looked uneasily into the dark eyes of the man of Darakon in front of him. He held out his pale hand and shook it. "Yes," he said.

"Then let us find a place to get some fires going," Corvaire said. "I'm sure your men would enjoy some reprieve from their sopping clothes. A couple of the soldiers looked at Kellen whose clothes and socks were probably mostly dry under his fine tunic.

"Very well," he growled under his breath.

Chapter Twenty-Six

Thick air heavy with worry within the walls of the castle lit with warm blue light. Around every corner lay a still silence as if a king lay dying. Silent prayers from long-dead soldiers seemed to whisper from underneath the stones—praying for the king to live, let the king live . . .

Stone's pale body moaned deeply and then gasped for air. Gracelyn's hand shook as she wiped away the cold sweat that beaded down his face. Hydrangea rocked in a chair in the corner of the room with heavy eyelids, but every time Stone groaned from the sickness, she was startled back to alert. Lucik stared at him as Gracelyn washed his arms with a cool rag, and Mud who was laying on the table by his side—he whimpered softly throughout the night.

"I can't tell if he's getting better or not," Gracelyn said. "Just when I think his fever is breaking it seems to get worse."

"He's not dead yet," Hydrangea said, not meaning to sound so grave, but Gracelyn shot her a cold glower. "I meant that to be a sign he might be improving."

"Well he's not goin' to die," Gracelyn said, looking down at Stone's closed eyes which twitched through the pain.

"We need to be prepared," Lucik said, "there's a chance he won't . . ."

"Just stop it please," Gracelyn said through her tears. "He's going to pull through. The prophecy said he's the one to stop this war. He's got to make it." She leaned closer to his face. "You hear me, Stone, you have to make it."

※

You have to make it . . .

He heard the faint voice call out through the darkness. The voice was distant but familiar. It was as if he'd heard that voice before. It was a warmth in the darkness that made his heart slow and he took a deep breath.

"Gracelyn . . ."

Feeling his bare feet touch the cold ground he couldn't see beneath them, he took step after blind step. His fingers were spread out wide at his sides attempting to feel something . . . anything . . . He yearned to hear her voice again. He ached to hear her words again.

"How do I get out of this place? Has Arken trapped me here? Wake up, Stone. For the love of all things holy, wake up . . ."

In the darkness he could not feel with his fingertips, he saw his friends' faces fogging in his mind. He remembered Gracelyn's smile, her cheerful, chipper attitude and her raw power when the time came. He saw Adler's sneer—that same smirk he always showed just before he was going to say something snide or rush into battle as Stone's side. Ceres' hair gleaming in the sunlight crossed his mind, and he remembered the way she narrowed her mossy green eyes when she told Stone how dumb he was acting, or when she was about to have words with Adler for being crude.

He thought of Corvaire and Marilyn, and he missed the Old Mothers Seretha, Gardin and Vere. The way they died by the heat of the Neferian's fire would be carved into his memory for the rest of his life. He'd never seen such raw power.

Step after step he walked alone. Hoping for something to scrape against his fingers or call out back to him as he yelled out for someone to help him, someone to find him.

Then, to his right, he saw a dull glow, like sunlight creeping into a hole in a cave above, beaming down on something vague behind a wet rock. He'd turned to walk toward it before he even realized he had. There was nothing else, it was only that glowing beam lighting an object that was round and still. As he approached it, he saw it was a person kneeling over.

His steps slowed as he saw that the person was holding something that was hidden to Stone. It was on the other side of what looked like a broad-shouldered man. He heard something then . . . the man was sobbing.

Stone swallowed hard, and then spoke. "Excuse me, sir . . ."

There was no reply, the man only continued to cry.

"Sir, are you well? Do you know where we are? Do you know what this place is?"

Taking slow steps, Stone walked to the side of the man, and while the man seemed not to notice him still, Stone soon saw what the man had cradled in his arms.

His knees nearly buckled, and he covered his mouth with his hand as he gasped. Within the man's strong, pale arms was the body of a boy. His body hung limp and his head was careened to one side with his eyes closed.

The large man's head was still down as he sobbed. The boy's body was that of a boy no older than twelve, and as Stone leaned in to look at the boy's face, he felt as if he'd seen the boy before. His eyes were closed by his black hair which was long but strewn over the side of his face, carved into a widow's peak at the top of his forehead.

The large man's sobbing stopped abruptly, startling Stone back to stand up straight.

The large man lifted his head, gazing out into the darkness, seemingly not noticing Stone standing directly in front of him.

"Who's there?" the man growled.

Stone didn't move a muscle, but he couldn't look away from the man's dark green eyes the color of the leaves of an evergreen at dusk. His strong, broad nose sniffed, widening his nostrils.

"I can't see you, but I know someone is there."

At the man's forehead was a very prominent widow's peak with thick, black hair pulled back and he had strong black eyebrows. His arms and chest were bare, and Stone's jaw dropped.

He looked into the man's scanning eyes, and then he looked down to the dead young man in his arms. And as he saw what lay beneath the boy, Stone's hands flung up to cover his mouth and his vision grew wet with tears. His lips quivered behind his hands as he sniffled and sobbed. He shut his eyes hard and heavy streams of tears rolled down his cheeks.

The strong man seemed to have forgotten about Stone's presence and leaned down and kissed the boy on the forehead.

"I love you, son," he cried. "I'm going to miss you more than anything. You'll always be with me, and I'll always be with you."

Stone's chest heaved as he cried.

The man's tears fell onto his son as he lowered him into the wooden box.

"No," Stone said. "He's not dead. He's not dead!"

The man gently lay the boy into the coffin, and with his strong hands on the wooden side, his head slunk as he cried.

"I'm sorry I failed you, I'm so sorry, son."

Stone swallowed and took a deep breath.

"I'm here, father. I'm not dead. You didn't fail me. I'm still here."

But the man only continued to cry.

"I'm alive, don't leave me down there in the dark. It's so lonely down there. I don't want to be alone in the dark again . . ."

He reached over to touch the man on the shoulder, but his hand slipped through it like dry sand, and as the large man stood to walk away, he melted away slowly like the sand in an hourglass, fading away back to the darkness.

"Don't leave me," Stone cried. "Tell me who you are. Tell me where you are." His lips quivered again. "Tell me who I am . . ."

A sharp voice behind him made Stone snap around, wiping the tears off his cheeks quickly.

"I had a change of heart," the voice said.

"Leave me alone, Arken."

"You asked for you father, so I gave you a look at him," Arken hissed with a grin. "The resemblance is strong in your kin. You look more and more like him every day."

"Where is he?" Stone asked.

"Now, now," the Dark King glowered. "You had your chance, remember? All you had to do was give me the Majestic Wilds and you all could have had your families back."

"Why are you doing this to me? Just to torment me?"

"I wanted to see your face," Arken said.

"Why?"

"You act as though you and your friends are the only ones who've lost ones you love?"

Stone didn't respond.

"You know how many years my body has walked this world? I don't. I lost count many years ago. But I've lived many times the span of a normal man's life. So, don't tell me about loss. Everyone and everything I've ever loved has died. From old age or a spear in the belly. Every, single, one is gone. And you stand here crying because your father is still *alive*?"

"Yes, that is why I cry. Your loss is not greater than anyone else's, and when I kill you, you will have no more grieving to do, and no one will mourn your death."

"I think you may be mistaken," Arken said. "I've done nothing for my people but try to give them the lives they deserve. They deserve so much more than what the old kings and the Old Mothers of this land cast down upon them. I'm saving my people!"

"By killing these people?"

"If that's what it comes to," Arken said. "If all I need to do is make way for my people to return to our lands, then that is not too high a price to pay. Tell me, Stone, how far would you go for your friends? How far would you go to save their lives?"

"As far as I needed."

Arken smiled again as his leather cape's tails rustled in the darkness.

"We are not so different, you and me. It's a shame we must meet again, and I will have to kill you. I rather enjoy you as I said. Someone who seemed so weak has proven to make it through far more than any other man could."

"I'm nothing like you," Stone growled.

"We're the same boy. Just born in different times, and under different mad kings. You're welcome for the gift. Thought you might like to see your father's face once before you die."

"I'll not die by your hand, Arken. I'm coming for you, and when I do, you'll wish you'd died all those years ago when the old kings defeated you."

Arken scoffed at him, spinning as his cape flung behind him and he vanished into the darkness.

Stone got one last look at the boy in the coffin before it faded away too.

※

GRACELYN SCREAMED as Stone sat up from the table gasping for air. Her scream woke Lucik and Hydrangea, who both leaped to their feet, rushing to the table.

Stone choked on his dry mouth as he took short gasps of air.

"W—water," he muttered.

"Here, here," Hydrangea said, putting up a mug to his lips. "Drink slowly, slowly."

He wet his mouth and gulped down some of the water, choking on it. His eyes were wet from coughing, but he heard that same voice he'd heard in his dream, or whatever that was.

Turning to his right, he saw the reddened, hazel eyes of Gracelyn glaring at him as if she hadn't seen him in a year's time.

"You—you look terrible," he said to her, as she wrapped her arms around him, squeezing tightly. "I can't breathe."

"I thought you were dead. But I told you not to die. I told you that you couldn't die."

"I heard you, Gracelyn," he said. "I heard your voice in my darkness . . ."

"Thank you for listening," she said as she pressed her lips to his cheek. "Thank you for not dying."

"I'm not dead yet," he said as they both released their arms from one another. "We've got too much work to do before I sleep for good."

"You need rest," Lucik said, checking for a fever with her palm on his brow. "It's been a long night . . . for all of us."

Stone saw Mud panting at the end of the table, wagging his tail energetically.

"Oh, come on up here, boy," he said as Mud leaped onto the table like a clumsy puppy, licking Stone's cheeks and sitting sloppily on his stomach. "Easy there, I'm happy to see you too, boy. I'm very happy to see all of you."

Chapter Twenty-Seven

"Two days . . . Two more days of this?" Adler said not nearly under his breath enough. Two soldiers of Verren sneered at him, and one cleared his throat and spit by the early morning fire.

Dozens of horses grazed and drank by a nearby waterhole next to a cluster of rocks slightly off to the north. Tents had been erected overnight. Ceres hadn't slept under a dry canvas tent since their escape from Atlius, and even though she was surrounded by soldiers—and she most definitely hated soldiers, she appreciated reprieve from the cool wind and rain.

Campfire smoke drifted among the tents as the golden sun rose.

"I'd take two days of warm food," Ceres said, "and no worry of throat-slitters running into our camp in the night."

"Right." He winked. "Now we camp with the slitters . . ."

Corvaire approached from the front of the camp with a large satchel bag slung over his shoulder. His long black hair whipped over his shoulder and his beard had grown into a frayed, grizzly texture. He heaved the bag over and plopped it next to their fire, startling Marilyn, who's head was resting on Ceres' lap.

"Hmpf, sorry," he said. "We head out shortly. Just spoke with Kellen, he's telling his troops to saddle up. We'll ride again within the hour."

"Gonna be a lot slower journey with all these steelheads around us," Adler said.

"Like I said, I told him we'd give him two days to try to convince us that he could escort us to the mountain."

"But we're not gonna let him, right?" Ceres asked with slender, lowered blond eyebrows.

Corvaire grinned and nodded.

"How are we supposed to get rid of them?" Adler asked. "Just tell them we're going to be on our own way? Thanks for the food . . .?"

"He agreed to our two days too," Corvaire said.

"He'll take our terms over his *king's*?" Adler said as he stood up and brushed the dirt from the back of his pants.

"Let's say it was more about us buying time," Corvaire said, watching the dozens of soldiers around them sulking around, doing their preparations to ride out.

The saw Kellen was coming back to their ranks with a pair of soldiers carrying their helmets. Kellen wore a long gray robe with a red satin scarf around his neck, and he carried a long, thin curved sword sheathed at his hip.

"We're making initial preparations," he said. "Make sure you're ready."

"All right, I'll make sure to pick up my pack and mount my horse," Adler said. "Can you give me three minutes?"

"Hilarious," Kellen said with a cold glare. "You'd make an impeccable jester."

"Actually, I'm a hunter," Adler said with narrowed eyes.

"Impressed, I assure you," Kellen said as he turned to

speak to the others. "We've *real* hunters out now gathering food for the journey. They will catch up with us later on the road."

Ceres snickered at Adler. "They're prob'ly hunting more than elderly squirrels."

"Pff, what'd you know about hunting?" he asked.

"If you come back with one more turtle to cook, I'll—"

Ceres was silenced by Marilyn's elbow in her ribs.

Kellen leaned down to speak to Ceres. "I've got orders to escort you to where you need to go. But I'll just say here and now, I'm not interested in you two bickering like brother and sister . . ." he turned to walk back to the front.

"Brother and sister?" they both said in disgust at the same time.

Something happened that stopped every soldier in their position.

A low horn blew to the south. It rang out from the top of the low hill, but still the highest position in that direction.

"A scout," Corvaire said. "Get your swords . . . Sounds like something is coming."

Kellen ran over to the side of the road to see the scout waving his arms after blowing the horn. He was signaling the convoy, but Ceres and the others didn't know what it meant.

"We ride northwest if anything runs afoul," Corvaire said. "You hear me? Northwest through the grass."

Each of them stood, ready to draw their swords. Adler ran over to the waterhole to get their horses.

While Ceres was watching Kellen and the scout communicate by over one hundred feet, she felt a tugging on her sleeve. She looked over and saw Marilyn gathering a piece of paper she'd been given by one of the soldiers the night before, and with a quill dipped in a small jar of ink she wrote the words, *I don't trust this man, nor what is coming over that hill.*

"Marilyn, you know what's coming?"

Marilyn nodded with wide eyes. She wrote, *Greed. Greed for Power.*

Kellen seemed content with the signs they'd sent back and forth.

"Over a dozen men in robes on horseback," he said to the two soldiers with him.

"What banner do they fly?" one of them asked.

"No banner," Kellen growled, looking back at Corvaire. "But by their clothing I know *why* they've come . . . Ready the troops, and get those warders ready . . ." He stormed off as the two soldiers rushed into the ranks shouting orders.

"Mount your steeds! To arms! Warders, front and center!"

"Warders?" Adler asked with a furrowed brow under his brown hair. "Didn't know Kellen brought warders . . ."

"Only one thing you really need them for," Corvaire said, and a blue glow twinkled in his eyes.

The scout rode quickly down the mountain back toward them as two long lines of soldiers on horseback were formed, and one woman and man in long gray robes with long staffs stood behind the ranks. Ceres couldn't see their faces, but they were ready with their arms out wide at their sides. Ceres thought of her parents, readying her Indiema.

The scout rushed back into the ranks shouting, "Sorcerers, fifteen of them! Wizards approach!" Not long after he returned, Ceres could see the riders in robes coming over the hill. Each of them wore black and had white steeds.

Corvaire stayed on the road with the others.

"What should we do?" Adler asked with his Masummand sword in hand.

"Look at how they ride," Corvaire said, almost in admiration. "So casual. They're not afraid of the army before them. They'd kill all these men with a mere muttering of strange words under their breaths. Kellen has no idea how to fight them."

"So . . . what do *we* do?" Corvaire asked.

"Adler," Ceres said softly. "Look at them, don't you recognize them?"

Once she asked those words he seemed to grasp what was approaching.

"Yeah, I remember now. It's them again . . ." he said in a cold tone.

"Go no farther," the captain of the soldiers of Verren called out once they were thirty yards off. The banner of Verren whipped in the wind on spears above the army. The red V with the solid golden stripe across it was known everywhere in the Worforgon—no one could mistake it.

"Soldiers of Verren," the woman at the center of the fifteen riders called out. Her head was pale and bald, and she had bone earrings in both ears and a circular one in her nose. "I am Paltereth Mir. We seek out those who rode the plains alone in the wind and rain. I see they ride with you now."

"What's your business out here in the Argoth?" the commander asked. "Don't know who you're talkin' about. Now ride off. We are soldiers of Verren, sworn to King Roderix II, true king of the Worforgon. Ride off and no harm will come to you."

"True king," Paltereth said back snidely. "Everyone's got their own king around here. King Roderix, King Tritus, the Dark King . . ."

"The Vile King," Adler yelled back from behind the ranks.

The soldiers looked back at him in surprise at his sudden brashness, but once they looked back at Paltereth and saw the disdain on her face, they all knew it to be true.

"Salus Greyhorn, the *Arcane* King, is indeed king to many of us," she said proudly.

The soldiers of Verren shifted uneasily in their saddles. Many murmured about the Arcanic Mages that were before them.

"But who we hail to has little to do with what we must do," she said. "It is of utmost importance that those of the Darakon line and the two young ones who ride with them reach the mountain of Elderon with much haste. Who escorts them there is of no importance, but my king has tasked us with ensuring they make it, and quickly." She turned her head slowly to peer between the horses to fix her eyes upon Ceres'.

Ceres felt a cold creeping up from her toes and into the follicles of her hair, tightening them on her scalp.

"This isn't good," she whispered, realizing she'd lost her Indiema, so she quickly regained it, ready to cast out a spell if it came to that.

The commander heaved his chest out and drew his sword, causing more rustling within his ranks as the horses snorted and stamped their hooves. "We are under orders by King Roderix II to take the travelers where they must. Your aide is not needed. We will escort them to where they must go. You may ride on now."

The Arcanic Mages shuffled, hefting their long, metallic-looking black staffs with many shades of precious stones inlaid in them. There was a very long moment where Ceres' palms sweated, and she could tell Corvaire felt uneasy by his eyes darting around at the many about to die for the right to protect them.

Adler glared at Kellen, who was standing next to the commander, fidgeting with his hands. Somehow Kellen caught the glare and looked over at Adler, who cocked his head as if pressing him to do something. Kellen seemed to shake off the nerves with a loud clearing of his throat.

"A-hem," he coughed. "Mages of Salus . . . let me be the first to offer my sincerest . . ."

Paltereth whispered a handful of words and her staff glowed a dark shade. Kellen choked on his words, unable to speak, clawing at his lips.

"Warders!" the commander burst out.

Both warders chanted, but then two of the Arcanic Mages cast spells and the warders' staffs shook and trembled. They both gripped them nervously in both hands as they shook violently.

"I'm not here to harm you," Paltereth said in a low, hissing tone. "If I cared to, you'd all already be dead. Your blood would boil, every hair on your bodies would burst into searing fire, and the bones in your body would break and snap like kindling."

"You attack the army of Verren," the commander said. "You've declared war upon King Roderix II! Riders . . ."

"Hold, hold," Paltereth said, holding her staff out harmlessly, sheathing her sword and wiping her pale hand over her bald head. "I didn't come here to fight." Kellen regained his voice and the two warders' staffs were calmed. "If you wish to die today, then die you will."

A young girl in dirty blond hair burst through the ranks to stand in front of all the riders of Verren, including the commander and Kellen.

"Ceres," Adler muttered. "What are you doing?"

"Your King Salus gave us his offer," she said with fists clenched. "Stone never accepted. We don't need your help. We aren't going to give him the new Majestic Wilds. They are not for him."

"We aren't here for that offer," Paltereth said. "Our king bade us to take you to the mountain. Something is coming." Her voice hissed and her dark eyes narrowed. "The dark in this land grows, and our king knows there is only one chance at stopping it. You must make it to the mountain. There is little time."

"What is coming?" Ceres asked. "Tell us all, right here and now so we can decide if your words be true."

Paltereth looked uneasy being put on the spot so in front of the dozens of riders of Verren. She turned to and briefly discussed it with the Arcanic Mage next to her. Once she seemed to have decided, she turned back to Ceres and her white steed neighed loudly.

"Your war," Paltereth said. "Your war has seemed to be your everything. But the world has yet to hear its true name."

"Why do you speak in riddles?" Kellen asked, but buckled backward at a false wave of her staff, glowing in darkness.

"What do you mean?" Ceres asked. "We are at war with King Arken. Everyone is."

"Not yet," she said with a dark glower. "The true beginning to the war is coming. And once it begins, there is no going back until the bitter end."

"What true beginning?" Ceres asked with her arms out wide, yelling for all to hear.

Paltereth seemed irritated by the young girl's persistence. "You need to get back to Endo Valaire. We will keep you alive until that time. For what exactly will happen our king cannot see. But what he can see is . . . What is coming will be like no other war for ten thousand years . . ."

Chapter Twenty-Eight

"It seems we have no choice then," Ceres said in a strong voice. She turned to Commander Rourke. "With your permission I would ask that these Mages of the Arcane aid us in our travel as well as with your forces."

"But I—" Kellen protested.

"I'm not speaking to you, chancellor," she said. "These soldiers do not fight for you. They fight for the king, and for their leader."

Commander Rourke glared uneasily at the fifteen mages on white steeds peering coldly back at him with their dead eyes.

"If that is your wish," he said. "My orders are to accompany you to where you must go. Under any other circumstance, I would never ride next to those of the Vile King, but if you allow us to escort you past the promised two days then we will allow this."

"I allow you to escort us to the mountain," she said, causing Corvaire to groan. She turned back to face the mages. "I allow you both to take us safe to the coast. Under the terms that you do not cause harm to one another, and your camps remain separate from one another. Do you agree to my terms?"

Paltereth nodded her head low and the commander let out an '*Aye.*'

Ceres returned through the uneasy soldiers on horseback and picked up her bags.

"What have you done?" Adler asked, touching her back gently.

"Saved all these men's lives," she said casually. "These men, innocent or not, would all die in cold blood this day if they were to enter into battle with Salus' mages. You know that. Corvaire knows that."

"But . . ." he said warily, "what happens when they get to Endo with us? Neither has said a word about after we get to there. What will they do then? And what about this new war that witch speaks of so vaguely?"

"Don't matter," Ceres said, and leaned to whisper into his ear. "We'll have left them all far before we get to the mountain."

Adler drew back with wide eyes.

"But . . . how?" he whispered back, and with Corvaire paying close attention to their words.

Ceres smiled wryly and winked at Marilyn, who winked back.

※

BACK ON THE damp road west under the warm afternoon sun, the four of them were in the center of a long procession of military and magic. On their right rode the commander of the troops of Verren, and on their left was Paltereth Mir of the Arcanists.

Ever since the mages had entered the convoy, Ceres and the others had hardly spoken a word to one another, because of the prying ears of the mages. The soldiers had their weapons ready to draw while they rode.

It was a long six hours under the warm sun and thick air. Marilyn rode upon Corvaire's horse, and Ceres didn't know if she appreciated not having to hide in the plains and keep a watchful eye for unwanted parties, or she'd rather not have to worry about the dozens that surrounded them.

Kellen rode at the front of the line of horses, and Ceres supposed it was because he wanted to be as far away from Paltereth as he could, without simply fleeing that is.

Adler kept giving Ceres curious looks throughout the day, obviously wanting more information about what they'd talked about just before the mages rode into the caravan. Paltereth even shook the Commander Rourke's hand, but Ceres assumed a promise of a mage of the Vile King's held about as much weight to it as a bucket full of water with a hole in the bottom.

As evening approached later, they set up their camps. They found a wide, flat patch of grass with a clear stream next to it. The soldiers camped on their right side in their tents of canvas and had scattered fires. To the left side the mages sat in a ring around a single warm fire that held a violet hue at its center. They didn't have tents either, instead they pitched square roofs of a white cloth material similar to linen, pitched upon poles of dark wood. Each of them sat up with their legs crossed. They drank a strange tea that Ceres thought smelled of tar and moss.

While in the middle of the encampment as the horses neighed peacefully under the shining moonlight, and with each of them having warm meat in their bellies, Adler finally felt comfortable enough to ask the question.

They all sat close together, as if keeping each other warm in the cool night breeze.

"Marilyn wrote it out to me last night," Ceres said. "She

woke me in the middle of the night."

Marilyn nodded.

"While she was down in the cells of Atlius, and after they'd removed her . . ." Ceres gave her a somber glance. "She found there was another magic wielder in the cell across from hers. And since they assumed with no tongues, none could cast without words, the guards left them mostly alone."

A soldier walked by, and Ceres stopped talking, prodding the fire and sending out a fake shiver. The soldier walked past and back out into the tall grass.

"She wrote that the man's name was Maniigus. He was a warlock from Mÿndmorden. He taught her things in secret."

Marilyn's head slunk.

"What kinds of things?" Corvaire asked in a low tone.

"How to cast spells without speaking," Ceres said uneasily.

"What kind of magic did you learn down there, Marilyn?" he asked with a raised eyebrow.

"She told me it's called the Seliax."

"The Seliax?" Corvaire said, grabbing Marilyn's arm. "What were you thinking learning that?"

She glared at him.

"She said he promised it would help her grow her tongue back, so that she could once again use the Elessior."

"What's the Seliax?" Adler scratched his head.

"Doesn't matter," Corvaire said.

"It seems to," Adler replied.

Corvaire sighed. "It's similar to the Arcanic magic, except it was manipulated by a cult like group ages ago called the Aigons. Where the Arcanica uses water and poison, the Seliax used *shadow* and poison."

"What's that mean for Marilyn?" Adler asked.

"They use movements with their fingers and hands to cast, because the Aigons took vows of silence," Corvaire said, glancing on his sister with another deep sigh, and gently put his hand on her shoulder. "Those kinds of magic, although powerful, are like a disease . . . a disease with no cure. She will carry it with her forever."

"She learned it so that she could get back to her Elessior," Ceres said. "She knows the potion now that would grow back what was taken from 'er. Once we're at Endo she can concoct it."

There was an uneasy silence as the campfire popped and crackled.

"Also," Ceres said. "Maniigus taught her a handful of spells, including one that makes you the same shade as the shadow itself, or the night."

"That's how we're going to get away from them?" Adler asked. "You're going to camouflage us?"

"She said it's more than that. It'll actually *turn* us into the night . . ."

"I don't know if I like the sound of that," Adler said, shifting uneasily on the log he sat upon.

"We won't have to worry about created noise as we travel or even about the horses' hooves. We should be able to ride straight down the road without even the mages noticing us."

"They'll notice us being gone," Adler said.

"I don't like any of this," Corvaire said, shaking his head low, muttering to himself.

"So, once the sun's up, then?" Adler asked, with a furrowed brow, and popping his knuckles.

"If we can find a dark patch of shadow, we'll be able to hide within without being seen," Ceres said, and Marilyn nodded.

"No, no, no," Corvaire said. "I don't like any of this, not one bit . . ."

"It's either that or we take all of these people with us to the city of the Majestic Wilds . . ." Ceres said pointing out at all the tents and troops. "I don't see any other way . . . Do you?"

"You'd be breaking the vow you made to them," Adler said snidely.

"You think I give one shit about lying to soldiers and dark mages?"

Corvaire and Marilyn both smiled at her.

"No, no I don't think you do," Adler laughed.

"So that's that then," Ceres said. "The only question left is . . . when?"

Marilyn then pointed to the fire, and then up to the moon, nodding her head.

"Tonight?" Ceres asked.

Marilyn nodded.

"Shouldn't we plan this a bit better before we . . ." Adler said.

"If she says tonight, then I think we should trust her," said Ceres. "It's still early, and if Paltereth says that we need to get there with such urgency, then maybe we should listen ta' her."

"We would travel much quicker without them," Adler said, looking to Corvaire for approval.

"If you say we ride tonight, sister, then we ride tonight."

"We'll need to wait until most of them are asleep," Adler said. "We'll need to ride hard to get as far away from here as possible in the darkness. Who knows how long it will be before they find we're gone. And they won't give up easily on us. After all, Gracelyn is up in Endo, and every king seems to want a piece of her power."

"What do we need to do to prepare?" Ceres asked.

"I suppose she just needs to cast that dark spell," Corvaire said. "And then the race begins."

"If Paltereth and the mages catch us," Adler said. "Only Crysinthian knows what they'll do to us."

"I know what I'd like to do to them," Corvaire growled.

"In another hour or so," said Ceres. "Most of the soldiers should be asleep. That would be our best hope."

The hour passed but felt more like five. Ceres nervously awaited the fires to slowly die down as the soldiers went slowly off to slumber. The ring of mages was no longer sitting but laying with their heads resting on their packs. Human after all, she thought.

"All right," Corvaire said. "If we're to do this. Then let's get it over with."

"No one move while she casts," Ceres said. "Don't want to give anything away, but she'll let us know when it's ready."

Marilyn sat upright in front of the fire they'd let die down intentionally, to reduce the amount of light.

She closed her eyes and held both arms out with her palms facing down, and her middle finger touched her thumb on her right hand and her ring finger touched her thumb on her left. Her right hand flipped upward, and her index finger slowly curled into her thumb also. She balled up both fists tightly, and then opened them both up fully with her fingers outstretched and brought both hands to the sides of her neck and then down to her chest where she pressed both palms flat against each other with her fingers pointed outward.

Opening her eyes, she looked down at her hands and gave them a loud clap, and then another. She stood slowly and took a log next to her and struck another log on the ground with it. She looked around and saw no stirring. With a nod to them, she picked up her pack and walked over toward Hedron.

"That's it?" Adler asked. "I don't feel any eviler yet . . . dark magic and all . . ." He shouted at the top of his lungs then. "You all are a bunch of dung eating, slimy tongued mother grabbers who wouldn't know how to read a book if they had a knife to their throats!" They all watched as nary a tent stirred and the mages lay soundly. "Kellen, I hope you fall off your horse and break your leg you coward!"

"Let's be on our way . . ." Corvaire said.

They all moved to the horses, stirring them up and saddling them.

"We need to be careful not to touch anyone," Ceres said. "They can't see us or hear us, but they can feel us."

They were upon the three horses, but this time they snatched a horse for Marilyn to sit upon, and Corvaire tied it to his horse to guide it for speed.

He placed her upon the horse, and she flattened her chest onto the back of its mane.

"Ready?" Corvaire asked, holding the reins tightly.

Each of them nodded.

As he whipped the reins, leading them toward the road ahead, Ceres let out a loud shriek of pain. Her hands twisted and her head shot back.

"Ceres!" Adler cried out, and Corvaire drew his sword looking around for what had attacked them.

She cried out again in agony and fell off Angelix's side as the horse seemed startled as well by her rider's agony. Ceres fell onto her side and Adler quickly leaped down to her aid.

"Ceres, talk to me. What's wrong?"

He grabbed her hands in his, and she twisted and contorted in pain as he inspected her for wounds. A few moments raced by as he searched her torso, chest, and back, but his hands were dry of blood.

"What is it?" Corvaire asked, still he and Marilyn were mounted on their steeds.

"There's no injury," he said. "I can't tell what did this to her. Poison? Could it be the Arcanist? Or . . ."

Corvaire's jaw dropped and Marilyn's eyes fixed upon her with a wide smile.

"Could it be?" Adler asked.

Ceres moaned and slowly stirred awake, holding her head as she sat up. "My head," she mumbled.

"What happened?" Adler asked, helping to keep her up.

"Are you injured?"

She moaned again. "A—Another one. There's another one now . . ."

"Ceres," Adler said. "Another what?" He looked up at Corvaire.

"Another one has been born . . . Another *Majestic Wild* has arisen . . ." she said with bloodshot eyes.

Corvaire leaped down and ran over to her. "Where, Ceres?" he asked urgently. "Where is she?"

Adler helped her up to her feet.

She looked around as if unsure where she was. Looking back and forth, and then turning back around, she pointed back down the road.

"East?" Corvaire asked.

"She's far," Ceres groaned, trying to shake the cobwebs away. "Far to the east."

"Let's go," Adler said. "The soldiers would never suspect we're going east. They'd go west for weeks before thinking we'd turn back around."

They realized that Marilyn had gotten down from her horse and was standing just behind them. She took out the same paper and dabbed her quill in the ink quickly and scribed, '*No. We must reach the mountain. That is our destination for the time being. We need to let Gracelyn and Stone know. It's too late to turn back now.*'

"Marilyn," Corvaire said. "Are you sure? This is a new Majestic Wild. What if someone gets to her first?"

She shook her head. '*It would take far too long by horse*, she wrote. *Quicker to fly from coast to coast.*'

"Fly?" Corvaire asked.

They all looked at her with wide eyed grins creeping up on their faces.

"Fly?" Adler asked with his eyebrows raised. "Did you just say, *fly?*"

PART VI
LOVERS AND KINGS

Chapter Twenty-Nine

※❀※

Elated, fatigued, and unsure of how they felt exactly about Ceres' findings, they rode west. Each of them was weary as they rode their horses westbound, as they found themselves trusting Marilyn's guidance but as they rode uneasily down the road past the groups of sleeping soldiers in camps and the mages that stirred under their canopies under the stark moonlight, they all knew there was no turning back.

A half hour passed as their haste had quickened and they rode hard. With still no horn sounded from them missing back at the two camps, Corvaire halted them to discuss what was next—after all, they couldn't ride all night and all day.

Each of them shifted eagerly on their horses, as the four horses breathed easy.

"If she's all the way toward the east," Adler said, gripping the horn of the saddle tightly. "How are we going to fly there?"

Marilyn took out her paper and after Corvaire helped her down, she began to write. *'Gracelyn.'* She held up for all to see, and they watched as she took the page and wrote more. *'Grace-*

lyn, as one of the Majestic Wilds has the power to summon Grimdore back to the mountain.'

"Grimdore?" Ceres asked, shaking her head in disbelief. She was embarrassed with herself she'd almost forgotten about the dragon that was Endo Valaire's protector, or she'd thought it had passed in the fight with Arken's giant Neferian in the battle that killed the previous Majestic Wilds. "The sea dragon? Is she recovered from the fight?"

Marilyn shook her head and shrugged her shoulders.

"It is the best bet we have," Corvaire said. "We've got to get word to Gracelyn to summon the blue dragon up from the sea, whether she's ready or not."

"Does she know how to call the dragon?" Adler asked. "Is it just one of those things she knows how to do instinctually?"

"Perhaps," Corvaire said, brushing his hair back and looking west. "It's a song she must sing. Its shouldn't be too difficult to find if they've found their way around the archives under the mountain."

"A song?" Ceres asked. "What kind of song?"

"It's a song in a language no longer spoken by man's tongue," Corvaire said. "The words are not recognizable, and Gracelyn may not even know what they mean, but those words carry far. It hasn't been sung that I know of in generations."

"Well," Ceres said. "We've got to get her to sing it, an' quick! There's another of the Majestic Wilds in the east, and who knows who out there have my power to sense out their births. We've got to get to her now!" She dismounted and her boots hit the still-damp ground. "Marilyn, can you send another scroll to them?"

'*I can try,*' Marilyn wrote. '*I fear my magic is weak because of the current spell.*'

"Then try you must," Ceres said with a serious glare into Marilyn's eyes the color of darkly shaded oak.

Marilyn nodded, standing in the middle of the road that

led east. She held her arms into her body, but Ceres could tell she was moving them in front of her. She stood there for a few minutes, and then took out more paper and tore it into a long, thin strip only an inch wide. After dipping her quill in the small bottle of ink she wrote quickly. Handing it to her brother he read it quickly and handed it back with a nod.

"Now what?" Adler asked as Marilyn looked up at the night sky filled with brilliant stars that framed a full, bright moon that emerged from behind a thick, dark cloud.

"I suppose we wait an' see if it worked," Ceres said.

"Should we ride while we wait?" he asked with his leg shaking nervously, still saddled up on Hedron.

"Just a moment," Corvaire said, scanning the skies as well. "We'll know soon enough if it worked."

"I hope it does," Ceres said, and then in a whisper she prayed. "Please, Crysinthian, if you're out there and you can hear me—please give her the strength to cast the spell. We need help. We can't stay out in the open with these mages chasin' us. Please . . ."

As if emerging from the dark itself, a raven swept out of the sky and landed on Marilyn's forearm, which she'd held out. The raven was huge for a bird, as it seemed scraggly, and Ceres noticed seemed to be molting by the fluffy feathers that stuck out from its back. It let out a deep caw as its obsidian black eyes looked around at them. It let out another *caw*.

Corvaire went over and helped Marilyn to tie the scroll to its leg as she had to prop up her forearm with her other arm under the weight of the bird. It was nearly two and a half feet long from beak to tail. Once the scroll was tied to its leg, Corvaire backed off and waved for the bird to fly off. It flapped its wings that reached a massive span over four feet together and took off back into the night sky, slipping between the lights of a cluster of stars and disappeared as quickly as it had appeared.

"You did it!" Ceres clapped her hands.

Marilyn placed a finger in front of her own mouth, shushing her.

"What's the matter?" Ceres asked.

"Can't you feel it?" Corvaire said. "The spell she cast before is fading away. Marilyn's not strong enough yet to cast both spells." He rushed over to her to help her back up on her horse.

"Maybe you should let her ride with me again," Adler said.

"I'm not going to disagree," Corvaire said. "We need to ride. We need to get as much distance as we can between us and those behind before Marilyn can regain her strength. For I don't think the mages of Salus or Rourke are going to give us another chance at this . . ."

They were quickly mounted and making their way down the dark road, whipping their horses' reins, and kicking their heels into the horses' sides.

Ceres leaned into Angelix's neck. "Ride girl, ride hard!"

※

EVEN IN THE damp woods at night, unable to get a fire going, and without a fresh meal to cook by a warm fire—he'd never remembered being so hungry in his whole life as he was after healing from the black death hornet's sting.

They prepared a whole meal of suckling hen, fresh green beans with butter and rosemary and fresh cream rolls, but he couldn't wait from the aromas that wafted from Lucik and Hydrangea's kitchen, so he shoveled handfuls of bread and soft cheese into his mouth.

The potion had worked so well even, that he found his legs strong under him as he walked, not achy and sore like a normal venom that powerful would do to the muscles in your body—he even ran part way to the house with Mud running happily next to him, smiling up at him.

"Slow down," Gracelyn said, placing her palm on his forehead to take his temperature. "You're going to upset your stomach."

"I'm fine," he said as he waved her hand away. "In fact, I feel great!" He gave Mud a piece of cheese from off the table.

"He's probably fine, dear," Lucik said to her after she leaned over while mixing the dough for the rolls, kissing Hydrangea on the lips. "You did well, he's alive, let's celebrate, why don't we. Why don't you go over and open one of those reds he likes?"

Hydrangea put down the pan she was tossing the green beans in and wrapped her arms around Lucik's neck.

"What a perfect day to have a party," she said, moving her feet, trying to get Lucik away from cooking, who laughed and tried to push her away. But Hydrangea pulled her away finally. "Can't you hear the music? Can't you picture the band playing while we're in some tavern back in Verren? The Tall Tale's maybe?"

"I remember," Lucik said with a wide grin. "How could I forget those nights?"

Stone had a mouthful of food still as he watched the two dance in the middle of the kitchen while Gracelyn went off to get the bottle of wine Lucik asked for. He swallowed the food down and grinned widely as they danced.

They laughed as they swayed back and forth, holding each other's hands as Lucik twirled Hydrangea, who spun gracefully.

With the bottle of wine in her hand and still a look of worry on her face, Stone stood and grabbed the bottle, putting it on the table next to them.

"May I have this dance?" he said playfully, bowing to her.

"You what?" she said a blank expression or her face, and then she raised an eyebrow. "Dance?"

"Come on," he said. "I bet you're a great dancer!" Stone held his hands out for her to take. "What do you say? We're celebrating tonight."

"Are you a good dancer?" she asked, with the blank expression washed away to a curious, playful grin.

"I have no idea!" He laughed.

She looked over at Hydrangea and Lucik, who were then pulled in closely to each other, dancing slowly. Laying both her hands into Stone's, he smiled a wide smile and bowed his head again. She moved his left hand to the side of her waist, and they swayed back and forth, with his feet moving fluidly beneath him to his surprise.

"You're not too shabby," she said, looking down at his feet.

"I suppose I'm not," he said.

They danced for a few moments that warmed Stone's heart to its brim. He felt as if it might burst out of his chest. Her face was close to his, and her wild hazel eyes glowing in the candlelight with vibrant browns, oranges, and greens. She laid her head on his shoulder.

"You know you scared me half into my own grave," she said, and he felt a calm affection between them. There was no tension, no worry. It felt as natural and comfortable as any memory he'd ever had.

"I won't do it again," he said.

"Promise?" she asked softly.

"Promise I won't almost die?"

"Mhmm."

"Sure," he said with a laugh.

They were startled alert with the loud sound of something shuffling on the window's edge. It came so swiftly and silently, even Mud was just stirring awake. The caw echoed loudly throughout the house.

"Another raven!" Gracelyn said, running to the window.

"What's the scroll say?" Lucik asked, as Gracelyn untied the scroll quickly. "Who's this one from?"

She untied it and the raven flapped its wings, flying off back into the tunnel that led out into the fresh mountain air.

"It's from Marilyn again," Gracelyn said with a smile, and as Stone watched her smile turned from white teeth showing to a frown of great worry, she held it out for Lucik to read as she looked deeply at Stone.

"They're in trouble," she said. "They're being trailed by not only Roderix's men, but also a pack of the Vile King's mages. We've got to get them out of there."

"Roderix and the Vile King?" Stone asked, watching Lucik's grim expression after she handed it to Hydrangea. "But we saved Roderix and Salus said he'd leave us alone while we decided to take him up on his offer or not . . ."

"That's not all," Lucik said to him, and Hydrangea handed it to him.

Toward the end of the scroll he saw the words hastily written in Marilyn's handwriting—*'another girl, Ceres sensed another Majestic Wild in the east.'*

His expression hardened. "How do we get them?"

"Read on," Lucik said.

'Gracelyn must summon Grimdore with the Song of Dragons.'

"Song of Dragons?" he muttered.

"Do you know the song?" Lucik asked Gracelyn.

Gracelyn hung her head with her fingernails scratching her cheek. "Song of Dragons, where have I heard that before? Oh, wait . . ." She snapped her fingers with her head perked up quickly. "I didn't hear it, I *saw* it! It's in a book in the library. I think I remember which one. I didn't read that part because I didn't understand the words, but something called the Song of Dragons sticks out in a book."

"Let's go find it now," Stone said. "If they're in trouble then we've no time to waste!"

Each of them rushed to the library, and Gracelyn led them up to the second level, and to one of the oldest sections where many of the books had no spines or covers.

She thumbed through the lines of dozens of books on the bottom shelf, as Stone bit his fingernails.

"Do you see it?" Lucik asked. "Can we help?"

"They all look the same," Gracelyn said, in a frustrated tone with herself. Then she stood back up and put her hand over her closed eyes. "I'm trying to remember something else about the book. What was it again? There was something special about it. Was it a picture, no, it was something like a texture that made me pick up the book in the first place."

"Was it, scales?" Hydrangea asked, pulling a book from the other rack to the right, also with a spine missing.

"Yes!" Gracelyn quickly took it from her hand. The cover and back cover were both textured with large scales of a soft, golden metal. She went through the pages quickly, looking for the part with, hopefully, the song they needed.

"Anything?" Stone asked.

"Here," Gracelyn said excitedly, halting turning pages and scanning some lines of letters that looked nothing like their language.

"Can you read it?" Lucik asked. "Can you sing it?"

"I couldn't before," Gracelyn said, but then her eyes glowed a bright blue, casting that light down onto the page. "But now that I know what this is . . ." She raised her head. "We need to go back out to the mountain."

"We can't go back out there," Lucik said.

"It's the only way the Great Sea Dragon Grimdore will feel my call."

"Grab your swords," Hydrangea said. "Who knows what might be out there waiting for us."

"Arken won't send anything out again," Stone said.

"How do you know that?" Gracelyn asked.

"He told me. He enjoys me too much to let something else kill me. He wants it to be him now. Dark is his mind, but he believes us to be the same."

None of them seemed to know what to say, so they instead went back out the tunnel that led to the mountain, with Mud at the lead, bounding through the tunnel. This time they took the left trail up and entered back into the burned-out city of Endo, where Seretha and the others were killed by Arken's Neferian, and Grimdore had retreated after narrowly escaping being devoured by it.

"Go ahead," Lucik said once they were back within the cities' walls. "Sing us the song."

Gracelyn lifted the book before her, and with her eyes glowing that same soft blue under the warm sunlight that was just rising over the Sacred Sea, she sang in a voice that wasn't entirely her own. Singing words that sounded like nothing Stone had ever heard, the words still rolled off her tongue delicately, yet intentionally, as if she'd known the words all her life.

Her song rolled through the city and off into the cool sea wind that rose up from the sea as it crashed into the rocks far below. The birds stopped their singing, and even landed in nearby trees and ledges. All the critters of the area left their caves and nests to watch Gracelyn as she sang the Song of Dragons.

For a moment, Stone even thought he could feel the rattle of the mountain moving to listen to the song. It felt as if the entire world was watching and listening.

Then with her voice hitting a single high note, she let it ring out, feeling like it was the only sound in all the Worforgon. Letting the note die down, she gently closed the book and there was an eerie silence, as if someone had just been laid out to rest. It sank into everyone then the eternity the fallen had entered into, and that they all would fall into.

The silence broke with a monstrous roar that made the birds fly back off into the sky frantically and made the beasts around scuttle back into their dark holes. It roared again from below and they ran over to the corner of the city, and as each roar intensified, they had to cover their ears as they ran.

They made it to the corner of the city as Mud had already gotten there, barking madly. And as they got there to look down they felt the strong gusts of wind fly up the cliff as the head and underbelly of the mighty turquoise dragon flew upward at a menacing, humbling speed.

It flew up overhead, flapping its enormous wings with thick muscles in its back glistening in the orange hue of the rising sun. It hovered above them, sending forceful wind down upon Stone and his friends, while Mud quit barking, perhaps remembering this dragon.

Grimdore slowly lowered herself to the grassy fields of the city.

She seemed even bigger than the last time he'd seen her.

"She's grown stronger," she muttered.

Her long white horns curled up from both sides of her massive head as smoke smoldered out of her mouth as she growled. Holding her wings out wide, they appeared larger than before, stretching out wider than the outer walls of the city. Her teal wings were reflective and marked with scattered black scales. A long red strip ran down her back to the long, curled white spike at the tip of her tail.

Gracelyn slowly walked forward to her. "She's beautiful," she said softly.

Grimdore's fiery red eyes glared at her, and after a loud snort, she lowered her head to where her snout was mere inches from Gracelyn, who touched it delicately.

"Ready to fly again, girl?"

Chapter Thirty

During the night prior, they'd ridden until their horses were on the brink of exhaustion, and they knew they'd gone as far as that night would take them. Off the road they'd found a gray rock that jutted out from the ground nearly fifteen feet tall. It was surrounded by a thicket of trees and brush rising from the grass.

Even Ceres knew that if it stood out that much to them, surely the soldiers and mages would spot it just as easily from the road. There was no doubt in their minds Kellen and Paltereth had noticed they'd fled. But they knew their best hope was of finding a shaded spot for Marilyn to rest that would be partially hidden. Corvaire and Ceres might hold off the many troops of Kellen and Rourke, but neither of them wanted to test their magic against the group of Arcanic Mages.

They turned and rode off into the grass, all of them tired and struggling to sit upon their saddles from aching legs from riding so hard throughout the entirety of the night sleepless. Riding underneath the shade of the canopy of the scantly leaved tree and entering the shade of the rock, they tied their horses. Adler sat with his back to the rock with a groan.

"I'm starvin'," he said, before gulping down water from his canteen.

"Me too," Ceres said after her stomach grumbled from his words.

"Stay in the shade," Corvaire said as he led Marilyn to a place to rest.

"What's the use," Adler said, kicking a rock next to his boot. "There's no telling when we're going to see them riding down the road like an army. Probably killed each other first, blaming the other side for our escape."

"We can bet on Gracelyn," Ceres said with a sigh. "We can trust Stone."

"Well, what then?" Adler said. "You know me, Ceres. I'm ready for a scrap anytime, but it's hopeless against all them. We have no idea what those mages of Salus are capable of."

"Maybe not," Ceres said, snapping at him. "But we sure as hell know what's *he's* capable of." As she said that Corvaire slipped low into the grass, back toward the road.

"Aye, we do."

The sun hung high overhead, the heat permeated the shadow. Ceres found herself dazing in and out as the light trickled through the branches overhead as they swayed back and forth. The chirping of crickets in a harmonious vibration felt like a soothing melody.

She awoke slowly sometime later, unsure of how long she'd dazed. Next to her, Adler snored softly. Marilyn still lay where Corvaire had put her to rest—sleeping soothingly.

Sitting up, she looked around, but couldn't find Corvaire. She stood, glanced around—still no sign of him. The four horses were still tied up and resting. "Where'd he go off to?"

Walking off on her own, she found on the backside of the stone was a pasture of lilies flowing in the breeze. It was beautiful under the warm golden sunlight. It seemed to stretch on for nearly a mile.

She knelt to pluck one from its stem. It smelled like fresh lavender, which her mother used to mix into the soap she made for them. Each of its pedals were a deep, lush violent at the center with pure white tips, and there was a rich orange color right in their center.

Smelling deeply with her eyes closed, it took her back home. Back to when she was a little girl, while her siblings ran around the yard and her mother made lunch and her father chopped wood in the back. She felt as if her heart was glowing, but then she felt a deep ping of regret in the pit of her stomach when she remembered she'd never see that place again—she'd never feel that safe, or that much love ever again.

Ceres stood, crushing the lily in her hand, tossing it away.

Then, Corvaire's voice called out loudly. She couldn't tell then what he was yelling, as he was clearly running, so she ran to the other side of the stone, and swallowed hard at the sight of them . . .

He was running through the grass, yelling, "Get to the horses! Get on the horses!"

Behind him, back on the road, just coming into view were the Arcanic Mages, with their horses in a full sprint—waving their wands above them. Adler was already helping Marilyn up to his horse for them to ride together, and Ceres could tell from his bloodshot eyes, he'd been awoken by Corvaire's yells, and saw the incoming mages.

"Marilyn," Ceres said, running over to her and grabbing her sleeve. "You've got to cast the spell. You have to cast the spell now."

Marilyn looked worried as she looked up to the mages. With her hands she motioned all around to the ground beneath them and to the trees above, shrugging her shoulders.

Ceres sighed deeply.

"What? She can't cast it again?" Adler asked.

"I think she's saying they already know where we are, and

we're only invisible in the shade or in the dark. They'd find us here, even if she cast it."

"Then we ride," Adler said, putting his boot in his stirrup.

"You ride," she said, glancing back at the mages as they plunged into the grass.

"What?" his eyes were angry. "Get up on your horse!"

"He can't fight them all alone," she said. "He needs me. Take her away from here."

"You take her away from here!" Adler steamed.

"You can't do nothin' against them without the Elessior," she said. "Now go."

"I'm damned tired of you saying that," he said. "You don't need blazin' magic to fight everything."

"You're good but you can't fight them in a sword fight, Adler!"

He grinned, "This isn't any old sword." He tapped the scabbard.

"What are you doing?" Corvaire yelled at them as he ran in. "You should be riding far from here? Go!"

"It's too late now," Ceres said. "We have to fight."

She looked past the mages and saw the men of Verren had just appeared on the horizon.

"Then we hold our ground," Corvaire said, drawing his sword.

"I don't know if we can beat them all," Ceres said. "Maybe if we can just kill the mages then we can renegotiate with Kellen and Rourke."

The mages' staffs beamed to light as they rode, each swirling in a dark cloud.

"That doesn't look great . . ." Adler said.

Corvaire's hand blazed to glow in a white heat that sparked from his fingers.

Ceres stood tall and took a deep breath, readying her Indiema to call forth Juniper's Red Haze, or Vines that Hold.

Only under the direst circumstance would she attempt Searing Flesh, for Corvaire's stark warning about that spell stayed deeply ingrained in her.

The mage's black clouds swirled and then burst forward at them, as Corvaire unleashed a blinding band of lightning from his hand. Marilyn was back down to her feet preparing another spell of the Seliax, and Ceres and Adler had to turn away, covering their eyes from the bolt.

By the time the explosion had died down, and Ceres' eyes were able to readjust, her jaw dropped, and she couldn't believe her eyes as a massive wall of thick ice had appeared between them and the mages. Corvaire's lightning had created a large crater in its side, but the wall stood nearly forty feet tall, and much wider.

From behind she heard the roar of the mighty beast. She turned and watched its shadow sweep over the lily fields at incredible speed.

It roared again as it landed behind the rock, each of them ran over as quickly as they could. She recognized it at once as the great sea dragon from Endo, and she at once locked eyes where her friend sat upon its back.

"Stone!"

She ran as quickly as her feet could carry her, with Adler just on her heels. Corvaire helped Marilyn around the stone as Grimdore looked down with her fiery eyes, seeming to recognize her friends and lowering her head with a low, yet soft rumble.

Stone leaped down from her wing and ran over to Ceres and Adler who all wrapped their arms around one another, holding each other as tightly as they could. He held them as if his family had returned to him after years apart.

"Your hair's longer," he said to her with a wide grin and tears in the corners of his eyes.

"Yours too." Ceres laughed.

"Adler, you've got a beard now," Stone laughed.

"Nice to see you too, pal. I see you're nearly clean shavin'. Had a rough go of things lately?"

They all laughed. Behind, and still upon Grimdore's back, Gracelyn cast another burst of ice from her hand, growing the wall wider on both sides.

"Well, I nearly died," Stone said. "But that's a story for another day."

Adler laughed. "I think we nearly died, what? A dozen times now since we last saw each other."

"I missed you two," Stone said. "I felt like I lost my family again when you left . . ."

"We're together now," Ceres said, embracing him again.

"I'd like to keep it that way," Adler said, looking back at the wall and the dragon with the three still upon her back. "Speaking of, we have a plan to get out of here with our heads still on our shoulders? Don't know if those mages of Salus are gonna like that barrier too much. See . . . they seem to want to take us to Endo, but they were too late, but the soldiers back there were brought by Kellen, you remember him right? Eccentric, kind of rat-like? Bad taste in clothes."

"I remember," Stone said as Corvaire led Marilyn over to him. Lucik and Hydrangea had climbed down. "Marilyn!" He ran over and wrapped his arms around her as her eyes teared up too. "You're alive. I didn't know to believe it, but it's true! Here you are! By Crysinthian, I can't believe it."

"Believe it," Corvaire said, who held out a hand for Stone to shake but instead he jumped at the tall, broad-shouldered man and wrapped his arms around him too. "It's quite good to see you, Stone. Quite good indeed." He smiled. "Lucik, Hydrangea, pleased to see you two as well. We'll need all the hands we can get if we're to fight the forces beyond that wall."

"We didn't come here to fight," Lucik told him.

"What do you mean?" he asked with a raised, thick eyebrow.

"She means the fight isn't here," Hydrangea said with her arms out wide.

"Where's the fight?" Ceres asked.

"You tell us," Stone said. "You're the one who's going to lead us to her."

"We can't all get up on that dragon," Adler said. "Surely . . ."

"Strange thing about that Song of the Dragon you told us about . . ." Stone said, looking up to the sky as another shadow crossed the lily patch, and then another as a pair of loud screeches roared as the two other dragons fell to the grass plains.

"I can't believe it . . ." Adler said with wide eyes, walking slowly forward.

"The song doesn't just call Grimdore," Stone said. "It's brought others as well. This one is named Y'dran, he's a fire drake from the north, and that one over there is Belzarath, she's an ivory dragon from the south."

"Incredible," Ceres said, in awe. "Breathtaking."

"They'll take us where we need to go," Stone said. "Shall we?"

"What about the horses?" Ceres asked.

"Hurry, Adler," Corvaire said. "Help me untie them quickly. We'll unsaddle them and rush them off. Any luck we'll see them again."

They ran off.

Ceres was admiring Y'dran's vibrant red scales along its slender body. It was smaller than Grimdore, but she supposed all dragons were. She'd never seen a dragon, other than a Neferian her size. Its eyes were a glassy white with thin slits of blue. Its belly was covered in orange and yellow scales.

Belzarath's ivory body was accentuated by the black horns all the way down her back and the gray webbing in her wings. Her red eyes with yellow pupils were piercing.

"Let's get ready to fly off," Lucik said. "Come with me, Marilyn, I'll help you up."

They walked toward the dragons as Ceres looked back and saw the black smoke of the mages creeping over the wall, even with Gracelyn adding more and more ice to it on all sides.

"After you," Stone said, "I've got loads to fill you in on, and I'm sure you've got lots of stories for me." He ushered her up Belzarath's wing and he followed her up, helping Adler up too. She wasn't as large as Grimdore, but the dragon didn't bat an eye at the three of them upon her back.

"So where to?" Stone asked her as Corvaire and the others mounted the two other dragons.

"Dranne," Ceres said.

"Dranne?" Adler asked. "Why there, another one of the warring kingdoms? After we saved King Roderix's life. And on the back of bloomin' dragons?"

"We'll head there first," she said. "Then maybe I can get a read on where the new girl is."

"Better than staying here," Stone said as he kicked the dragon's back and she flapped her wings. "Hold on tight. It gets breezy up there."

The ivory dragon lifted off with huge blasts of wind upon the grass. She carried them off into the sky just as the other two dragons flew off after.

Once they were high off in the sky, they saw the ice wall succumb to the black clouds of the mages, causing it to crash down in large chunks like a glacier breaking off into the sea.

The hair whipped through their faces and the warm sunlight caressed the skin on their face as each of them smiled at each other. Stone looked down and waved at Gracelyn who waved back enthusiastically.

"Together again," Adler said. "The Orphan Drifters Trio."

"We're not hidin' from dragons no more . . ." Ceres said, and then let out a loud holler into the air. "We're ridin' em!"

Chapter Thirty-One

❦

For what would've taken weeks to reach by horse, the three dragons however, fly so swiftly that within three days Stone saw his first glimpse of the great city of Dranne. They'd flown to the Gulf of Kanis, resting to sleep the night. It's amazing how deep a sleep Stone realized he could get when there were dragons around to protect you. The next day they flew over the dark water gulf with thousands of islands permeating its waves, landing on the other side for one more night of rest. Then they flew over the Durgish Mountains and into the plains that surrounded the Kingdom of King Bolivar Tritus and Queen Angelica Tritus.

From on high, gliding through the soft white clouds and blue sky the city looked like a never-ending sea of structures of dark gray stone and small huts. The small roads of the outer parts of the city cut jaggedly through the buildings and homes until they reached the inner wall of the castle.

The sun hung five fingers high behind them and the sky beyond Dranne was already darkening as they approached. Adler had told Stone the castle was called Pike Castle and had stood ever since the King Arken had been nearly killed, maimed, and banished off into the Obsidian Sea. Pike Castle was a series of growing light gray towers that grew in height until they reached the innermost white tower of the palace where a golden spike pointed up to the heavens like a divine finger of the gods. The towers had hundreds of windows with battlements and bartizans along them. The bartizans even rose high on the towers—only reason to have those that high would be from flying attackers, Stone thought.

They didn't need to get that close in the air to the castle before they could hear the alarms. Huge horns blew and the city stirred to life at the sight of the dragons. It was no usual display, Stone thought, but surely they'd be more startled to see a Neferian approaching than three dragons of teal, red and ivory—especially with riders on their backs.

"Expect a welcome party," Adler said, laying low on Belzarath's back as the wind rushed hard onto their faces.

"We may scare them all off," Ceres said, holding her blond hair back from whipping at her eyes. "If we're lucky. Or we can just simply explain that we mean them no harm."

"Don't know if they're going to believe that," Stone said, holding tightly onto a thick dragon scale and a black horn on the dragon's back.

"If we're given a chance to speak," Ceres said. "We can explain who we are. There's a chance they'll know who we are already, or possibly Corvaire."

"If we could reach the guild in the city," Adler said. "They'd help us find her. They know every nook and cranny of the castle."

"The queen knows who we are, I know," Stone said. "I'd gather King Tritus too after Gracelyn's magical attack on the two Neferian by the sea, and of Corvaire's defense of the people of Hedgehorn."

"Look!" Ceres pointed down to the south. "Riders!"

Stone looked and quickly spotted them. From their height

it was hard to decipher much about the pack of thirty or so riders.

"Can't tell who they are," Stone said. "But they're riding to the castle, and at an incredible speed for horses."

"Look though," Adler said. "No gleaming from the sunlight . . . No armor . . ."

"White horses, too," Ceres said.

"It's impossible," Stone muttered, with a hard swallow.

They heard Corvaire's voice yell over from the back of Grimdore. "Arcanists!"

"C'mon now, Belzarath," Ceres said to the dragon. "Fly swift, we need to beat them to the city."

The dragon's neck dipped as they felt a surge as they descended at an incredible speed, and each of them gripped more tightly onto the white dragon. Smoke smoldered out of the sides of its mouth.

"Can't be the same ones," Stone said. "No way they could ride as fast as a dragon flies."

"The Vile King lives in the south," Adler said. "But who knows where his followers dwell around the country? They can be anywhere . . ."

The three dragons glided swiftly down as the horns continued to blow and huge catapults were being loaded around the castle's battlements. Stone wasn't sure the catapults would be able to reach the outer limits of the city—in fact—how many surrounding homes had been built around the castle since a last dragon attack, he asked himself.

With mighty flaps of the dragon's wings and a loud screech by Grimdore that sounded for surely miles all around, they landed on the outskirts of the city of Dranne. They saw a convoy was rushing out of the palace gate with the sigil of the city raised along its ranks—a blue crescent moon and a grayish-silver sword on a white banner.

Stone saw the mages were still at least four miles off, so they had at least a little bit of a head start. They got down from the dragons as they each eyed the city warily, and the eyes of the city did the same upon them and their dragons. Surely no other person has ridden a wild dragon in generations, except the Runtue of course.

They waited in a line, side by side, waiting for the convoy to enter out of the city, which took the better deal of ten minutes. The crowds grew in the city streets during that time to thousands.

Corvaire told Ceres to seek out the new girl while and if she could. So, she stood there trying to feel out for her while the soldiers rode down from the palace.

Once the soldiers did reach them, they stayed on their steeds, and the man at the lead wore a golden helmet with silver and black sets of wings on each side. His face was grizzly and dark. His beard the color of snow and his eyes a piercing blue.

"King Tritus welcomes you to his city," the man said as more than a hundred soldiers poured out of the city on horseback.

It didn't look like such a welcome as a show of defense, so each of them waited for him to speak again. Stone and Ceres were glad that Adler kept his mouth shut.

"Welcome, Knight Drâon Corvaire, and welcome to you, Marilyn Corvaire the Conjurer. It has been many years since the great city of Dranne has welcomed you into its arms. Yet this is the first time you've brought dragons with you . . ."

"Commander Triog," Corvaire said. "It's good to see you still serve your king." He bowed his head.

"The years haven't been as kind to me as they have you," the commander said. "That Darakon blood in yer' veins."

Ceres pulled on Stone's shirt sleeve.

"She's here," she whispered. "She's here in Dranne."

Corvaire and Gracelyn's heads both turned slightly, as apparently they heard her as well.

"There are riders approaching," Corvaire said. "We wish passage into your city so that we may attend to some private business we have. We come in peace."

"Aye, riders," Commander Triog said gruffly. He spat on the ground. "That is why I cannot abide by your request to enter the city."

"But why?" Corvaire asked. "We are friends of Dranne. We are friends of your king."

"The riders of the Vile King and his black magic don't ride for Dranne, they ride for you."

"How do you know this?" Corvaire asked with a furrowed brow.

"They'd not dare come near this city," he said with a growl. "No Arcanist has stepped foot in this city for decades. And now they ride in a pack day and night the same evening that you approach our home? Turn back, Knight of the Darakon. Take your dragons someplace else. We have our own war to fight here. We need none of yours."

"The war we fight is coming to you, whether you accept that or not," said Stone, as the commander looked perturbed by his sudden interruption.

"What do you know of war, boy? We've been fighting wars longer than you've been walkin' on two legs. Just because an old tale says you're special, don't make it so. Special is a price you pay, honor is given to those who fight fer' it."

"We've fought the Neferian," Stone said with his fists clenched. "I've fought no legion of men, but we've fought off three of the dark dragons now. Our dragon behind us even lived after fighting one off. First to ever do so. So, you can go on about your honor, but what use is honor when everyone you know is dead? Burned alive but white-hot dragonfire and Arken stands over the ashes of your city."

The commander glowered at him and the other soldiers looked unsure of what to think about Stone. He didn't know if they'd ever seen a man his age talk to the commander of their army like that before and left with all his body parts still attached.

"I'm sure you know as well as we do that King Roderix sent out an army on its way here," Stone said, waiting to see the commander's reaction. He only groaned. "But are you going to fight them off *and* the dark dragons? We need your help. You must let us into your city. We'll leave as quickly as we can, but there's something of importance we must do."

". . . And that is?" he asked, leaning forward in his saddle.

Stone looked at Gracelyn, unsure what he should say.

"Listen," he said, "we . . ."

Grimdore roared behind them, sending many of the horses reeling back and sending many riding off. Belzarath and Y'dran roared right after. It was a piercing roar that thundered through the lands, and as Stone and the others turned back to look at the dragons, Mud barked as well, but not at the dragons, he was barking to the south. Stone saw the riders of Salus were still miles to the southwest, but as soon as he heard their roars, he knew what was coming from the dark clouds to the south.

A shattering roar bellowed from deep within the shadowy clouds, it cracked and broke at the tail of its call.

"By Crysinthian's beard," Commander Triog said with wide eyes. Then he glowered at Stone quickly. "What've ya' done boy? They've come for you! Fly away. Fly far away from here!"

"No," Stone said. "They're not here for me! That's what we heard from the Vile King's mages. They needed us to get here. They said the true war would start here."

The soldiers of Dranne flooded back into the city toward the palace.

"They didn't come for us," Ceres said. "They came here. They came to burn."

Then they saw it—and they saw him . . . King Arken upon the back of the great Neferian that was three times the size of Grimdore. It had grown tremendously since they'd last seen it.

"Into the castle!" Triog yelled. "Back to the castle. Protect the king and queen!"

The dark dragon was instantly recognizable to them. Its large, muscular crimson head cascaded to a smooth, huge black body with shimmering black scales. The webs of its wings behind its massively long arms held stripes like veins of gold in their matte black. A serpent like yellow filled its menacing eyes, and they could see Arken with his curled horned helmet and thick sword.

"She's here!" Ceres said. "She's somewhere in the city! We've got to find her!"

"I'll go with you," Stone said, running to her side.

"No," Gracelyn said in a hollow voice.

"We have to find the girl!" Stone said, with a confused expression and his arms out. "I have to find her."

"Ceres is a Litreon, you are not. You are the one told to lead to the Dark King's death," Gracelyn spoke as if her other side had taken over. "You will ride Grimdore. We will fight him together."

Corvaire seemed to not want to argue with one of the Majestic Wilds. "Lucik, take Hydrangea and help her find the girl, and quickly! Stick to the alleys." Lucik nodded and took Ceres' hand, leading her up to the city. Mud ran after.

Stone was stuck. He wanted to help both his friends, but those most wise were telling him that he needed to fight. *Why do we always end up splitting up? I hate this damned war! It's always tearing us apart . . .*

As Ceres and the others ran into the city that was swarming in a chaos of mothers pulling their children behind them—crying—the horns that blew all around the city, the rustling of frantic soldiers and even those carrying their grandmothers down roads filled with thousands of scared civilians.

"Look!" Adler said, pointing up to Arken. They quickly saw two more gigantic Neferian and riders flying from the clouds, flapping their scaly wings toward the great city. "More of them..."

"Up on the dragons," Corvaire said. "Marilyn, do you wish to come or stay?" She held her hand out for him to take and they all ran over to the dragons but then heard a familiar, ominous voice...

Stone stopped, slowly turning around to see a lone figure standing only six feet behind.

"It isn't too late, boy..." the voice rasped.

Stone instantly recognized the crooked nose, thin lips and dark, soulless eyes of the slender man in the dark robes and crown of bone and ivory around his bald head.

"King Arken Shadowborn has come to ravage Dranne," he said. "Only you can stop it, and I will show you the way... if only you ask..."

"I'm not interested in your offer, Salus," Stone said through his teeth. "Not then, and not now."

"Look to the sky, Stone. Don't you see what beseeches you? It's death. Pure death and anger. Power like this world has never seen..."

"I'll show him anger and death!" Stone said.

"I don't doubt the believed truth in your words, but I fear reality has not beset you. Say the words, Stone. Say them thrice and I will give you what you need to destroy him!" His empty eyes glanced over at Gracelyn as she sat upon Belzarath's back.

"I'm not giving them to you," Stone growled. "Crawl back from where you came from or fight with us."

"I don't *want them*," Salus rasped. "I want to join them as equals. Together we will be able to create a new world, peaceful and prosperous. A world where there are no civil wars, no Neferian, and one of freedom."

"I'm not giving them to you," Stone said. "Now, I've got a war to fight." He turned to run to the dragons.

". . . I know one of them is here . . ." the Vile King's voice was slimy and wretched.

Stone spun back around. "They are not yours! They're meant to be *wild*!"

"If you will not trade their friendship," Salus said with a wry grin, "then I will be forced to take it. It is far too late in the game for mere parlay . . ."

"You want to go to war with us?" Stone asked. "In the middle of all of this?"

"There is no want," Salus said. "The only ones to make it out of this Great War alive will be the ones remembered as saviors. What do you want your legacy to be, Stone? Tell me . . .?"

"My legacy?" Stone said with a scowl, turning back and mounting Grimdore. "I want to be remembered as a friend who didn't make deals with devils. That's what I want to be remembered as." He clicked his boot heels on Grimdore, and she took off back to the sky as he drew his sword—flying south.

"Then you've made your decision . . ." Salus said with a dark sneer as his Arcanic Mages rode up behind him on horseback. "If you won't join me, then you are against me . . ."

Chapter Thirty-Two

The sky turned a blazing fiery red as the sun fled to the west and the three dragons summoned by the Song of Dragons and the three Neferian led by the Dark King himself flew at blinding speeds at one another. Stone gripped tightly onto Grimdore's scales as she let out a deafening roar as he felt the heat forming from deep inside of her. Gracelyn held on next to him.

"You ready for this?" he asked.

"Don't know," she said with her hood and brown hair blowing wildly behind her.

Adler rode Y'dran to their right with Marilyn behind him, and Corvaire rode Belzarath to their left. The dragons snapped their jaws as the Neferian flew at them.

Dranne below sprang to light as torches burned, leading the way for those fleeing or running to their homes. The young ran with the elderly, and babies cried in their mothers' arms as the dragons screeched overhead. Stone saw the fires bellowing within the dark dragons' long necks.

"Remember, Stone," said Gracelyn. "My magic won't work

against Arken, or his against mine. But our dragon and his are vulnerable, and we are all vulnerable to dragonfire."

"Yeah, there's no escaping that . . . Well, here we go!"

Arken's Neferian opened its maw wide, showing its sharp teeth, nearly wide enough to swallow Y'dran whole, and Stone saw the white fires were brewing within, ready to spew.

Then Stone heard a voice in his head, as loudly as if someone was speaking into his ear.

'I didn't come here for you, Stone. If you get in my way, then this will be where your true grave will lie.'

He spoke back, "Fly far away from here, Arken, and I'll let you take your people back where you came from where you can live in peace."

'Peace . . .? I know no such thing while these villains live with their gold and castles, killing and defiling wherever they go . . .'

"I can't let you do this. I'm going to kill you if you attack the city."

'Then . . . Kill me!'

Arken's dragon spewed the blazing hot dragonfire at the dragons which all quickly dodged by veering to both sides, with Grimdore being the largest darting nearly straight down. Stone and Gracelyn felt the searing heat on the hairs on their arms singeing. The Neferian dropped too, and its fire blasted down upon an outskirt of the city.

Gracelyn cast a spell of ice to try to slow the fire, but it burned right through.

"He's strong," she gasped. "Much more powerful than the others."

"Well, we're lucky we have you then," he said.

The clouds burst with light, and Corvaire sent down a bolt of lightning between the three dragons which each of them roared and screeched as it hit the ground with a loud crash of thunder. The three Neferian separated, with the other two beginning circling the city on both sides.

"After the big one," Gracelyn said to Grimdore, who was still behind them. "Let the others chase the smaller ones. I want you to burn it alive, I want it to feel your wrath!"

Grimdore turned with a strong pulling jerk to the left, circling back.

"Grimdore may be smaller," Stone yelled, "but she's faster than Arken's. I've seen it before!"

Y'dran was chasing after one as the rider whipped the reins on his dark dragon. A dark mist hung about Adler and Marilyn as they flew after it, and the Neferian blasted a white inferno down upon the eastern edge of the city.

While the homes burned beneath them, the black mist blew unnaturally forward, against the wind and overtook the Neferian as it shrieked from inside the mist. White fires blasted up into the sky and around as the dark dragon seemed unable to escape the shadows.

Meanwhile Corvaire, as in the city of Hedgehorn, had summoned a swarm of wasps that flew after the Neferian to the west, which the rider glanced back at and then pulled the reins back and the dragon turned slowly, flapping its wings backward. With a crashing roar, it blasted the swarm with a wide swath of dragonfire.

Stone swallowed hard as he watched the fires burn nearly all of the wasps, as they were concentrated in a tight cloud, and few were left to buzz helplessly away.

Corvaire's dragon sent its own raging orange, yellow and white fires back at the Neferian, hitting it flush in the chest, and it let out a high-pitched howl. They couldn't tell if it injured the Neferian or not, but they all hoped.

While it was stunned, Belzarath crashed into it, cutting in deep with her claws, and biting at the base of its neck. Gnawing and scraping, it was vicious and the Neferian continued to shriek.

Arken's Neferian turned and made flight toward it, but it

descended as its wings were growing heavy. Sheets of ice were building upon both its wings and long arms. The dark dragon's strength kept breaking through it as the ice fell into the city, but the sheets grew larger, and quicker than it could shake them off.

Y'dran plowed into the side of the Neferian Belzarath was ravaging, and the ivory dragon bit at the other side its neck. Blood rolled down both sides of it as it fought, curling its neck down and snapping its jaws at the two. The rider, even in the madness, climbed from his saddle and was climbing over toward Adler and Marilyn.

"He's coming," Adler said. "Directly ahead. Should I get up and stop him? I'd love nothin' more!"

As Arken's Neferian struggled to keep flight, the third Neferian saw the battle and was flying back over the city to fight off the two smaller dragons. Adler was getting up from his saddle when a dark figure appeared on the other side of the rider, who spun to strike the featureless black figure and slashed at it with his long sword, but it passed through with only a wisp of smoke. The dark figure with no eyes or face took its own dark sword of smoke and slashed it fiercely.

The rider turned to look back at Adler with wide, confused eyes, and then his head slid from his shoulders and tumbled down the Neferian's back, followed by his body as the shadow figure gusted back into the wind from where it came.

Adler looked back at Marilyn, who was breathing heavily and was growing pale. "Marilyn, hold on! You did it, you got one of 'em!"

The two dragons continued their savage attack on the Neferian as it had clamped down onto Belzarath's shoulder and was biting ferociously down on it. Belzarath didn't shriek or moan, the dragon gnawed harder on the Neferian's neck.

With a strong flick of her wings Grimdore crashed into the Neferian with her sharp teeth digging into the Neferian's neck.

It released Belzarath and let out a frightening roar as it looked to be preparing to blast its white fire down upon them.

"Now, Grimdore!" Stone yelled. "Do it now!"

While her maw was clamped down onto the neck the other two dragons had been sinking their teeth deep into, Grimdore felt hot to the touch, and with an explosion of flames, an inferno of heat blasted out of her mouth. She blew the dragonfire for what felt like the longest moment of Stone's life, and when she calmed and he was able to open his eyes again, he saw the Neferian's wild eyes above give a longing, blank look down at him.

"Look, Stone." Gracelyn pointed down.

He looked and couldn't believe what he saw.

Twirling through the air, tumbling toward the city was the large, headless body of the Neferian.

"She did it . . ." he said with wide eyes.

And as its body crashed into a courtyard of buildings and the side of the cathedral, Stone looked at Gracelyn who had the same look on her face.

"They can be killed . . ." she said.

The three dragons released the head which went falling end over end toward the ground as the other Neferian readied its white fire to blast into them and Arken's shook the last of the ice from its wings.

"That's not going to make them happy . . ." Adler said. "That's not going to make them happy at all . . ."

<hr/>

BLINDED by and coughing on the musty smell of dragonfire, she ran through the alleyways of the city. A man running past knocked his shoulder into her in his frenzy as he went by, nearly knocking Ceres over, but Hydrangea caught her before she fell.

She shook off the cobwebs trying to sense where the girl was.

The girl, have to get the girl before this fight turns the city into another ruin like Aderogon.

The stone buildings on either side of them shook as a Neferian flew over with such fury, its roared caused small bits of rock to roll off the tops of the building onto them. It was chaos, as the dark dragon blew down upon the alleys before them a huge swath of white fire that killed everyone it touched and sent buildings crumbling to the ground.

Lucik grabbed both of them and pulled them around a corner as the hot gust of air shot down the alley they'd been in, and Ceres could feel the tips of her hair singeing.

"Which way?" Lucik asked after the hot air died down and Y'dran flew over after the Neferian and its rider.

Ceres took a deep breath and focused. She could feel the girl out there somewhere, like a thin piece of string connected them, even though she couldn't see it.

"This way I think," Ceres said. "To the northeast."

They quickly shot back down the alleyway the same way they'd been heading as the fires grew a few roads before them.

"I guess that means she's still alive," Hydrangea said as heavy beads of sweat slipped down her brow from the heat of the fires. There was heavy yelling up ahead and many people running past them, sobbing as the tears streaked down their faces dusted with ash. One man held his severed arm as he stumbled down the alley, and another mumbled as blood poured down the side of his face.

"This is insanity," Hydrangea said, following Ceres—all with their weapons drawn.

The dragons roared up above, in their swirling madness. They flew past in fierce flight, and Ceres knew not if each time they passed over if they'd spew down their death upon them, but she fought hard to push those fears aside and feel for the string. *Must keep feeling for the string . . .*

"We're getting close," Ceres said as they turned another corner, stomping through puddles and covering their mouths from the smoke and smell of charred wood and flesh.

The other two followed just behind, with Mud darting around the people who rushed past, trying to find a safe place to hide from the dragon battle above in the night skies. She watched as Stone flew above with Gracelyn on Grimdore's back, and that gave her hope. But then she watched as Arken's enormous dark dragon flew after with white flames bellowing out of the sides of its tooth-filled maw.

I have to hurry, she could be the key to fighting off the Neferian with Gracelyn if I can find her and tell her what she is . . .

A pair of children walked slowly by them, they were no older than six each and their eyes were wide on their dirty faces. The boy looked up at Ceres as he held what was perhaps his sister. They were alone, and that pulled at Ceres' heart. She knew the pain all too well of being alone . . .

"Keep going," Lucik said reluctantly. "We can't help them all. Our best chance of helping them is by finding her. *She could be the key.*"

"Here," Ceres said, stopping next to a charred garden box below a window framed by rectangular stones. Mud quit running ahead and looked back. Once his gaze turned back toward them, he growled low.

They all noticed Mud's instinct. Turning back around, they looked back down the alley they'd come from, but Ceres' string had turned to a thick rope and she turned another corner, not able to fight what was pulling her.

Mud ran to Hydrangea and Lucik's side, each of them holding out their weapons.

"What is it, boy?" Lucik asked, swaying her sword from side to side people continued to rush past her screaming for help and hobbling in pain. But they couldn't seem to see what he was barking at as Belzarath and a Neferian crashed into one another in an explosion of flashing teeth and claws.

Meanwhile Ceres had turned another corner as the then fat rope pulled into her chest as if it was tugging around her chest as if it was tightly wrapped around her.

A pair of eyes met hers in one of those longing glances they tell about in old stories. It was the sort of longing glance that seems to last for ages but is little more than a flickering moment in the grand space of time.

The eyes were gray, like an old wolf's—dim but wise, and those of a hungry predator. Her eyes dug deeply into Ceres' although they were twenty feet away, and Ceres didn't know exactly what to say, she was being pulled so whimsically into them.

Then the girl with red hair dusted in thick ash turned away and ran.

"Wait!" Ceres screamed, and ran after her.

Chapter Thirty-Three

Ceres ran as fast as her legs could carry her as she wove between those fleeing the city. All the while she kept looking over the crowd for the red-haired girl who seemed to be running from something—maybe even her.

But she couldn't help thinking of her friends back there in the alley with Mud, so she nimbly darted through the crowds, gaining speed upon the girl with the red hair, and the string was as strong as an iron chain. While in chase she quickly shot through an alley to the left, after seeing the girl turn down the road up ahead left. Ceres was accustomed to cities, and not standing out. She moved like a sharp wind down the alley, and as she turned right once more, she reached out and grabbed the red-haired girl by the wrist.

"Let me go," the girl fought with her gray eyes glaring into Ceres'. She thought she saw a flicker of warm golden light in them as the girl tried to tear her arm free.

"Wait," Ceres said, holding on tightly. "Wait jus' a minute. Let me talk to you."

"I've got nothing to say to you," the girl said, pulling her arm free, but Ceres reached out and grabbed her by both shoulders, holding her close to her, nearly shaking her.

"I've got somethin' to say to you, and you're going to listen!"

The girl's eyes narrowed, and she crossed her arms over her chest.

"I'm not going to hurt ya," said Ceres. "But I've come an awful long way to find you." She leaned in to whisper to the girl. "Listen. I know what you are. I know what you're becoming. I'm here with friends who can help you, but you must come with me now. There are other bad people that are going to be looking for you soon. An' trust me, you'd much rather be with us than with any of their rotten asses."

The girl pulled back slightly with an eyebrow raised. She almost looked sad as her pale skin flushed.

"You know what I'm talking about, don't ya? You see, I felt it nearly across the whole continent as soon as you . . . changed."

"That—that was only a couple days ago. How'd you?" the girl asked softly.

Ceres simply looked up to the sky at Stone and Gracelyn gliding upon the teal dragon.

"What's yer' name?" Ceres asked nicely, loosening the grip on her shoulders.

The girl seemed unsure to tell Ceres or not, pulling away as the frantic citizens of Dranne ran past them in all directions. One of the Neferian roared loudly overhead, blasting its white fire onto the southern part of the city.

"I'm Ceres. I'm from up north. Small town call Briewater on the coast."

"My name is . . . Rosen . . ."

"Well, Rosen, it's a pleasure to meet ya, and I'm sure we'll have time to get know each other, but I think it's best if we do that someplace far away from here . . ."

She grabbed her again by the wrist and tugged back toward the alley.

"I—I can't," Rosen said. "This is my home. This is all I've ever known. I can't just . . . leave."

"Ya got family here?" Ceres asked.

"Yes. A couple of aunts and an uncle, and my cousins."

"Where are they?" Ceres asked.

"At their home, I think. There's where I'm going."

"All right," Ceres said, letting go of her wrist. "My friends are right back there. Come with me to find them and then we'll all go with you to where your family is."

Rosen again, didn't know to trust her or not.

"Rosen, there's another one like you with us. Don't suppose you can feel her?"

"Another, like me?"

"She's the one up there fighting the Dark King himself. Her name's Gracelyn."

"Gracelyn?" she muttered.

"Come," Ceres said with her hand out. "Please . . ."

Rosen took her hand, running behind her down the dark alleyway, and with each step Mud's barks grew louder and louder.

They turned back right and entered back into the alley where Ceres nearly dropped her sword at the sight before them.

Black smoke swirled around violently in an unnatural circle of whooshing wind. Mud stayed back, barking madly as nothing beyond the dark smoke was visible.

"Lucik! Hydrangea!" Ceres yelled past the smoke. She saw a woman's hand reach up into the air, just above the smoke, and she could see it was Lucik's.

The rushing, swirling smoke faded away, and once it did, Lucik dropped to her knees and Hydrangea lay on her side on the ground groaning.

Ceres looked up and saw a face she'd not wished to see again.

"Salus," she growled.

"Who's that?" Rosen asked, with a faint tremble in her voice.

"That, Rosen, is the Vile King."

"So that's her?" Salus sneered. "Excellent."

"You can't have her!" Ceres said. "We made no deal with you."

"The deal is dead." Salus, glared Rosen up and down, brimming with pride.

Beyond him, his horde of Arcanic Mages flooded in, each of them with their mad eyes leering at Rosen.

"What did you do to them?" Ceres asked, watching Lucik helping to get Hydrangea back up to her feet, which she did with a groan.

"It matters not," Salus said. "I got my answer from them. I was only asking where you'd gone off to. But I should have known you'd just come to me."

A dark form blew past Ceres' leg and she quickly realized it was Mud running at the king.

"No!" she cried, but with a swipe of his hand before Mud was even halfway there, the dog flew sideways into the stone wall to the right, landing next to Hydrangea and Lucik, whimpering.

"Ceres," Rosen said. "He's one of the ones you said would come, isn't he?"

"Aye," Ceres said with a nod. "He's a sorcerer, and those behind him are his cronies."

"Please tell me you know how to fight them?" Rosen said hesitantly. "I don't want to go with him."

A pair of dragons roared overhead and one screeched in pain, and another burst of dragonfire exploded to the east.

"I know a little magic," Ceres whispered uneasily. "But I've got nothing to defend us against him."

Rosen gasped.

"The only ones who can fight him are up there," Ceres said.

With a quick movement between them and the Vile King, something shimmered as it flew through the air, end over end. The sword was flying at him with great speed, and Hydrangea was left with her arm extended out as she'd flung her blade at him.

Hope returned to Ceres as she and Rosen watched, ready to jump into battle.

The blade stopped though, hanging in the air, and then it slowly turned to face back at them. Salus had his aged, wrinkled hand out as black smoke overtook the blade. From the dark cloud that hung between them, the sword shot out, and Ceres cried out as the sharp blade stuck into Hydrangea's chest, piercing through her as the blade's bloody tip stuck out of her shoulder blade.

She dropped to her knees, looked up at Lucik, whispered something, and then fell to her side limply.

"No!" Ceres shouted. "No!"

"She . . . she's not breathing," Lucik cried, running her trembling hands along Hydrangea's face, neck and chest—unsure what to do. When she pulled her hands back, they were covered in blood.

Ceres swallowed hard. For the first time in a long while, she was truly scared. She could tell she was breathing rapidly, and her hands shook.

Please, Crysinthian, show me a way through this. Please, please . . . tell me what to do . . .

"Hydrangea," Lucik cried with her forehead pressed to her lover's. "Wake up, wake up. Don't do this. Please, wake up. You can't leave me like this . . . You can't leave me alone . . ."

"Now," Salus said as his mages crept through the night alley like shadows themselves behind him. "Come to me, child. Come and I will cause no harm to anyone, including yourself. I only wish to speak with you. I believe that we may work together to create a better world . . ." The corner of his mouth curled up.

Lucik knelt, sobbing over Hydrangea, cursing the Vile King's name. Mud whimpered and his legs moved slowly as he lay on his side. Rosen reached out and held Ceres' hand.

"I have to," Rosen said with tears streaming down her cheeks. "There's no other way. He's going to kill you all."

"You're not going with him," Ceres said, with tears of her own filling her eyes. "I'll lay down my own life before he lays his weasley fingers on you."

"I have to," Rosen cried. "But I don't want to . . . I'm scared."

"Me too," said Ceres. "Me too."

Salus slowly moved toward them, like a ghost his long robes floated him over the stones on the road.

"I'll treat you well," he said with a raspy voice. "You'll have everything you ever desired, and more . . . I'll show you places and things no one in these miserable lands could ever dream of. The power we will have together when the Majestics Wilds and the Arcane King are finally united. You'll see, and you'll show the others what they can become."

"The . . . Majestic Wilds?" Rosen muttered to herself. "Yes . . . Now I'm beginning to see."

"What?" Ceres asked, as she was looking down at Lucik, but then her head turned to look over at Rosen whose red hair was flapping behind her.

"Your magic is not enough to stop his," she said as the hairs on Ceres' arms straightened and tingled. "But deep down . . . I know that mine is."

"Yes," Ceres whispered. "You are powerful enough to stop him."

But how could she know?

"Take your men and leave this place," Rosen said. "This is my home, my city, and I'll not have you take me from it."

"I'm only leaving with you," he growled, pausing between them and Hydrangea's fallen body. "Come, child . . . There is no other way."

In a flash of light, from behind him Lucik's sword glimmered in the reflection of blazing golden light from Grimdore's fire above. Arching through the air silently it cut through his hand that was outstretched at Rosen. As the blade cut through, his hand fell to the ground, leaving blood spattering on the road.

He grimaced with a shriek, turning toward Lucik who prepared to cut his head off next. Yet the Arcanic Mages stirred to life behind them and black mists quickly overtook her, raising her high up into the air.

"Wicked witch," Salus spat as he held his forearm as the blood gushed out, and he slunk back. A pair of mages quickly attended to his wound. His face was twisted, and he looked darker and much older and frailer than just moments before.

Lucik hung in the air in the pillar of smoke, she fought but then groaned in pain, cursing the Vile King. She twisted and shook as the smoke started to tear into her.

A pair of pale skinned mages with dark eyes approached Rosen.

"Come," one of them said with a hiss.

"Rosen . . ." Ceres said nervously. "Help her."

Each of the Arcanic Mages grabbed one of her arms, pulling her toward them, but then they quickly stopped. Not only did they stop, but they quit moving all together.

Lucik's groans turned to screams of pain as the smoke darted around her.

"I told you," Rosen said through teeth clenched. "You're not taking me with you." She turned her body and both arms of the mages broke like glass and cold wisps rose from their elbows where they'd broke from.

The rest of the mages' glares fell upon Rosen as she walked slowly toward them with her long red hair whipping behind her.

That a girl. Give them hell. Kill them all!

"You kill these people because of me?" Rosen snapped. "I don't even know them. But I for sure don't know you . . ."

The mages pulled their injured king back within their ranks.

"We are taking you whether by will or force," one of them hissed.

With a quick movement of her hand, and a whisper from her lips, "*Thyfonus Bitternex Onum.*" She cast out a burst of icy wind at the mage, blasting into him and knocking him unconscious, nearly frozen solid.

The mages quickly abandoned their attack on Lucik as her body fell from twelve feet high to the ground next to Hydrangea as she winced from the fall. The bright blue blast that Rosen had cast full of icy shards and shimmering snow, returned to her hand where it lay in a soft aura of blue light.

The mages moved like snakes around one another in the narrow alleyway, drifting in and out of the shadow.

"Return to where you came," Rosen said in a voice far more mature than she'd sounded only moments earlier. "Or all your fates will be like these three . . . frozen and broken . . ."

"Get her!" Salus' voice called out from behind the mages. "Bring her! Kill the others!"

Their staffs moved about them and another group of them pulled their thin swords from their sheathes, many of them snarled with their yellowing teeth.

"Rosen?" Ceres said with haste.

The Majestic Wild held her arms out wide, as the mages' spell was creating a dark shadow above them that was turning the city to a deep place devoid of light, and Ceres could feel the shadow creeping toward them.

Rosen clapped her hands. "*Polaris Nor Ravenus.*"

The shadow fled as the bright white light of her clap illuminated the alley as if a white, shining sun rose directly overhead, and then Ceres felt the rumble of the ground. The mages seemed to sense it too, and as their shadow had fled, they all scattered to find the light they lost.

The light faded, and the shadows returned quickly but not before *they* came . . .

Their growls were monstrous as their long teeth shown from their maws. Ceres ran to Mud, pulling him close to the side of the alley as they ran by. Their bodies were huge and covered with icy, white fur as the mages struggled to cast another spell, and half of them fled back down the alley.

"Incredible," Ceres muttered as the bears rushed past at blinding speed, crashing into the mages, biting and clawing. The thousand-pound bears easily tore into their ranks as the mages screamed and cried out in pain while the pack of eight bears crushed and sliced the Mages of the Arcane.

Mud whimpered in her arms and Rosen stood at the mouth of the alley with her arms still in front of her from the clap and an icy orb formed around them. Mud was injured but nothing seemed to be broken as she lay him back down and ran to Lucik.

"Where are you hurt?" she said. "Tell me what to do to help you."

Lucik lay on her back next to Hydrangea, with her silver hair strewn on the stones beneath her. Blood trickled from her mouth as her face was growing pale. Her head was turned sideways, looking at her lover who lay next to her, dead.

"Lucik," Ceres cried as teardrops fell onto her friend's chest. "I'm here. Tell me what to do."

The icy bears continued their attack upon the mages as Lucik lifted her left hand and took Hydrangea's.

"It's funny," she said. "I'd give anything to bring her back."

Ceres choked from her tears.

"I don't even mind me dying," Lucik said as tears rolled down the sides of her eyes. "I just don't want her to be taken. She was my everything. She was my sunshine, my life. She had so much left to give this world . . . I . . ."

"You do to," Ceres said. "We need you. We need you . . ."

"My body is broken," she coughed. "I feel that something has burst inside of me."

"No, no, no . . . We're going to get you out of here . . . You're coming back to Endo with us. We can heal you back at the mountain."

"Child," Lucik said, taking Ceres' hand in her other hand.

Ceres wept, "Yes?"

"I—I just wanted you to know that you will become a great woman someday. Your strength, your spirit . . . I saw it in you the first time I lay my eyes upon you. The others are going to need you. Stay strong for me, will you do that for me? Take care of them."

Ceres nodded, biting her lip.

Lucik turned her head to look back at Hydrangea whose bright blue eyes gazed up lifelessly at the starry sky.

"I've never seen anything so beautiful," Lucik cried. "I'm sorry I let you down, bunny. I'm sorry I let you . . ."

"Lucik . . .? Lucik?"

Ceres watched as her body fell limp, but her eyes remained fixed upon her fallen lover's. Their fingers were intertwined, and they lay together on the cold stone. Ceres sobbed with her head lowered as Mud hobbled over and with a whimper, he rubbed his muzzle against her arm.

She turned and wrapped her arms around him. "Thank you," she said. "I know, boy. I'm going to miss them too."

Rosen stood behind her, silently, sniffling.

Ceres looked up to see the icy bears stood over the pack of bodies torn apart with dead mages with contorted faces. Then a wind blew in and the bears faded off like glittering, white dust.

Chapter Thirty-Four

❧❧❧

Once the Neferian's severed body and head crashed down into the city—never to fly again—Stone and the others' hope soared, as Arken's Neferian and the other's wrath doubled. While the three dragons were more agile than the much larger dark dragons, Arken seemed to know how to spew his revenge upon them, by lighting up the vast city in white dragonfire.

The dark dragons blew huge blasts of it upon sections of the cities, causing infernos to blast through entire roads and squares full of people running for their lives in terror. Stone knew what the Neferian's fire did to people, as he'd seen it up on Endo when Seretha and the past Majestic Wilds were burned down nearly to the bone.

Stone kicked Grimdore's back as he watched the dark dragons spew their vengeance upon the city.

"So many are dying," Gracelyn yelled to him as the wind flew past and the teal dragon's wings flapped mightily, trying to keep up with the Neferian. "I can feel their anguish, their pain. We've got to stop him. He's bent on destroying the entire city!"

"We can't let him do that!" Stone yelled back to her. "Can you use your magic to stop him?"

"My magic is weak now from the first attack," she said. "I need time, and now he's too swift!"

The other two dragons were in pursuit of the other Neferian on the other side of the city as they spat their own fire at the dark dragon. Even when their flames did hit the Neferian's scales, it seemed to not even notice as it continued its barrage upon Dranne.

Arken whipped the reins of his mighty dragon as his leather capes tails whipped behind him. He leaned forward in his saddle as he whipped with one hand and held his great sword in the other. The Neferian veered left, to the west, and toward the castle at the center of the city.

Catapults released their fiery rocks coated in tar at the dark dragons as it approached—which it easily evaded as they flew past. Heavy spears whizzed through the air at it, and Stone was astonished at its ability to swerve through the onslaught from the soldiers below.

Grimdore let out a blast of her dragonfire at it from behind, but the fires didn't even seem to harm the dark dragon's tail as it continued its flight toward the highest pillars of the Castle of Pike.

Arken approached the castle and turned to fly around it, and as Grimdore flew toward the highest spire, Stone found himself looking into the eyes of King Tritus himself, with his Queen Angelica standing next to him. They were behind a thick glass within their throne room, and Tritus looked as mad as a rabid dog as he barked at the other subjects that scuttled behind him in the room.

"What are they doing in there?" Stone asked, as Grimdore turned to follow Arken. "Why aren't they fleeing deeper down into the castle?"

"Perhaps they think they're safe in there," Gracelyn said.

"Maybe they think Arken can't get to them. I see wardens behind them, casting a spell of protection."

"They can't stop him," Stone said, looking back at her.

"If they can't," Gracelyn said. "Then where is there for them to run to?"

"We've got to get him, we could knock him off his dragon. Or you could use your magic," he said.

"My magic doesn't work against him, remember, only his beast."

Stone pressed his chest down onto Grimdore's back. "Get me close, girl. Get me as close as you can. I'll take him out. I'll cut him from his dragon . . ."

The two dragons wound around the tower the royal pair were holed up in, and as Grimdore flapped madly to catch up to the dark dragon, they spun back around to the side where King Tritus stood just on the other side of the glass.

All within the palace chamber, as well as Stone and Gracelyn held their breath as Arken's dragon spewed its white dragonfire onto the side of the tower. Its flames ripped through the night air, fully engulfing the tower's southern face, and the palace's room was hidden behind the flames.

Grimdore crashed into the dark dragon, as it was more focused on destruction than the teal dragon in pursuit. Stone held on from the great impact that shook both dragons with incredible energy, but once Grimdore started clawing and biting, he started to get up from the dragon's back.

The flames died down and once they faded, they could see the glass and stone of the tower were charred and burned, but the glass seemed to be intact still, as King Tritus yelled with his sword held high above him.

Gracelyn grabbed Stone's wrist as he went to make his way to Arken.

"Not yet," she said with wide eyes.

"What do you mean? When else?"

"Something's wrong," Gracelyn said. "I can feel it. Something has happened, something . . . with great sadness."

"There's going to be more sadness if I don't stop him," Stone said, pulling his arm away.

"Please, Stone, listen to me . . ."

He turned back to her with wet eyes from the heat, his pale skin was singed in black soot and his hair blew untamed in the hot wind. "I have to do this. I can end this war, right here, right now."

"But it's not now," she said, holding on tightly to the dragon's scales as Grimdore attacked the Neferian, yet the Neferian dug its thick claws into the stones of the tower, and Arken's focus was upon the palace chambers. "Please, Stone. If you go, you're going to die."

"My life for his," Stone said. "I'm willing to make that sacrifice."

"But I'm not!" Gracelyn cried. "I can't lose you like this. Arken's got something planned. We need Grimdore to stop him, not you."

Belzarath crashed into the other side of the Neferian, biting and clawing. Corvaire gave them both a warrior's look as the dragon tore into Arken's dragon savagely.

King Arken whipped the reins of the mighty beast, and with a great roar from its maw it pulled back, jerking Grimdore and Belzarath from it, and pulling down huge chunks of stone from the tower as its claws had dug deep within them.

Flapping its mighty wings, it forced both the dragons back.

"Fire!" Corvaire yelled, and both dragons spewed their fires upon it, but the giant wings repelled most of the fire back at them.

The dark dragon flew into the tower again, sinking its claws in deep, this time above the glass.

"He's going to tear the tower to pieces." Stone shook his head.

Corvaire's hands illuminated in white light, as a bolt of lightning crashed down toward the Dark King, but he had a spell of his own ready.

A thick sheet of ice had formed to the top of the tower as the lightning struck into it, shattering the ice and sending crystals falling in the night sky like a snowstorm.

The dark dragon pulled again with the thick, sleek muscles in its back glistening, and Stone watched in horror as with the stones tumbling down, the thick sheet of glass broke from the tower, and the Neferian roared.

King Tritus yelled out from the tower. "I'm not afraid of you! Come fight me like a man! I'll show you what a true king's wrath is!"

"I don't want you to fight," Arken said down in a stark, commanding voice as the dragons flew to attack the Neferian once more. "I want you to die with your wrath."

"No . . ." Stone said with his mouth agape, watching the Neferian's neck begin to glow with white fire through its black scales.

Queen Angelix's gaze met his as she mouthed the words, "Save them. Save everyone . . ."

The Neferian screeched as its fires tore into the palace, burning everything within.

"No!" Stone yelled as he watched the king and queen be blown back into the tower as their flesh was burned from their bones. He looked at Corvaire who's face turned flush. "You devil! You killed her!"

By the time the Neferian had spewed his last bit of flame the inside of the tower was a raging inferno that went floors down and the top of the tower was a giant blaze of white flame.

Arken spun and looked down at Stone.

"He deserved to die," he said. "They all do." He whipped

the reins and burst off the tower flying over the two dragons, back off toward the south.

"After him!" Stone yelled, kicking Grimdore.

"Stone," Gracelyn said, touching the back of his shoulder. "He's retreating."

"We can't let him win, not again . . ."

The mighty Neferian flew off at great speed high up into the southern sky as the other Neferian and the rider flew up from the city to join him. Y'dran came up behind Grimdore and Belzarath as they flew after.

"We can't match their speed," Gracelyn said, squeezing his shoulder. "I'm sorry."

Stone looked back at Corvaire and Adler, each of them with looks of defeat on their faces.

"We should find the others," Gracelyn said softly.

Stone squeezed the dragon's scales tightly as his knuckles grew white. He clenched his teeth and fury raged within him—an urge for revenge was welling up inside of him.

"We should find Ceres," Gracelyn said. "I felt a new power appear down below. She might need our help . . ."

He thought of Ceres, his oldest friend, and if she was in trouble, then he would be at her side.

"Grimdore," he said with a sigh, "take us down, girl."

The three dragons descended back to the outskirts of the entrance to the city where they'd last seen Ceres, Lucik, and Hydrangea. The two Neferian flew high in the clouds until they disappeared back into the smoky clouds.

The dragons landed and the five of them got down from them. People continued to flood from the city that was lit by dozens of fires scattered throughout Dranne, including the one that blazed at its highest peak.

They were almost all covered in blood and ash—women, children, men with burns that melted their clothing to their skin.

"This is madness," Adler said in shock. "When is enough going to be enough for him? How many have to die?"

"He won't stop until everyone bows to him," Gracelyn said. "He's going to go after all the kings and queens, until every living soul lives in fear of him."

"We've got to find Ceres," Corvaire said. "Come."

They all ran off behind him through the crowds, as Adler helped Marilyn along. Calling out her name in the crowds, they were all looking for her blond hair to be rushing out of the city with the crowds.

"Ceres," Stone yelled. "Lucik, Hydrangea, where are you?"

They continued through the city, looking down alleyways, but mostly continuing deeper and deeper straight into the madness. Calling out their names, Stone grew frantic, worrying that maybe the worst had befallen them, or even that they were outside the city with so many other thousands of people.

But then he heard something.

"Wait," he said, halting the others. "You hear that?"

Past all the chaos, yelling and homes ablaze he heard a faint dog's bark.

"That's Mud," he said with renewed energy. "I know his bark anywhere. This way!"

They all ran behind him dodging the people that were running across their path then on their way away from the fires. The bark was getting louder.

Stone fell to his knees when the dog hobbled toward him, he looked white as the dog was covered in ash.

"Mud," he said, petting the dog gently. "You're hurt."

Mud turned, and barked at them, facing back the way they'd come.

"Take us to them," said Stone.

They ran after the dog who limped, leading them through alleyways.

But when they turned that last corner, they all stopped in their tracks.

Stone gasped.

"Oh no," Corvaire said grimly.

In the faint light of the intersection of two alleyways, and on the other side of a pile of bodies in dark robes torn to shreds was Ceres on her knees sobbing over two lifeless bodies.

"No . . ." Gracelyn cried with her hands over her mouth. "No . . ."

"I couldn't save them," Ceres sobbed. "I couldn't save them . . ."

As they walked over the pile of dead mages, Stone saw the girl with the long red hair standing just behind Ceres. Her hands were behind her back and she was swaying from side to side.

Corvaire knelt and checked the bodies of their fallen friends. Once he was sure they'd passed, he groaned and hit the stone ground with his fist. His head slunk and he hit it again.

Stone went to Ceres who rose, he held his arms out for her, and she held him tightly, crying hysterically into his shoulder.

"I'm sorry I wasn't here," Stone said.

"Me too," Adler said as he wrapped his arms around her too.

"There's nothing you could've done," she said, sniffling. "He was too strong."

"Ceres," Gracelyn asked. "How did you fight off Salus and those Mages of the Arcane?"

Ceres pulled away from them, wiped her nose, and looked at Rosen.

All of them then examined the girl with the flowing red hair, gray eyes, and freckles on her cheeks.

Gracelyn walked slowly over to her. "Do you know who I am?"

"You're like me," Rosen said, brushing her hair back behind her ear. "Aren't you?"

"Yes."

"What are we?"

"We're two of the three," Gracelyn said.

"But I don't think I want this," Rosen said, and Gracelyn put her hand on her arm gently.

"Neither do I. But fate chose us . . . We don't have a choice, we were never given one."

"But I like my life," Rosen said. "I don't want to be around all this death . . ."

Something flickered in her mind.

"Aunt Daphne . . ." she muttered and started to run off.

"Go with her," Corvaire told them. "Marilyn, help me with their bodies . . ."

Rosen ran from alley to alley, brushing past those still fleeing from the city, with Gracelyn, Stone, Ceres and Adler chasing after her. Mud limped behind.

Eight or so roads down they turned a corner, and Rosen stopped quickly. Before them was an entire street burned away by white dragonfire. Not a single house or shop was left standing as the flames burned away the last of the wood and smoke billowed up from them high up into the sky.

"Is one of those her home?" Gracelyn asked.

Rosen folded her arms around herself and her head lowered as she started to sob.

"Which one is it?" Gracelyn asked.

Rosen pointed to the one before them, and two homes to the left.

"How many lived there?"

Rosen extended all five fingers on her hand.

Stone's heart sank and he swallowed hard.

"I'll go look," Adler said, walking off toward the home.

Gracelyn rubbed Rosen's back as Adler returned minutes later.

He stood before Rosen and sighed deeply. "I'm so sorry . . ."

Rosen turned and burst into tears.

"Rosen," Ceres said softly. "I'm so . . . ."

Rosen pushed Gracelyn aside. "This is your fault!" she said with menacing eyes. "I should have come here like I wanted to!" She was striding toward Ceres, shaking her finger at her. "I could've saved them! I could have saved my family, but you took me away!"

"I—I didn't know." Ceres shook her head.

"It's not her fault," Gracelyn said. "You know whose fault it was."

"Who then?" Rosen demanded, spinning back to Gracelyn. "Who killed my family? Tell me!"

As the flames ripped through the city, with the king and queen murdered, and thousands still fleeing or struggling to put out the scattered fires that tore through the city, Stone took her by her arm and spun her gently toward him.

"The Dark King killed your family. And if you come with us, we will help you get your revenge. We will all get our revenge."

The End

Continued in Book IV:
The Fallen and the Flames

Continue Reading

The story continues in Book IV
The Fallen and the Flames

Author's Notes

Things seem to be intensifying, and with the decades old feud and civil war seemingly over, what could happen next when things seem to be spiraling out of control and enemies appear around new corners…?

Alright, enough with the promotion for the next book haha. That actually might make its way to the blurb for book 3. Hmm?

This book, to be honest, was much more difficult to complete for so many reasons in 2020. I've also realized that for my writing style- middles are hard for me.

Middles of individual books, and the middles of series. They say that every author knows the beginning and end to each book, but the middle is where the true meat of the story is.

I pushed through like I always do, as I'm a completionist… That's a word right?

But once I got toward the end I just sprinted through in a week or so. If you've been following me, you know that I love writing endings.

I'm planning two more books in the series, hopefully not

three, because I feel whatever the last book in this series is gonna be pretty long because there's a lot more story to fit in before Stone finds the end to his path.

I'm planning on pushing through the next two books fairly quickly, hopefully having them both out by summer next year.

I'm thinking about having Corvaire on the cover of book IV, maybe him and Marilyn?

Peace fellow humans,
C.K.

About the Author

Having grown up in the suburbs of Kansas, but never having seen a full tornado or a yellow brick road, he has been told more than his fair share of times while traveling, 'You're not in Kansas anymore.' He just responds, 'Never heard that one,' with a smile.

In the 'burbs' though, he found my passion for reading fantasy stories early. Reading books with elves, orcs and monsters took his young imagination to different worlds he wanted to live in.

Now, he creates his own worlds. Not so much in the elves and orc vein, but more in the heroes versus dragons one- there's a difference, right?

Yes, he grew up with The Lord of the Rings and tons of RA Salvatore books on his shelves, along with some cookbooks, comics, and a lot of video games too.

Other passions of his are coffee, good beer, and hanging around the gym.

To find out more and learn about what he's working on next please visit CKRieke.com.

C.K. Rieke is pronounced C.K. 'Ricky'.

Go to CKRieke.com and sign-up to join the Reader's Group for some free stuff and to get updated on new books!

www.CKRieke.com